PILLOW

TALK

Jeanne McNamee

Pillow Talk

Aubrey and Nick Henson live what appears to be a dream life with their two children on the cool waters of Mystic Island, New Jersey. But all is not well in paradise. After fifteen years of marriage, the couple is on the brink of divorce … until Nick mysteriously develops parasomnia.

As a parasomniac, Nick sleepwalks but appears alert and present. As his true feelings for Aubrey emerge, from a place deep within, Nick begins to treat her in a manner reminiscent of the man she once fell in love with.

Aubrey, a nurse, eventually diagnoses Nick's illness but debates telling her husband about his disorder, much to the dismay of her lifelong best friend, Libby White. Her decision to hide it leads to ongoing deceptions.

Their night *dates* seem to be bringing them back together, and their marriage appears to be healing itself … until Aubrey suddenly finds that *she's* the one in this marriage who's in for a rude awakening when Nick discovers the dark secret she's been keeping.

Nick and Aubrey's story will intrigue and enchant—and make readers wonder if love gets in the way of life … or if life gets in the way of love.

McNamee, Jeanne; Pillow Talk

McNamee, Jeanne; Pillow Talk (p.3) c. 2019

Ebook ISBN # 978-0-9984118-6-6

Paperback ISBN # 978-0-9984118-7-3

Other Novels by Jeanne McNamee

My Sister's Secrets

Karma Debt Book One: The Awakening

Karma Debt Book Two: The Revelation

And

Coming November 2019:

The First Noel

CONTENTS

DEDICATION

For My Daughters,

Ashley, Allison, and Katie:

To Each of You . . .

I love you, I value you, & I am eternally proud of you.

xoxoxo

ACKNOWLEDGEMENTS

Thanks to my readers and followers on Facebook, Goodreads, Twitter, and Amazon. I am so grateful for your loyalty and support!

To my friends and extended family; love and thanks for continuing to read what I am writing. I'm so lucky to have each of you in my corner.

Special thanks to Michele Daniels for traveling with me to book club gigs and acting as my personal assistant. Also, thanks to my friend Gigi Larsen, for dropping all your Christmas obligations to read this in an evening, when I desperately needed feedback—you rock! I love both of you, ladies!

Gratitude and love to my friend, Dawn Marshall. Thanks for being my videographer, photographer, and Thelma to my Louise. I couldn't imagine this ride without you.

Tons of thanks to my editor, Julie at Beach House Editors (www.beachhouseeditors.com). As it turned out, this was such a difficult story to tell. You were spot on in your suggestions to invest the reader in Aubrey's outcome. You have been—and continue to be—amazing. I can't tell you how much I appreciate how much of your own personal talent and patience you invest in me to help me tell my stories. Thanks for your understanding as I tried to make this story the best it could be!

I'd be amiss if I failed to send an angelic shout out to my *Badass Manifesters*: (alphabetically) Ashley Gordon, Valeri McLaughlin, and Colleen St. Michaels. Thanks for putting together the *Align Retreat* of 2018. In past novels, I've acknowledged a doctor who healed my body and a counselor who healed my mind. Today, I shout huge thanks and send love from my heart to these incredible women for helping me to heal my soul. I am, indeed, aligned. You all rock!

My heart is full of love for my parents, Gene and Kathy Anderson. Thanks for cheering for me on this journey.

As always, thanks to our children: Jim III, Ashley, Allison, Katie, Bob, Josh, and Zack for your perpetual support and love. Also, a huge shout out to my sons-in-law & daughters-in-law (and to my "almosts") who support and love those that mean the most to me; Alexis, Vin, Jeff, Tom, Natalie, Dani, & Tori. I love you all.

Huge Nana hugs to my grandchildren who fill my heart with joy … Eli, Kenzie, Sydney, Nora, Cameron, Carter, Juliette, and Lucy.

Last—but never least—thanks to my husband, Jim. I'm sorry for all the nights my *parasomniac-self* has woken you (and kept you awake for long periods of time, as I kissed you all over your head to profess—over and over again— my everlasting love for you). As you are aware, that's where the idea for this novel was born. You've been a great sport. I love you.

Prologue

Once upon a time ... Now, isn't that the way all stories—or, at least those ending in *happily ever after*—naturally begin? I used to think so, but that was back when I was young, naïve, and believed in the notion of people actually living *happily ever after*. And, that was long before, well ... *my own* marriage happened.

I'm reasonably certain that the beginning of my story is no different than most of my married, female counterparts. Feeling like a twenty-five-year-old princess, I showed up at the church on my wedding day in a white bridal gown mimicking the one I'd dreamt of wearing since I was just a little girl. There were friends, flowers, family members, and magnificent, thundering church organs. Oh, and, of course, not to be forgotten ... there was also a groom.

I was entirely prepared to present myself to the man of my dreams, knowing he'd already assured me: I was the woman of his. If I'm to be honest here, and, with all that's happened, I'm really trying to be ... I technically wasn't *pure* enough to be wearing white, to begin with, but, to be fair, no one was aware of that fact more than my husband-to-be.

No, Nick and I had consummated our relationship long before I made my appearance at the back of that church, hooked on the arm of my father, fifteen years ago. We both more than understood—I wouldn't be the nervous bride hiding out in the bathroom on our wedding night.

The truth was, back in those days, we simply couldn't keep our hands off each other. We'd met in our last year of college at Rowan University. I was a Democrat, and Nick was a Republican (I didn't hold that against him, and later converted him). After a few dates, and not too long after we'd met, we were headed home on board a Greyhound bus from a political rally we'd attended together in Washington D.C.

After a long day of mutual flirtation, we'd ended up having sex in the bathroom at the back of the bus. Who would have believed Bush and Gore could ever have been that arousing? We realized we were kindred spirits. Well, I guess at that time, kindred … at least on a sexual level.

And so, the *sex challenges* began …. We were doing *it* in all kinds of crazy places. It was our game: always daring one another into the next insane location to have sex … and whichever of us was the first to decline to do the deed—in the selected setting—would forever be crowned *the loser*.

Forever is a big sentence. It almost rhymes with *life in prison*.

Considering the stakes, in a brief period of time, we'd managed to christen most of southern New Jersey. It began on the toasty-warm roof of the local baseball league dugouts, just after sundown. If that wasn't enough, we'd gotten sand in our most personal crevices on deserted beaches in the middle of the night, as the waves rolled onto the shore. And we didn't apologize when we tainted a park bench on a local fishing pier. Nick and I both broke out in poison ivy after rolling around on a blanket we'd carelessly tossed on top of a bed of pine needles, off a random back trail in the Pinelands. We even managed to have sex in motion while riding a Ferris wheel on Morey's Pier in Wildwood. On that particular occasion, we'd both agreed … it'd felt like we were flying.

Our adrenaline rushed, our hormones steamed, and our hearts raced as we tangled our limbs into crazy positions … all in the name of taking a risk and pushing our passion for danger over the top. The danger lay in our mutual fear of getting caught.

It wasn't until we'd hit the skies, on the way to our honeymoon, when we were finally able to claim membership into the ever-elusive *Mile-High Club.* At thirty thousand feet, inside of a bathroom onboard a 737, we finally knew how it really felt to have sex while flying. I'd like to say the sex graduated into a more mature *making love* at that point in time, but it didn't. Let's face it, when you're in a three-foot by three-foot bathroom, with one foot propped on the toilet seat and your backside teetering on the edge of a two-foot-long countertop doing *it* … it's just sex, pure and simple. *Lovemaking* would have been a far too proper term.

All these years later, it's hard to believe that it was Nick and me. But it's true. Once upon a time, I adored him. With thick black hair, sapphire eyes, and a body that would make any red-blooded heterosexual gal drool, Nick was irresistible. He was sexy in so many ways. Quite frankly, to other women, he probably still is.

Mostly, I believed him to be absolutely perfect because he was so totally in love with me. He was mine, and I was his, and we were both fully convinced our love would last forever.

If I recall correctly, the *sex challenge* game ended not long after we'd married, when Nicky challenged me to have sex on a church balcony. I'd refused. As adventuresome and daring as I was, that was just too weird and over-the-top for me. Sex in God's house? Not on your life. So, technically, I caved first ... Nicky won.

I stopped calling him *Nicky* a long time ago. It was probably around the same time I stopped loving him. Well, I guess, theoretically, I still *loved* him. I just wasn't *in love* with him anymore. We'd lost each other along the way somehow. It was so long ago, I'd really stopped being convinced we'd ever *had* each other in the first place.

After graduating from college, each of us got a real job, we bought a house and got married. We did all the things you're supposed to do when you become an adult. We thought we were on the responsible and perfect road to happiness. But, after we'd added two kids and a dog, our attachment—and our affection—for each other became blurrier.

At the end of the day, we'd landed ourselves on the expressway to boredom. You know the thing no one tells you about when you're getting married and settling into adulthood? It's that taking on all those grownup responsibilities doesn't mean you have to stop having fun. It was definitely a real-life lesson we'd collectively somehow managed to miss out on.

Don't get me wrong. There were some playful times after we got married. Like just after we'd bought our new house ... before kids. There was this one time when we were painting the dining room, Nick had accidentally knocked over about a half a gallon of gray paint. It quickly spread across the hardwood floor. I started to give him a hard time, you know, *money doesn't grow on trees* and all that. So, he'd grabbed me, stripped off the romper I was wearing, while kissing me all over my face, and lowered my naked body right on top of the spill. Well, one thing led to another and the next thing you know we were rolling around on the chilly floor, leaving painted impressions of our derrières —and other unmentionable parts—on the hardwood. Afterward, and by the time we'd returned from washing the paint from our bodies, the imprints on the floor had nearly dried. In spite of myself, that memory still makes me smile.

Ultimately, we'd ended up having to carpet the dining room. Both our dining room table and china cabinet were situated on top of the rug—covering the evidence of our abstract portrait from that afternoon romp—clear up until the day we sold it. Who knows? Maybe it's still there. How odd would it be if *that* had actually outlasted *us*?

In recent years, more times than I'd care to admit, I've wished I could go back to our old house to pull the carpet up, just to make sure our body art was really there. To prove to myself that it'd actually ever happened at all. That those two crazy-in-love people were really Nick and me.

Which brings me to now ...

And, to what I've done.

Some might consider my actions to be worth prosecuting or, at the very least, deem them morally obscene.

Some might declare me desperate, a disgrace, and even a liar.

Or, perhaps, in the most minimal terms … a liar by my omissions.

In that regard, I should apologize for the things I've done since I'm not particularly proud of them. But I can't.

I'd even considered defending myself now by saying I did what I did for my kids. But, truthfully? I didn't.

The fact is—even though I understand anyone who hears my story will believe me to be nothing short of a criminal—all I really wanted was to feel loved, less lonely, and desirable again.

I wanted to *belong* with somebody. *To* somebody.

I wanted to feel completely invested in something again. I missed having a partner, a lover, and the apparition of a lifelong best friend.

So, before people judge me, I welcome them to try jamming their feet into my shoes. What if this was *their* life? I'd tell them to consider what they'd do … how far they'd go. What if the marriage in which they'd been investing all their efforts into—for the past fifteen years—was going entirely off the rails? Would they pull out all the stops? Bend a moral rule or two? Think about it.

Either way, whichever camp people fall into—*she was wrong … she was right*—this is *my* tale and the story of how it all ended.

As for me? I hate to say it, but I really do have to admit … I'd do everything exactly the way I did it, all over again.

Chapter One

Aubrey Henson tip-toed to lean across the stainless steel sink and gaze out from the garden-style, panoramic kitchen window overlooking the lagoon. She was grateful for the beautiful view from their reverse living home. The kitchen, great room, and dining room were all located on the upper floor, affording all the best views from the rooms where they spent most of their time. The bedrooms and laundry room were one floor down, and a bonus room and two-car garage were located on the lowest level.

Chunks of ice still bobbed on the surface of the chilly salt water. The mooring whips, which, during the summer season, attached to their pontoon boat to keep it from crashing into the dock, were nodding in the air looking like abandoned fishing rods. The January sky was gray, and the worst of winter was just getting started. Even the cheerful, white kitchen cabinets circling the room, matching those which made up the island in the center, couldn't adequately brighten the dreary space.

Waterfront living had been a dream for Aubrey and her husband, Nick. They'd been thrilled when they'd sold their first house, after just five years of marriage, and moved into their new home on Mystic Island, New Jersey. It had been an even a greater rush when they'd purchased their twenty-four-foot pontoon boat, and first pulling it up to secure it to their brand new dock. Aubrey could still picture the way Nick had looked at her when he'd smashed the pre-scored bottle of champagne on the bow, officially christening her the *Aubrey Lyn.*

For many summers now, they'd boated, swam, paddle boarded, kayaked, or simply entertained friends and family on one of the three multi-level decks facing the lagoon. The feeling of the warm sun on their skin, the smell of barbequed chicken on the grill, the sight of boats meandering past their dock in the *no wake zone,* the sounds of ships' bells clanging, and the taste of the salty breeze had all blissfully teased their senses during the last ten summers.

In contrast, the winters were always rough here. Seemingly endless days of sunless, dismal skies, coupled with the cold, damp sea air, always brought Aubrey down. December's dark days rolled into a bitter, cold January which only served to further dampen her mood.

After ringing in the new year, the realization had hit her … in spite of multiple counseling sessions she and Nick had attended over the last several months, each one more disastrous than the last, her marriage was very much on the metaphorical rocks. Aubrey had no idea how things had completely fallen apart. Absorbing *that* reality dragged her spirit to a whole new low.

A while after Aubrey poured her freshly brewed coffee into a mug, Peyton came moping into the kitchen. She waved her hand toward her mother's cup. "Mom, I'm beat. Can you pour me a coffee, too?" Without waiting for an answer from her mother, she strolled over and grabbed a box of cereal from the pantry, stopped at the refrigerator for milk, and headed for the table and the stack of bowls and spoons that were waiting there.

Aubrey's thirteen-year-old brown-haired, brown-eyed first-born was a challenge, and they'd suffered more than their share of arguments. Consequently, Aubrey was learning to pick her battles. She shook her head and rolled her eyes before grabbing another cup from the cabinet and filling it with coffee. "You know I don't like you drinking coffee, Peyton. It's too much caffeine. You're too young."

Delivering the cup to the table, Aubrey was not at all surprised when Peyton offered no more than a twist of her mouth and a shrug of her shoulders. The truth was … on the first day back to school following their long holiday break, Aubrey hadn't expected much in the way of conversation from her teenage daughter.

Walking away to retrieve her own coffee, Aubrey sighed as Peyton propped the cereal box against the floral decoration in the center of the table and stared at the back of the box. There was no way she was actually reading it, as she'd done this enough times in the past to have memorized the text.

Just as Aubrey brought her cup to her lips, Teddy walked into the room. Named after her dad, Theodore Simon, at ten years old, he was the spitting image of Aubrey. Well, except for his eyes … they weren't the color of caramel like hers. Instead, they shimmered deep, crystalline blue, identical to those of his father.

Placing her cup back onto the dark granite countertop, Aubrey realized it would likely be cold by the time she was able to drink it. It was only a touch above warm right now. This was the story of her life.

Crossing the room, she tousled Teddy's thick blonde hair. "Hey, kiddo, good morning."

Teddy glanced up at her, squinted his eyes, and grinned. "I don't think it's so good, Mom. I wish winter vacation wasn't over."

Grateful for his congeniality, Aubrey pulled him in for a hug. "Look at the bright side, honey. At least it's already Tuesday, and this is only a four-day week for you. Go ahead and grab whatever cereal you want for breakfast. Bowls are on the table."

As soon as Aubrey had finished delivering marching orders to Teddy, Nick walked in, appearing tired. It was no surprise. Aubrey knew Nick hadn't slept well, as his tossing and turning had served to continuously awaken her all night.

Aubrey guessed he must have had meetings lined up. Nick didn't usually go to the office in a full suit and tie. Today, carrying his leather briefcase, he was all decked out in a dark gray Brooks Brothers 1818 Fitzgerald fit two-button suit and tie. In black Gucci loafers and a shirt the color of Hydrangeas, which lit up his eyes, Nick dazzled. Well, that was right up until he spoke, reminding Aubrey exactly why she didn't like him very much anymore.

Not looking directly at her, which was typical of how he behaved toward Aubrey lately, Nick cleared his throat before speaking. "I know I said I'd get the kids to school today, but I have an early meeting I have to get to. You'll have to take them."

For the last several years, ever since Nick had taken the position of CEO at a prestigious accounting firm, he'd become so unreliable. Aubrey had to restrain herself from stomping her foot like a child. "Darn it, Nick! I told you I was meeting Libby for lunch today. I have errands I have to run this morning. If you'd told me last night, I'd have taken my shower already. Now I'll have to run the kids, come back to get a shower, and I won't be able to finish all I needed to do."

Nick walked over to the table where the kids were sitting. Apparently not knowing what to expect, even the dog ran under the table and cowered. Aubrey could tell Nick wasn't listening anymore. Instead, he was merely waiting for her to stop talking so he could say goodbye to them.

Standing behind Peyton's chair, he shot back over his shoulder, "So, cancel with Libby. She'll understand."

Slightly raising her voice, Aubrey said, "I'm not canceling. We have reservations in Philly. You know we do this every year on the day the kids go back to school after winter break! This isn't fair, Nick." Confrontation made her stomach hurt, so it was not a surprise when she suddenly began to feel knots forming in her gut.

Libby White and Aubrey had been best friends since high school. Libby had been Aubrey's maid of honor at her wedding and was Peyton's godmother. She was the only person in the world with whom Aubrey could share her darkest secrets … and fears.

She literally *needed* this time. It was the equivalent of free therapy. Not only that, she knew Libby felt the same way. Besides,

Libby was divorced and had recently begun to date a new guy. Aubrey couldn't wait to hear all the gory details so she could live vicariously through her friend. Sadly, it was something she'd perfectly mastered lately.

Aubrey watched as Nick kissed Peyton on top of her head. "See you later." Back when they were all happy, he used to add little nicknames. He'd called her *kitten* or *princess*. These days, Nick was so miserable, it felt as though he hated them all.

Peyton smiled weakly. "Bye, Daddy." While her relationship with her mother appeared to drain her these days, Peyton seemed to still be willing to put her efforts into attempting to reclaim her position as *daddy's little girl*. No doubt, Peyton had no clue as to why she'd fallen from grace. Aubrey felt sorry for her. Actually, she felt sorry for all of them.

As Nick rounded the table, he threw his free hand in the air. "I don't know what you want me to do, Au-brey. You always start this crap with me." He shook his head and waved her off. "You'll just have to figure it out."

She shuddered. Aubrey hated how her name rolled off his tongue like Draino these days. Hearing him say it felt caustic to her ears. It was a far cry from when they'd first fallen in love, and Nick would speak her name … back then, it'd almost sounded like the melody to a song just floating in the space between them.

When Nick approached Teddy, his son perked up. "Hey, Dad! Guess what? I just finished building my model of Hogwarts Castle in Minecraft last night! And, I did it in survival mode!" Teddy beamed.

"Uh, huh. I'll see you later, buddy." Nick leaned down and pecked his son on the head.

"I'll see you later, buddy?" Aubrey's tone clearly indicated she was more than annoyed. "How about saying, *hey, Teddy, we don't play video games on a school night, remember, buddy?*"

Teddy shifted his gaze from his dad to his mom and back again.

Aubrey knew she sounded whiny, but she was sick and tired of always being the bad guy. Nick was barely home anymore, and when he was, he acted as though he were one of Peyton and Teddy's friends, leaving the crappy discipline stuff for her to handle. That, or he'd ignore the children altogether.

Nick rolled his eyes, clenched his jaw, and shook his head as he crossed the kitchen. "I'll see you all tonight."

As usual, there'd be no kiss goodbye for Aubrey. Nick had stopped doling those out months ago.

Hearing the door slam, Aubrey turned her attention back to the kids. "Get your backpacks. We need to get going. Meet me at the front door in five."

Agitated, Aubrey almost failed to notice the tears in Teddy's eyes. "Hey, Ted, are you okay? What's up, kiddo?"

Teddy's lip quivered. "Are you and dad going to get a divorce?"

Crossing over to the table, Aubrey saw Peyton raise an eyebrow and glance in their direction. She leaned over and placed her hands on each of Teddy's shoulders to squeeze them. "No, sweetie, we're fine. Sometimes moms and dads just fight about things. It'll be alright."

The lie tasted like straight vinegar crossing her lips. Aubrey hoped Teddy wouldn't ask her to stick out her tongue like she'd done to him when he was little. If Aubrey had thought the kids weren't telling the truth, she'd ask them to stick out their tongue. If Peyton or Teddy were lying, they'd reluctantly only show the smallest piece of their tongue through pursed lips. Knowing that meant they weren't answering truthfully, Aubrey would proclaim she could see *the devil dancing* on their tongue. If they opened their mouth wide and stuck their tongue way out, Aubrey knew they were telling the truth and would announce *there's no devil there!* It was a trick used on her, as a child, by her own mother.

Swinging his legs around to the side of the chair, Teddy wrapped his arms around Aubrey's neck. "Please, Mom. Please don't divorce my dad. When Billy Ray's mom and dad got divorced, they fought so much he used to come to school with stomachaches every day. I know dad can be mean, but you have to promise me you'll still love him and stay married to him." Teddy leaned back, with eyes locked on hers and tears streaming down his face, waiting for his mother to reassure him.

The lump in Aubrey's throat throbbed, and she could feel Peyton's stare boring a hole into the side of her face. Billy Ray was one of Teddy's best friends. She knew all about the horrible divorce between his parents. Everybody did. Aubrey had literally witnessed Billy's little arms stretched out as one parent pulled his one hand and the other parent tugged on the other at the end of a school function, each wanting the little boy to join them for photographs, and neither backing down. It looked as though they might literally rip the boy into two pieces. That poor child stood between his parents—who were supposed to protect him—with his eyes pinched closed, no doubt to block out the stares of the other appalled parents and his peers who were witnessing the spectacle. Eventually, Billy Ray's dad just disappeared from all school events.

Lately, Nick was behaving so selfishly and emotionally removed she wasn't sure that he wouldn't just do the same, leaving both her *and* their children. After all, Nick had already halted his attendance at their sports and school functions more than a year earlier. Still … her own miniature devil danced and practically pirouetted its way out of her mouth. "Oh, honey, I promise you, we'll be okay. I will do anything I have to do to keep our family together. Anything."

Swiping his hands across his wet cheeks, Teddy nodded. "I know you will, Mom. I'm just scared. I can't be one of those divorced kids. I just can't, Mom. I'll try to be really good. I won't play video games at night anymore. Just, please … keep our family together."

Wrapping her arms around her son, she said the only thing she knew to say. Aubrey promised, "Teddy, that will never happen to us. We're going to be just fine."

She leaned back, stared him in the eye, and nodded her head. "We *are* fine. Let's get going now. You're going to be late for school." Aubrey stood and pulled Teddy to a stand. "Go on. Get your stuff together." Glancing over Teddy's shoulder, Aubrey didn't miss

Peyton's reaction as she shoved her chair away from the table, stood up, and frowned, before following Teddy downstairs.

Aubrey hustled down the steps behind the children, stopping in her bedroom to grab her purse and change out of her slippers. She was upset about Teddy and annoyed with Nick as she scurried into their walk-in closet to snag something to put on her feet. Out of the corner of her eye—on Nick's side of the closet—she saw his planner on the floor. Aubrey assumed it must have fallen from the side pocket of his briefcase. She hurriedly picked up a pair of her riding boots before scooping up the leather-bound book.

Tossing the planner onto the top of Nick's dresser, Aubrey quickly moved to sit on the bed to put her boots on. Once she had one boot on, Aubrey made her way to the door, hopping along as she tried to finish pulling the second one onto her foot. She grabbed her purse from the hook on the back of the bedroom door and started for the hallway. But something stopped her and caused her to take pause. Then, for reasons she couldn't explain, she turned back to retrieve the planner, opening it to the month of January.

Scanning the pre-printed time slots for today's date, the hair on the back of Aubrey's neck stood up when she saw the eight o'clock A.M. entry … *John Jackson, Esq.*

Aubrey's heart skipped a beat, as she closed the book and backtracked to toss it back onto the closet floor where she'd found it, so Nick wouldn't know she'd seen it.

Her thoughts paralyzed her with fear, and her insides tightened. In spite of the promise Aubrey had just made to her son, the sick realization came over her … *Nick was actually filing for divorce.*

Chapter Two

After dropping the kids at school, the drive to meet Libby in the city afforded Aubrey time to think. While she knew things weren't going well, she never believed Nick would go behind her back and—without warning—contact an attorney. Even though she feared the whole *divorce thing* was fast approaching, Aubrey thought they'd sit down like adults and talk about it before either would move to hire representation. It made her feel ill. Even as she spoke to Teddy this morning, seeing him so upset made her realize that she and Nick just had to try harder to make their marriage work. As Aubrey made the promise to Teddy that she'd do whatever she had to do, she'd decided right then and there, she'd talk to Nick tonight.

When she finally arrived at the restaurant and found a parking spot, Libby was waiting in the vestibule. Their table was ready, and an overly friendly hostess led the way before leaving menus and telling them a server would be with them shortly.

Aubrey had barely seated herself when a wide-eyed Libby blurted out, "Aubrey, you look absolutely spooked! Are you alright?"

"Shhh," Aubrey warned. "The people three tables over just turned around when they heard you say that." She settled herself on the chair.

Lowering her voice, Libby leaned in. "Well, you're so pale. Did you run somebody over on the way here? What's happened?"

Aubrey shifted on the seat, barely able to speak the words that nauseated her. "As we speak, I think Nick is consulting with a divorce attorney. I knew nothing about the whole thing before this morning. I saw the appointment written down in his planner."

"You've got to be kidding me. Without telling you?" Libby was shaking her head. She swept a handful of her chestnut hair around to the front where she began to twirl it. Aubrey couldn't help but notice, in her Bohemian cream-colored cheesecloth smock and deliberately worn out, torn blue jeans, Libby looked as though she may have fallen right out of a nineteen-seventies fashion magazine.

"Yes, without telling me. Nick bailed on taking the kids to school this morning after he said he would take care of it. He knew I had plans with you today. I went into our closet to get my boots, and his planner had been left behind on the floor. My guess is it fell out of the outer pocket of his briefcase, and he didn't realize it. At first, I'd just tossed it onto his dresser so he could find it when he got home. But something told me to go back and look at it. So, I did. Sure enough, he had an appointment with an attorney at eight o'clock this morning." Aubrey slouched against the back of her chair.

Libby's emerald eyes widened. "Well, maybe it was something for work. I mean … Nick wouldn't file for divorce without saying something. Right? You guys have been going to a counselor. It doesn't make sense."

Aubrey's mouth was as dry as the dust in an old boarded up house. She didn't know what to think. "Actually, Nick bailed on the last two counseling sessions. I guess I should have known something was up. All I know now is that Nick was supposed to take the kids to school as of last evening. By this morning, he had a meeting that he was all decked out for … a meeting that clearly wasn't on the calendar at the end of his day yesterday when he'd agreed to take the kids to school." She picked up her napkin from the table, unfolded it, and dropped it onto her lap.

Libby cocked her head to the side. "Do you remember the attorney's name? Like, did you google him?"

Pulling her phone from her purse and entering her password, Aubrey answered, "No, but I can do that right now." Her hands were shaking as she searched for *New Jersey lawyer John Jackson,* and found his website. Her heart sunk like a lead balloon into the pit of her stomach as the site's homepage loaded, confirming her worst fears. Mr. Jackson was indeed one of the area's finest divorce attorneys. Aubrey passed her phone across the table to Libby.

Glancing at the screen, Libby slapped her free palm against her forehead. She handed Aubrey's phone back to her. "Oh, my gosh … I can't believe this. What a jerk. Don't people usually sit down and say, *hey, I want a divorce.* Isn't there some etiquette for this? I mean, what would Miss Manners say?" Libby paused and narrowed her eyes. "What are you going to do?"

After throwing both of her hands in the air, Aubrey buried her face in them. "I have no idea. I mean, I knew this was a possibility at some point this year, but I didn't think it would be now. I don't know, Libby, maybe Nick was just waiting for the holidays to pass. The Christmas decorations were just packed away two days ago. And, now, here we are."

Libby raised her shoulders. "Well, there is a bright side you know."

Shifting in her chair, Aubrey raised her eyebrows. "Bright side?"

"Sure." Libby's voice was a matter of fact. "If he divorces you, you'll be able to meet someone else and finally have sex again. There's that."

Aubrey's mouth and eyes opened wide, and it took a minute before she could even speak. "Libby!"

Laughing, Libby shrugged. "What? It's been how long … like seven months since you've *done the dirty*. Jeez, Aubrey, you're going to shrivel up down there."

Pointing at Libby, Aubrey stammered, "I … uh … can't even believe you just said that to me."

When a waitress arrived at their table, they were forced to discontinue their conversation. Once she'd taken their drink order and walked away, Libby spoke first. "Oh, come on, Aubrey. You don't want to be with Nick. So, what's the big deal? Why not go for the divorce and free your lady bits?" This time, Libby threw her head back, laughing.

"I can't believe you're behaving so insensitively to this. This is my life. My husband is divorcing me, and my best friend is making jokes about my lady bits. There's something wrong with this scene." Aubrey slouched further down into her seat and closed her eyes. She'd known Libby long enough to understand that she tended to use humor to deal with the unpleasant parts of life, but Aubrey wasn't in the mood for it today. Still, she knew the value of their friendship. Libby was the kind of friend Aubrey could call and say, *There's a dead body* and Libby would respond, *I'm on my way. Do I need to bring one shovel or two?*

"Oh, come on, Aubrey." Libby rolled her eyes. "I didn't mean anything by it. I just think you've wasted more than enough time trying to fix something when only half of that something is in your control. Nick's been terrible to you—and the kids, for that matter—for a really, really long time now. What you're doing is like trying to glue a broken vase back together when one of the pieces is missing. It's never going to be the perfect vase that it was before you dropped it. And, it'll never hold water again. Frankly, I'm not sure why *you* haven't consulted an attorney. Look at the life you've been living. I mean Nick's been downright nasty to you. He totally ignores you most of the time. You live like a single mom. What kind of life is that anyway?"

Aubrey knew Libby was right. The truth was, Nick was no more than her roommate, and Aubrey was living the life of a single mother. She'd become the chief cook, activity director, and taxi driver a long time ago. So long ago, she could hardly remember the time when she'd last considered her and Nick to be a real couple, nevermind a team. Still, it was hard for Aubrey to accept the idea that she would end up divorced. And, it was frustrating because it wasn't like there was a big thing that had happened. You hear about couples who have affairs or one of the partners drinks too much, overspends, gambles, or something like that. None of those things applied to her and Nick. Like a houseplant that dies because no one remembered to water it, Aubrey and Nick's marriage just wilted away one day at a time. Nowadays, it felt like everything Aubrey did only served to irritate Nick.

Aubrey shrugged. "I guess I just thought that counseling would help. That was easier to believe than accepting I was going to be divorced. I mean, I imagine at some point I realized it wasn't *really* helping. But …" She closed her eyes and shook her head. "The kids will be devastated. Nick and I went back and forth with each other this morning, and Teddy was a wreck after Nick left. He begged me not to divorce his dad."

Libby took a deep breath, exhaled, and reached across the table to grab Aubrey's hand. "Oh, honey, kids are resilient. You know that. It's quite likely they'll adjust to divorce long before you do. And, at the end of the day, kids grow to *like* having two Christmases. It's sad, but it's true."

Drawing her hand back, Aubrey twisted her wedding ring around her finger. "I know. But I'd believed I'd had the fairytale. I guess I just thought that we were going through hard times like other couples experience. Marriages rebound. I didn't think we were at the end of our time together. Or, at least I hadn't fully accepted that we were. Oh, I don't know, Libby. It's one thing to think about divorce or even to talk about it … it's quite another to be faced with the reality of it coming to fruition."

The waitress returned and placed a glass of wine on the table in front of each of them. She asked if they were ready to order. Libby told her they needed a few more minutes. The girl smiled and told them to take their time. The restaurant wasn't crowded at all, so it didn't appear as though they really needed to rush anyway.

Often the more practical one of the two, Libby raised her eyebrows. "You know, you're not even crying about this. Not one tear. Do you think on some deeper level you really understood this is where your marriage was going? Maybe even *wanted* it to go?"

Aubrey took a sip of wine before returning the glass to the table and sliding her fingers up and down the stem. "Well, sure. I was thinking about it just this morning—before I saw the planner. It still doesn't make it easy. And crying? You know better than anyone, I've cried buckets over slowly losing Nick … what we had … who we were. I've had more than one funeral, followed by a personal pity party, for my life's dreams."

Libby's voice was soft. "I know. I know you have and I'm sorry. But, if this is a bankrupt situation you're in … then, I think you need to stop investing yourself in it. You have too much life left to enjoy. You need to return to living it."

As much as Aubrey hated to admit it, she knew Libby understood better than anyone. Before she'd moved to her house on the outskirts of Philadelphia, Libby had been happily married, living in the suburbs of New Jersey. Well, at least she'd *thought* she was happily married.

About four years ago, Libby was in Aubrey's shoes. Or, almost. In Libby's case, she'd been blindsided when her husband, Austin, came home from work one evening and announced he didn't want to be married anymore. It wasn't that he'd found someone else. It wasn't even as though they'd fought a whole lot. They'd just sort of fallen into a pattern of coexisting, and Austin didn't want to do that any longer. Libby had offered to go to counseling. He'd declined, saying he just didn't love her anymore. At the time, Libby's kids were only ten and six years old. Her daughter, Elizabeth—Lizzie—was fourteen now, a year older than Peyton. Libby's son, Brody, was about to turn ten ... just like Teddy. Lizzie and Brody had turned out fine and seemed to be pretty well-adjusted.

Austin was fair in the divorce, even signing over their summer beach house to Libby since the kids were with her more often. It was located in Mystic, just two streets away from Aubrey's place. Things never became horrible. Therefore, Libby had maintained an amicable relationship with Austin ever since. Friendly divorce at its finest.

The waitress returned and dropped a bread basket with butter onto their table. They ordered another round of wine, a couple of salads, and a tuna wrap to share.

Aubrey folded her hands and rested them on the table. "Enough about this, for now. I need some happy stuff. Cheer me up. Tell me about mister new guy. I've been dying to hear about him."

Leaning forward, there was enthusiasm in Libby's voice as she shifted her attention to her own exciting life. "Oh, my God, he's amazing." Her eyes were wide as she held both hands in the air, fingers spread open. "His name is Jed. And, oh, Aubrey, he's fabulous. A perfect specimen of a man." Now, Libby was grinning and nodding. She looked as though she had a secret she wasn't giving up. But, Aubrey knew Libby, which meant *that* wouldn't last for long.

Tilting her head, Aubrey held up one finger. "Wait. Jed? Like the Beverly Hillbillies?" Smirking, gladly leaving her own problems behind for the moment, Aubrey started to bounce up and down in her seat, as she began to softly sing, ♫ *Come and listen to a story 'bout a man named Jed, poor mountaineer barely kept his family fed ...* ♪

Libby smacked her hand on the table. "You are darned right, *mountaineer ... mountain man* is more like it." She wagged her eyebrows up and down. "This man can sure fill out a pair of blue jeans ... back *and* front." Libby howled.

Aubrey closed her eyes and covered her ears, before returning her hands to rest on the table. "Jeez, Lib, I don't need to know all that. I do expect to *meet* him someday and to have to look him in the eye. You're too much."

"Speaking of too much ..." Libby pointed down at her own lap and raised her eyebrows. She started spinning her finger around in a circle, nodding, and pursing her lips. "He's definitely got more than any woman needs." Giggling, she leaned in again and swung her head from side to side, her hair sailing back and forth.

"Libby!" Aubrey looked around to see who might be listening in. Fortunately, the tables surrounding them were now empty. Still, she moved forward to whisper. "Did you actually *sleep* with him? I thought you said you've only been on a few dates?"

Libby answered using her best Mae West impersonation. "Oh, honey, there was no sleeping going on." Her laughter pliéd in the air.

"You broke all the rules. Don't you remember the rules? About the bases? First date: no base. Second date: first base … I mean, don't you remember the baseball diamond of dating rules?" While Aubrey was slightly shocked, she was more than a little amused, too. After all, she'd had her own experiences with adventurous sex, but she'd been far younger. Aubrey wanted to believe she'd do it a little differently at this age.

Mae West was back. "There were no thoughts of baseball rolling around in my head. Just muscles, sweat, and his …"

Aubrey winced and held her hand up. "Alright. Alright. But, I think you need to remember those rules until you determine if he's a potential serial killer or something."

Libby closed her eyes and dropped her head back. "What a way to die." She chuckled as she scooted herself upright.

As it turns out, it was just in time. The girl showed up with their food and refills on wine.

As soon as the waitress was out of earshot again, Aubrey spoke. "Just don't be foolish. And, it wouldn't hurt to use a little more discretion … play hard to get … you know what I mean."

Libby waved her off. "I'm forty-one years old. *Hard to get* is for the young girls. I'm erring on the *easy to get* side of life these days. That's why my folks named me Liberty … I'm all about freedom. Oh! And, I'm seeing him again tonight. Ooooh, Lord!" Grinning ear to ear, with eyes bulging, she hovered over her plate and sloppily jammed a forkful of salad into her mouth.

Aubrey laughed. "Yeah, right. Freedom. Your parents named you Liberty because you were born on the Fourth of July." She shook her head and twisted her mouth to the side. "Just be careful, would you?"

After they'd finished lunch and moved on to commiserating about the perils of raising teenaged girls, they finally parted ways at the front door of the restaurant because they'd parked in different garages. Aubrey told Libby she'd see her a week from Saturday in Mystic. January thirteenth was Brody's tenth birthday, and Libby was having a party for him. Actually, Aubrey's fortieth birthday was the day before, on January twelfth. Considering the circumstances, she already felt disappointed because she believed it was going to be a dud.

On the drive home, the reality of her circumstances set back in, and Aubrey ran through every possible scenario in her head. The more active part of her imagination had Nick waiting at the dining room table with divorce papers laid out in front of him. Another had Nick sitting on the end of their bed with a packed suitcase at his feet and a stack of divorce papers in his hand.

Aubrey drove as though she were on autopilot and couldn't stop her tears as memories began to chase her home. There was the time that Nick created this whole elaborate scavenger hunt to surprise her with a trip to Honolulu for their anniversary. She'd literally jumped into his arms when she found the tickets tucked inside their wedding album where he'd hidden them. The final clue Nick had given to her? *Tangible memories of the best day of Nick Henson's life.*

Recalling the times they'd taken their boat out at night, dropped anchor, and made love under the stars were the scenes flashing in Aubrey's mind. Then, Aubrey experienced a vivid replay of Nick standing next to her hospital bed, leaning in close, with their hands tightly laced together as they each held their breath waiting for Peyton to take her first and the shared joy when they heard Peyton's first cry and the tears they'd both shed when that beautiful sound bellowed across the room. The way Nicky's hand shook when he cut Teddy's umbilical cord, as though it were his first time doing so. And, the memory of standing outside the kids' bedrooms, quietly listening, as Nick sang them to sleep, warmed Aubrey right now.

Before this moment, Aubrey believed she wasn't in love with Nick anymore. But, digesting the prospect of their life together as being *over* was suddenly becoming more than she could handle. Over was just so final.

As she swung the car into the driveway and turned it off, Aubrey paused and wondered if it could be possible——no, even probable— on the very day Nick had likely had taken steps to file for divorce, she may very well have come to the realization … she was actually still *in love* with her husband.

Chapter Three

To Aubrey's surprise, Nick wasn't waiting for her when she got home. Not in the dining room, not in the bedroom. In fact, the house was empty.

Peyton and Teddy got in from school shortly after Aubrey had arrived home. Aubrey and the kids sat down at the kitchen table to eat a pizza she'd picked up. While the kids chatted about their respective days back at school, Nick got home and came into the kitchen and joined them. While he'd seemed distracted all through dinner, it'd been a shock when he'd sat down at the table with them at all. Typically, unless it was a special occasion, he either wasn't home or he'd make a plate for himself and head straight to his home office with it.

Studying Nick's demeanor, Aubrey wondered if he was just having dinner with his family sort of *trying them on* before giving them away. She did that with clothes before donating them. Aubrey would sometimes toss a dress into a bag as she cleaned out her closet at the end of the season. Suddenly, she'd second guess herself on one of them and retrieve it to try it on, only to confirm she really didn't want it and throwing it back into the bag again.

After everyone finished eating, the table was cleared, and the dishes were loaded into the dishwasher. As usual, Peyton took off to lock herself in her room, and Teddy followed not too long after. Nick grumbled something about work to do as he'd poured a glass of red wine. Picking up his glass and heading for the door, he didn't wait for Aubrey to respond.

Aubrey tapped her fingernails on the countertop and hesitated before speaking to Nick's back. "I thought we could revisit counseling. You know, we canceled the last couple of appointments." What she'd wanted to say was *you* canceled a few appointments, but she'd decided better of it and used the blameless *we*, instead.

Nick slowed his pace at the doorway, never even looking back at Aubrey. "I'm not wasting any more of my time."

"But, the kids …" Aubrey's voice broke. "Nick?"

He didn't so much as pause. Without answering, Nick shrugged and quietly walked away.

As the evening wore on, Nick never resurfaced. There was no mention of divorce or the mysterious last-minute appointment with the attorney this morning. Aubrey couldn't imagine what was looming and had felt on the edge of her seat. To her, it was like huddling in the bathtub waiting for a tornado that never materialized. But, enough fear had built up inside, as though it had.

Once ten o'clock rolled around, Aubrey finally exhaled. After spending the rest of the evening in front of the television in the living room, convinced there'd be no divorce conversation today, Aubrey decided to head to bed. Needing to silence her thoughts, she welcomed the idea of deep sleep and peaceful dreams.

Aubrey flipped the light switch on as she walked into their bedroom, but quickly turned it off again when she realized Nick was already in bed, sleeping. It caught her by surprise since he never came to bed this early. In fact, he'd often stay holed up in his office until nearly midnight.

As she quietly crossed the room to the bathroom, Aubrey wondered if perhaps Nick wasn't feeling well. He was a creature of habit, so she suspected something was going on with Nick for him to already be sound asleep at this hour.

Aubrey's uneasiness heightened. Part of her wanted to wake Nick up and ask him if they could just start over ... just forget all about this miserable time they'd been having. In the real world, she knew it wasn't that easy and—more likely than not—just too late to turn back time. After the memories of their good times came flooding back this afternoon, she'd realized how much she'd missed him. His touch. Their intimacy. Even Nick's coldness earlier didn't seem to erase Aubrey's yearning. Rather, at the time, it had just served to crush her spirit.

Ducking into the bathroom, Aubrey closed the door before turning on the light. Having just come from the complete darkness, she squinted at its brightness. The tile floor was cold on her bare feet. The pajamas she'd taken off this morning hung on the back of the bathroom door. Aubrey shimmied out of her clothes and finished getting ready for bed.

Leaning in over the sink, she looked at herself in the mirror. Aubrey was tired and the face staring back at her reflected that more than she'd have liked to admit. Her *elevens* were deep today. Using her thumb and forefinger, she stretched the vertical lines between her brows, smoothing them. Aubrey frowned, shook her head, and turned away from the exhausted version of herself.

She turned out the light before opening the door. Aubrey was quiet when she slid into bed, rolling onto her side, careful not to move her body too close to Nick's. His slow and steady breathing served to congratulate her on not waking him up.

A dream began to entice Aubrey into a deeper realm of sleep, but her eyes shot open when she suddenly felt Nick's arm wrapped around her middle to drag her closer to him. Her heart shot into her throat, and she felt like all four of her limbs were cemented in place. Drowsiness prohibited her from thinking quickly. Before Aubrey could grip what was happening, Nick purred behind her as he nuzzled his face into her hair.

"Hmm. I'm glad you finally came to bed. I've been waiting for you." Nick kissed her neck.

Blinking three times, Aubrey reassured herself she wasn't sleeping. This wasn't a dream. Nick—who hadn't so much as touched her in more than seven months—was now grinding his pelvis against her backside.

Nick lifted a lock of her hair and started twisting it around his finger. "Do you know you're the best thing that's ever happened to me? I'm so lucky I have you."

Aubrey didn't move and didn't speak. She couldn't seem to find her voice. *What on earth is going on here?* She wondered. *Exactly what is Nick up to?* She concluded he must've had more wine tonight than she'd realized. Way more.

Seeming to ignore the fact that Aubrey was speechless, Nick continued, "You are so sexy. I love how you feel." His hands followed the suggestion of the sentiment.

Unable to take it anymore, Aubrey rolled to face Nick. Thanks to a touch of light radiating through the blinds from a nearby streetlamp, she could just about make out his face in the dark. To Aubrey's shock, his expression was warm. Nick's eyes seemed a little glassy, but he was looking at her in a way Aubrey hadn't witnessed since … she couldn't remember when.

Aubrey's eyes narrowed and, to her own surprise, her voice quivered. "What's going on, Nick? What's this all about?"

Propping himself up on one arm, with his cheek resting on his open hand, Nick used the other to run his fingers across Aubrey's face. "Can't I just appreciate my amazing bride?" Nick sighed. "God, you're beautiful." He leaned in and landed his lips on Aubrey's.

She wanted to protest, demand Nick explain himself. Make him describe where this renewed affection was coming from … accuse him of being drunk. Aubrey wanted to argue that just because he wanted her now … didn't mean she wanted him. She'd been rejected by Nick time and time again over these last few years. There'd been many occasions when she'd snuggle in close to Nick's back, hoping and praying to rekindle some sort of connection with him and he'd literally shrugged her off and—without so much as looking at her—mumbled *goodnight*.

Aubrey had finally learned to close herself off from his coldness. Over time, like a trained dolphin, she'd mastered the ability to stop reaching out. It'd saved her tons of disappointment and those God awful feelings of utter rejection. There were plenty of times when she'd needed the closeness Nick was offering to her now, but he hadn't cared. On too many nights to count, Aubrey had stared at the ceiling, her body yearning for Nick's, as he'd slept only inches away from her.

In spite of all that, right now, Aubrey's desire took over. She *had* wanted him. Until tonight, Aubrey hadn't even realized how desperately she'd missed being touched. His touch. So, she arched her back and devoured his kiss. God help her. Aubrey wanted it all and was willing to leave the explanations for another day.

Without warning, Nick suddenly rolled away. He lowered his head back onto his pillow and stared at the ceiling. Aubrey's heart skipped a beat before he reached over, grabbed her hand, his smile glowing in the darkness. "You really are terrific, Aubrey."

There it was … her name … dancing in the air like a melody from a favorite old song. Nothing corroded the space between them tonight.

Aubrey turned her head to face him, to tell him how badly she wanted their old life back, to tell him she's missed how they used to be the perfect *us* … to tell him she'd realized, only this afternoon, how much she still loved him. Nick's eyes were closed. She could tell by his low, rhythmic breathing … he was fast asleep once again.

The bitter, moist air stung Aubrey's exposed face as she stood just outside the back door, wearing slippers and her winter coat waiting for Snowball, their nine-year-old Bichon Frise, to do his business. Yes … *Snowball*. Snowball is the kind of name you get when you think it's cute to let your four-year-old name your puppy.

Mystic was a quiet town with very few year-round residents. However, during the summer months, all the Shoobies came to town, and every house would be occupied. *Shoobies* were what the locals called the summer tourists. They were so named nearly a century ago. Back in the nineteen twenties, daytrippers arriving by train at 'Jersey shore resorts carried their lunches in shoeboxes. They clogged the sandy beaches but, since they brought their own food, they weren't supporters of local businesses. Even though that was no longer true, the locals continued to call the summer tourists *Shoobies*.

When all the summer houses were rented out to the Shoobies and porches and decks were full, if Aubrey had to call Snowball inside, she would try to just whistle for him or even whisper his name to avoid having people attempting to get a glimpse of the dimwitted lady who gave a dog a name like *Snowball*.

Today, it was freezing, and summer was a long way away, so Aubrey held the door open and shouted, "Snowball! Come on, boy!" Within seconds, he was running toward the door, seemingly smiling, as he always did. Aubrey tossed him a treat as he ran by her and into the house.

Nick was in the shower when she'd come down to let the dog out. Aubrey felt an odd, unexpected excitement about seeing him this morning. Unsure about whatever had come over Nick, she was more than receptive to it. While it surprised her, the pure joy Aubrey had felt when Nick held her last night was worth the consideration. She actually felt some sort of hope that their marriage could be saved. Aubrey was more than a little bit puzzled as to how her emotions seemed to do a one hundred and eighty-degree turnaround in little more than twenty-four hours.

Holding her cup of coffee with two hands, Aubrey leaned against the kitchen counter. Peyton rolled in—her testy teenage attitude intact—and sat down to have breakfast at the table. She hardly noticed her mother's overly friendly tone when Aubrey had offered a *good morning*.

Teddy and Nick arrived in the kitchen at the same time. Teddy was talking away about video games, and how he was going to Brody's birthday party on Saturday. Aubrey could tell Nick was only pretending to listen. Sadly, it was something she, herself, had been a victim of and had become more than accustomed to. Luckily, for their son, he didn't seem to notice.

Allowing Teddy to settle into his chair, Nick made his way around to say goodbye to Peyton before walking back over to the head of the table where Teddy sat. Aubrey stepped forward and smiled, waiting for her turn, as Nick bent to kiss Teddy's head.

When he straightened back up, Nick appeared surprised to see Aubrey standing in front of him. Aubrey's smile faded as she noticed the look of utter confusion on Nick's face. When the furrowing of his brows further transformed into an annoyed frown—as though she was blocking his way—Aubrey stepped aside, and Nick silently pushed past her.

And, for the first time, Aubrey realized … Nick had absolutely no idea what had transpired between them in their bedroom last night.

Chapter Four

The week had flown by. There'd been no more late night encounters with Nick, and Aubrey couldn't believe exactly how much time she'd spent, during the course of the week, wishing there had been. She especially hoped for some interaction with Nick tonight, on her birthday.

But, Aubrey's birthday had started out as the disappointment she'd expected it would be. When she woke up this morning, Nick had been long gone. He didn't usually go to the office so early, so it felt deliberate. After that one brief—but treasured—night with Nick, all the days since had already been an enormous letdown.

After Aubrey dropped the kids at school, she'd spent the entire day running errands, which included getting her hair done and pampering herself by getting a manicure and a pedicure. When she arrived home, most of the house was dark. There were no surprises, no *Over the Hill* or *Lordy, Look Who's Forty* signs. No Nick.

Aubrey pushed the front door open with her hip while balancing a paper bag full of groceries in one arm and a bouquet of flowers in the other. The flowers were for Aubrey. She'd treated herself to fresh flowers for her birthday. Once inside, Aubrey pushed the door closed with her heel. Using her elbow, she flipped on the light, illuminating the foyer and the stairwell, before heading up the steps to the kitchen.

Upstairs, Peyton was sitting cross-legged on a chair at the kitchen table, with her hair tied up in a messy bun, doing homework. Aubrey placed the bag of groceries and flowers onto the countertop and noticed a cake in a box from *The Bake Works*.

"Peyton, where did this cake come from?"

Looking up, it was the first time Peyton even acknowledged Aubrey had entered the room. "Oh, hi, Mom. Dad brought that home. He just left a few minutes ago to pick up Chinese food for dinner. By the way, happy birthday." Peyton went back to focusing on her homework.

Sighing, Aubrey turned away. "Thanks." When she'd dreamed of having a daughter of her own, this wasn't the relationship Aubrey had imagined. However, she was grateful for all the articles she'd read online, which reassured Aubrey that the *teen years* were the hardest times for mothers and daughters and that this phase would eventually end, and they'd have a real chance at a better connection. She sure hoped so. Frankly, Aubrey couldn't imagine it getting much worse.

Reaching into the cabinet under the kitchen sink, Aubrey pulled out a vase. She rinsed it out before placing it under the running faucet to allow it to fill. She had trouble containing how annoyed she was feeling. *Chinese. Nick's favorite. My birthday. Great.* Considering the way things had been between them, Aubrey knew she should probably just be grateful Nick had done anything at all. As she turned off the water, Aubrey silently vowed to try to make the best of it.

She carried the vase to the island, pulled the cellophane, cone-shaped sleeve off of the bouquet and placed the flowers into the water. As she hastily arranged them, she heard Nick coming through the front door downstairs. She slid the arrangement across to the middle of the island, centering it.

As Nick scaled the stairs, Aubrey took out two wine glasses and filled each one with a higher than average amount of wine. She couldn't help but hope that Nick might over-indulge once again. After all, it was her birthday, and just maybe he'd not only warm up to her again—but Nick would actually remain awake this time.

When he entered the kitchen, Nick put the cardboard box filled with Chinese takeout onto the counter, and without even looking at Aubrey said, "Happy birthday, Aubrey. Wow, forty, huh?" To say it was disingenuous would be an understatement.

Nick glanced over to where Peyton was sitting. "Peyton, go get your brother. Tell him dinner is ready."

Peyton, knowing better than to protest, hopped up, scooped up her books and went to find Teddy.

Aubrey tried to be friendly, in spite of Nick quite literally ignoring her. "It smells good. What did you get?"

Nick pressed his lips together, raising an eyebrow. "Chinese? You know, the usual stuff we get when we order take-out." He rolled his eyes, shook his head, and proceeded to put dishes and utensils onto the counter, next to the box.

Feeling deflated, Aubrey cursed the lump that immediately made its way into her throat. "Okay. Thanks." It was all she could manage without coming undone.

Teddy came running into the kitchen with Peyton in tow. "Happy birthday, Mom!"

It immediately lifted Aubrey's spirits and made her smile. Teddy was so innocent and sweet. He was always like a bright ray of sunshine for Aubrey. Rarely ever giving her a hard time, his love was so pure and kind. "Thanks, sweetie. Dad left some plates over there."

When Aubrey turned to point in the direction of the plates, she realized Nick had already filled his and was making his way toward the door. "Nick? You're not eating with us?"

With a furrowed brow, Nick sighed. "Umm, that would be a *no*. Jeez, Au-brey. What do you expect? I have work to do. I'll come down for cake later."

Aubrey tried again, motioning toward the island. "But, I poured a glass of wine for you." It sounded almost like a question. *Please come back?*

Balancing his dinner in one hand, Nick crossed over to where the glasses rested side-by-side and picked up one of them. Slightly raising it in the air, Nick smiled weakly. "Cheers." He started to walk away, then hesitated and turned back. Aubrey's hopes jumped up a notch—that was until Nick spoke. "Oh, and there's a present for you over there, next to the box." And, before Aubrey could say anything more, he was gone. She took a deep breath and exhaled.

Teddy and Peyton finished filling up their plates, took them over to the table, and sat down. Before making a plate for herself, Aubrey reached behind the box and picked up the generic, dull, solid pink gift bag Nick had left for her. She glanced over at the table. "Go ahead and start eating. I'll be right there."

She peered inside the dollar-store quality bag. There was a glass-jar candle and nothing else. No tissue paper. No card. Aubrey pulled the candle from the bag. It was baby blue in color, which matched absolutely nothing in their house. Aubrey thought to herself, *oh, it's a boy!* Twisting the lid off, she drew the jar up to her nose and sniffed. Instinctively, Aubrey scrunched up her nose, throwing her head back, while simultaneously whipping it over to the side. The smell was more than offensive. It reminded her of those stinky little blue *deodorizing cakes* that hung over the rim of the toilet bowl back when she was growing up.

Aubrey turned the candle upside down to see if there was a hint as to where Nick had purchased it. She recognized the tag on the bottom. It was from their drugstore. The price? A whopping $4.99. Aubrey quickly put the lid back onto the candle, placed it back into the bag, and returned the gift to the back of the counter.

As Aubrey filled her plate, she wondered why Nick had bothered to get her anything at all. He had to know she'd realize that absolutely no thought went into that present. Nick hadn't even bothered to remove the price tag or properly wrap the gift, for that matter. Aubrey joined the kids at the table, and her heart was as heavy as ever.

Even if Nick didn't believe he loved her anymore, they were still married. Aubrey *was* the mother of Nick's children, and this *was* her fortieth birthday. He could have done a little something special. It made her sad. Nick was more than aware that Aubrey believed that the worst thing one human being could do to another is to devalue them. She knew Nick no doubt understood completely—with this thoughtless gift—he'd done just that.

The second Aubrey finished eating and placed her fork on the empty plate, Teddy jumped up from the table. "It's time for cake. I'll go get dad."

Peyton sat at the table scrolling through her phone. Aubrey got up and cleared the dishes, placing them into the sink. She fished through the junk drawer and found a numeral four candle, and a numeral zero candle. Aubrey removed the cake from the box and pressed the candles into the icing on top of it and placed it on the kitchen table. She collected the lighter, dessert plates, forks, and a cake knife and put everything alongside the cake. Feeling just a little bit sorry for herself, Aubrey thought, *at this point, I may as well light the candles and sing happy birthday to myself.*

As Aubrey sat back down at the table, Teddy came in, dragging Nick behind him. "Light the candles, Dad!"

Nick picked up the lighter and held it over the four and then over the zero. A bright-eyed Teddy started singing, *Happy Birthday to you ...* while Peyton joined in, everyone but Aubrey seemed oblivious to the fact that Nick was staring out of the windows and only moving his lips, but not really singing.

After Teddy finished with an elongated and drawn out … *and many mooooore*. He knelt on the chair next to Aubrey and said, "Make a wish, Mom. Go ahead! Blow out the candles."

Aubrey did as Teddy requested. She closed her eyes for a moment, opened them, and blew out the candles, sending two small streams of smoke swirling up into the air.

Nick could have won an award for speed cake cutting if there were such a thing. In no time flat, he'd cut half the cake and divided it into four slices, putting one on each plate that Aubrey had placed on the table. It was no surprise to her when Nick picked up one of the plates of cake, grabbed a fork, and silently walked out of the kitchen.

Aubrey didn't try to stop him this time. Instead, she desperately hoped that her birthday wish would come true and she'd be spending time with the sweeter, more lovable *Nicky* later on tonight.

Chapter Five

Balloons, tied to the roadside mailbox, pirouetted in the wind in front of Libby's beach house. A sign reading *The Party is Here* was staked into the flower bed of rocks in the front yard.

Aubrey put the car in park and reminded Teddy to grab the gift as he opened his door to run inside to join Brody at his birthday party. Peyton tagged along today to hang with Lizzie since there was little else to do on a winter Saturday on the island. She disappeared so fast once they entered the house, Aubrey wasn't even sure Peyton had said a proper *hello* to Libby.

Teddy dropped their gift for Brody on a table, which already held several other presents. He ran off to join the other kids in the noisy family room downstairs. Aubrey made her way to the kitchen to see what help she could offer to Libby.

Standing at the sink, Libby looking frazzled. When she caught sight of Aubrey, she shook her head. "Twelve ten-year-old boys. What was I thinking?"

Aubrey laughed and opened the refrigerator, retrieving a bottle of white wine. She pulled two glasses from the wine rack and filled each halfway, and handed one to Libby. "Here's a little calming remedy. What can I help you with?"

"Thanks." Libby took a sip from her glass. "Everything is pretty much done. I just sent the magician and his assistant downstairs, so we should get a break for a good thirty minutes." Even if they're not any good … I'll settle for the well-paid babysitter. She crossed over to stand at the top of the steps, craning her neck down the stairwell to listen for the kids. Libby gave Aubrey a thumbs up. "Yup. We're in great shape. It's quiet. Mister Magic has all their attention. That guy is worth his weight in gold. I was pretty sure they were going to tie me to a stake and set me on fire if I didn't have something more to entertain them soon. Gosh, the winters are brutal down here. Letting those boys play outside wasn't even an option."

Aubrey was nodding, "Tell me about it." She reached out and pulled two chairs away from the counter. She climbed onto one stool and motioned to the other. "Join me at the bar. Take a load off."

Once Libby was seated, she raised an eyebrow and asked, "So, what happened with the attorney thing? Did Nick actually file for divorce? I can't believe we haven't had a chance to talk all week."

"Well, we did *sort of* talk … you did send me a birthday text yesterday. As far as Nick filing, I don't know what's going on with the mystery attorney visit. I'm not really sure. I came home from our lunch, and Nick was at work, as usual. Later on that night, he showed up and had pizza with the kids and me. I walked around on eggshells all that evening expecting … I don't know what. And, he actually ended up going to bed before me." Aubrey shrugged. "Go figure. He hasn't mentioned anything all week. Maybe he was waiting until after my birthday? I really don't know."

"Wow. That's so weird." Libby crossed her arms. "Did he even do anything for your birthday?"

"He gave me a cheap drugstore candle that smelled like toilet water freshener. And, he did get me a cake and take out Chinese—which is Nick's favorite, not mine. But, I wasn't expecting anything, anyway." Aubrey paused when her eyes filled up and failed to support how brave she was trying to sound. She tightened her jaw and began again. "The kids had presents and cards for me. That part was nice. But, if it weren't for them, it was pretty clear … Nick wouldn't have done anything for my birthday at all. So much for celebrating my fortieth and my grand admittance into old lady-hood!"

"Ah, Aubrey, I'm sorry. I'll take you out next weekend to celebrate properly." Libby tucked a piece of hair behind her ear. "I figured I would have heard from you if he'd filed, but I wasn't sure if not hearing anything meant you weren't in a position to talk. So, I guess this coexisting thing you guys have had going on continues?"

"Well, actually, something bizarre happened at the end of the day I saw you … when I found out about his attorney visit. I got into bed that night, and just as I was falling off to sleep, Nick woke up. He was hugging me, nuzzling my neck … he even kissed me." Aubrey paused to allow that to sink in.

"Wait. What? Nick kissed you? And, I didn't get a call about this?" Libby's eyes were wide open, her mouth matched them.

Aubrey was nodding. "It's crazy, right? He was telling me how much he loved me. He must have had more wine than I thought. I think he might be drinking in his office or something."

"Crazy is an understatement. Holy cow, he's been downright cold—nevermind, cruel—to you for almost a year. Now, he shows up as mister lovey-dovey? What *is* that?" Libby held her palms in the air. "What did you do?"

Covering her face with her hands, Aubrey peeked through her fingers as she spoke. "I kissed him back." She uncovered her face, and she was cringing.

Libby half laughed, half choked. "You did what?"

"Kissed him back. I did. I couldn't help it. It felt so good." Using the stem, Aubrey twirled her wine glass in circles. "He tasted so good."

"Are you sure you weren't dreaming?"

Nodding, looking like a bobblehead, Aubrey said, "I actually had to reassure myself of that very thing. I was laying there simply blown away. Part of me wanted to tell him to knock it off, but the other part of me had missed his touch so much … I let it happen."

Libby's eyes appeared permanently frozen in a *surprise* position. "Well, what did he say? I mean, all these months later, he really just came out of nowhere … pretending everything's been fine?"

"Actually, that's exactly what he did. One minute I was drifting off to sleep and the next, his arm was wrapped around me, and he was pulling me in to spoon with him. He had his hands all over me and then … he just kissed me."

Leaning forward, Libby whispered, "And, *then* what?"

"And then, nothing. The next thing I knew Nick was sound asleep again." Aubrey shrugged. "I'm telling you it was truly like something out of the twilight zone. So much so, as I was trying to get back to sleep, I was asking myself if it had ever happened at all."

Libby was squinting as though she were trying to wrap her head around what Aubrey had just said. "Well, what did he say the next day? I mean, how has the rest of the week been? You said he all but ignored your birthday …"

Aubrey smacked her hand on the counter. "That's just it, the next morning he was miserable Nick again. He hasn't touched me, come near me, or even acknowledged I'm alive."

Taking a sip of her wine, Libby swallowed and tipped her head to the side. "And you haven't asked him about it?"

"No. And, I'm really not sure why. I guess it's possible I'm afraid Nick will deny it happened. I needed it to be real. I couldn't have guessed how lonely I was, until those few minutes of togetherness. I really, really miss being part of an *us*." Aubrey's eyes filled with tears. "Darn it. I felt like I'd already mourned the loss of my marriage. But, I realized that the feelings that came with the combination of fearing Nick had filed for divorce and enjoying his touch again meant—that for me— this isn't over. Last night, when I blew out the candles, my wish was for a little glimpse of the old Nick again. Even that didn't come true." She wiped away a tear that had escaped.

Reaching across the counter to grab a box of tissues, Libby scooted it over next to Aubrey's glass. "Sadly, I know how you feel. It stinks to love somebody and have no idea how to rewind the clock. Maybe you should take a second look at counseling. Maybe a different counselor?"

Taking a tissue from the box and dabbing her eyes, and then her nose, Aubrey shrugged. "Nick already told me he's *not wasting any more of his time.* That's a quote. If you could see how he treats me … just hear how he says my name when he's sober, it's like he's repulsed by me or something."

Libby leaned over and grabbed Aubrey's hand, squeezing it. "I just know that at the end of the day, you have to believe that you did everything you could because the pain of losing someone you love so much is only truly consoled by the notion that you went down fighting."

"I know …"

Before Aubrey could say anything further, Mr. Magic showed up in the kitchen to say his goodbyes and collect his payment envelope. The volume on the lower level was already rising.

As Libby walked the magician and his assistant to the front door, Aubrey got up, threw her tissues in the trash, and put their wine glasses in the sink.

Libby returned and put her arms around Aubrey. "We'll talk more, later. You're going to be alright."

Aubrey nodded and cleared her throat. "Okay, you lead the way, Lib. I'll help you with the little monsters." As Libby led the way down the stairs, Aubrey followed and realized her friend was absolutely right. She wasn't giving up Nick so easily. While she might indeed go down, Aubrey was going down with all the fight she had in herself. No matter what Aubrey had to do, she *was* keeping her promise to Teddy.

Frighteningly enough, Aubrey had no idea how her circumstances were about to challenge that very notion.

Chapter Six

On Sunday morning, Aubrey arrived for work nearly fifteen minutes early. She always liked to have a few minutes to herself before hitting the ground running for her twelve-hour shifts. As a nurse on the mental health floor at Atlantic City Medical Center, there was never any guessing what any given shift would throw at her. It was undoubtedly one of the most rewarding—albeit exhausting—jobs she'd ever had in her life.

Sundays were always challenging. With the opioid crisis setting up one of its largest addict populations right here in the state of New Jersey, their unit was guaranteed a handful of weekend bingers in the emergency room, lining up to be admitted.

While Aubrey always tried to keep her work life and personal life separate, she found herself continually repeating self-reminders as to why she'd chosen this particularly intense field of nursing to begin with. Not that she'd ever needed an actual reminder. No, Aubrey could picture the day that caused her to redirect her sails toward this career, as though it were only yesterday.

Overall, it'd actually been a series of events, set in motion during Aubrey's junior year of high school, which collectively caused her to change the course of her life forever.

In high school, Libby and Aubrey had been good friends with another girl named Meredith Baxter. They could have been—should have been—best friends forever. The three girls had been inseparable in their freshman and sophomore years, calling themselves *The Three Muska-dears*—a name Aubrey's father had dubbed them, saying they were the female version of *The Three Muskateers.*

Sadly, it was just about halfway through their junior year when Meredith, unintentionally, began to fall away. She'd been injured in a cheerleading accident in the autumn of that school year. After a few months of narcotics, her injury had healed, so her doctors abruptly stopped prescribing her the pain medicine. Her parents ended up having to send her to rehab because the withdrawal from the drugs had been so severe. Meredith returned home sometime around Christmas, presumably cured.

The *Muska-dears* were back together over the holiday break from school, but that had ended up being short-lived. Meredith wound up being grounded by her parents because she'd stolen pain medicine from her aunt's medicine cabinet on a family visit there on New Year's Day. Her mother had found the bottle, with her aunt's name printed right on the label, buried in Meredith's underwear drawer, so there'd been no denying it. That seemed to be the official beginning of when everything started rapidly rolling downhill for their friend.

By the time spring rolled around, Meredith had been behaving erratically for several months. Libby and Aubrey tried to talk to her, but she'd repeatedly denied anything was wrong. She'd lost a lot of weight, and the girls had caught her in a number of lies. Sometimes they were lies that didn't even matter. It was increasingly disturbing.

Meredith would make plans and then cancel them, using one bad excuse or another, or worse, fail to show up without giving any notice at all. Both Libby and Aubrey had been struggling to remain friends with Meredith. Sadly, they were all far too young for any one of them to understand where the road Meredith found herself traveling on would eventually lead.

The icing on the cake—literally—came that summer. Libby had a slumber party, inviting five of her friends to sleep over, for her seventeenth birthday. Libby, Aubrey, and—when she showed up— Meredith, had planned the party and handmade the favors. Three other girls from school, Sandy, Pam, and Michele, each being more casual friends, joined in on the fun.

On the evening of the party, the girls hung out in the family room at the back of the house. Later, they enjoyed pizza, soda, popcorn, and of course chocolate cake served with ice cream in the dining room. Afterward, Libby opened her gifts, all of which were in the form of birthday cards with cash enclosed. That's the way birthday presents were done in high school.

Toward the end of the evening, the girls all snuggled into their sleeping bags on the family room floor to watch *Forrest Gump*, which had just been released on VHS tape about six weeks earlier. In the middle of the movie, Meredith said she'd left her hair tie in the dining room and went back to retrieve it. She'd returned, and no one had thought anything of it … that is, until the following morning.

Libby and Aubrey went to the kitchen to set up a continental breakfast for Libby's guests. Overfilling their arms to their elbows with orange juice, bagels, English muffins, cream cheese, and fruit, the girls hobbled to the dining room to place all they'd each been able to carry onto the table. When the girls turned the corner to enter the room, Libby gasped as she emptied the food she held onto the table. Her birthday cards were scattered across the surface, apparently having been rummaged through. She'd left them neatly stacked in a pile the night before. Some had been half placed back into their envelopes, others were just tossed on top of their envelopes.

Aubrey could still remember the look on Libby's face as though it had been tangibly imprinted on a photograph she'd viewed from time to time over the years. The disbelief mixed with hurt had been palpable.

Libby slowly picked up one and then another, realizing instantly that the cash had been taken from them. While she and Aubrey rapidly concluded it was unlikely, Libby quickly checked with her parents to be sure they hadn't taken her money. Of course, they hadn't.

While Libby was checking with her parents, Aubrey had returned to the family room. Knowing she'd stolen from her own family, Aubrey had looked directly at Meredith when she'd announced to the group that Libby's birthday money had been taken from all the cards and asked if there was any chance any of the girls knew what had happened to it. Aubrey watched Meredith's face turn crimson before she shifted her eyes to the floor. All of the others shot shocked, puzzled glances back and forth.

Later, one of the girls did come forward to tell Libby she didn't want to start any trouble, but a wad of money had fallen from Meredith's sleeping bag when she'd been rolling it up. Meredith had quickly stuffed it back inside the bag, before glancing around the room—appearing to try to see who might've been looking her way.

Convinced Meredith was the thief, from that day forward, Aubrey and Libby avoided her. It was actually pretty easy because Meredith didn't really try to hang out with them after that day, anyway. Meredith's actions told them she'd realized they'd both concluded she was the thief. Aubrey never figured out why Meredith didn't just go home, once she'd taken the money. She could only guess that Meredith must have believed if she stayed, it would seem less likely she'd be nabbed as the suspect. Leaving would have proven she'd been guilty beyond any doubt.

After that summer, Libby and Aubrey returned to school for their senior year. They'd both been saddened and horrified when they saw Meredith again for the first time. When she'd actually showed up for school, she'd looked like the stereotypical junkie portrayed in the movies. If her anorexia hadn't given her away, her soulless eyes would have. Immature and cruel boys at school had taken to calling her Mere-death because she'd looked so bad.

Aubrey, knowing what she knew today about the lengths an addict will go—and how low they'll stoop—to get their drugs, finally understood how Meredith's eyes had likely become so darned empty.

In the spring of senior year, Aubrey arrived at school on the Monday after spring break, with a solid commitment to the trajectory she was on, to become a civil engineer. College applications were out, and her grades were looking impressive, leaving her without any doubt that her dreams for her future would be realized. That particular day, April fifteenth, was unseasonably cold for a mid-April morning.

As Aubrey had walked through the doors of the east wing entrance that day, almost instantly she'd noticed that the bustle in the hallways had been different. There were a lot of whispers, and people had seemed to be staring directly at her, as she made her way through the halls on the way to her locker. Before she got there, Libby—with red and swollen eyes—came running up to her and grasped Aubrey by her arms. All Aubrey could remember now was the way Libby had been shaking her and repeating over and over, *did you hear? Did you hear?* Before finally dropping the bomb … *Meredith is dead. Oh, God, Aubrey … she's dead.*

Aubrey's breath left her, and tears had burned her cheeks as she and Libby had clung to one another. A guidance counselor had come along and taken the girls down to her office. She'd delicately explained how Meredith had overdosed on heroin.

Aubrey eventually learned that Meredith's mom had found her the day before Easter Sunday, sitting upright against the headboard on her bed, blue and unresponsive, with a needle still sticking out of her arm. At the time, Aubrey remembered thinking … *Meredith was crucified by a demon no one else could see.*

Along with their parents, Aubrey and Libby attended the funeral. There was a rose-colored closed casket with Meredith's sophomore picture in a white frame on top. Aubrey figured her family chose that picture because the tenth grade was the last time Meredith looked anything like herself. They handed out little purple memorial ribbons with straight pins because that was Meredith's favorite color. There were a lot of people wearing purple and too many to count were crying … no, *sobbing* is a better term. Aubrey and Libby joined them. Meredith's mom kept telling kids, as they came through the line with wishes they could have done more, no more could have been done. She was asking them, if they wanted to honor Meredith's memory, not to ever begin using drugs and to value life. When Aubrey and Libby got to the front of the line, Meredith's mother was kind enough to wish them well. No one mentioned how they'd both fallen away from Meredith. Many years later, Aubrey would realize how hard that must have been for Mrs. Baxter. She was burying her daughter, and the two remaining Muska-dears would be going off to college in the fall.

Not long after that day, Aubrey returned to the counselor's office and began the process of completing new applications to colleges to obtain a degree in nursing. Realizing she couldn't save Meredith, she knew she wanted to spend her life helping those who wanted to be saved, in memory of her friend.

All these years later, at this point in Aubrey's life, she'd already had more than one patient return to the crisis unit at the hospital to tell her they were sober because of her. Their stories about getting an education, finding true love, or becoming a counselor or nurse themselves never failed to warm her heart. Aubrey more than understood, she was exactly where she was supposed to be.

She often wondered, and today was no exception, why she never seemed to be able to find those feelings of belonging in her own home anymore.

Bad heroin laced with fentanyl had come out of Camden again, and addicts were overdosing all over southern New Jersey today. In their hospital alone, they'd had four patients brought in unconscious, each remained in a coma in the Intensive Care Unit. As of when she'd left the hospital, it didn't look like even one of them was going to make it. Six more overdoses—all revived with Narcan—ended up on her unit, and Aubrey had spent all day trying to stabilize the two who'd been assigned to her. As always, she'd said a little prayer asking Meredith to keep watching over them.

She hated what was happening with the drug epidemic, but more than anything, Aubrey couldn't stand the lack of resources available to help these addicts. She knew they could get them clean, but if they couldn't get them into long-term inpatient care somewhere—before insurance companies forced the medical staff to release them onto the streets—they'd be right back out there using again.

Aubrey was more than aware they'd have to un-politicize healthcare before any real changes would occur. In the meantime, she was committed to remaining down in the trenches with these poor souls, trying to save the ones she could and trying to buy another day to say goodbye for the families of the ones they couldn't.

Grateful when her shift was finally over, Aubrey was making her way to the time clock to punch out when she noticed a young girl sitting all alone in the solarium. Instead of sitting in a chair, she sat on the floor, wrapped in a blanket in front of the full-length windows, staring out into the darkness. As Aubrey moved closer, she recognized Cindy, a girl who'd been on the crisis unit enough times to be labeled a *frequent flyer*.

This was probably Cindy's sixth or seventh time here. Aubrey knew that most of her family had given up on her, as happened with so many addicts. Family members would just become mentally and emotionally exhausted. In Cindy's case, it just so happened her best friend had been clean for about five years. So, every so often, she could drag Cindy back to crisis to attempt sobriety once again. Aubrey knew that the more people who fell away from an addict's life lessened their chances to ever recover successfully. She felt terrible for Cindy because she'd burned so many bridges.

Anxious to get going home, an exhausted Aubrey continued to head for the employee exit. Cindy didn't even move to see who was passing her by. Aubrey realized that, sadly, she was probably rather used to people passing her by. It made Aubrey take pause. What were a few more minutes?

Turning back, Aubrey walked over to where Cindy sat. "Hey, Cindy. It's nice to see you here *trying* again."

Slowly, Cindy raised her dark, pitted eyes to meet Aubrey's. "Hey, Aubrey. I didn't know you were working tonight."

Aubrey nodded. "Yeah. It was a pretty busy shift. I didn't spend any time at the nurse's station. Why are you out here all alone? It's late."

"Actually, I wasn't here all alone." Cindy shifted her gaze back toward the window. "There were a few other people out here. They were eating snacks from the vending machines over there." Cindy pulled her hand from under the blanket to motion toward the corridor where a red soda machine could be seen glowing in the dim light. "That's how you can tell who the people are who still have family who care about them."

Aubrey furrowed her brow. "I'm sorry?"

"The people who have money for snacks from the vending machine … that's how you can tell." Cindy sighed. "They're the people who are brought here by family. Family who still pray for them … who can't sleep at night wondering where they are or if they're okay. Family who wait endless hours in the emergency room with them, hoping this time *their* addict recovers. And, when their addict is admitted here to the crisis floor, well, they hand them twenty dollars, so they have money for snacks. The snacks. They just scream out to the rest of us in the room *somebody still loves me.*"

Sitting down on the closest chair, Aubrey put her hand on Cindy's back. "I'm sorry, sweetie. I'm sorry it's all so hard for you."

Cindy offered half a smile. "It's okay. I guess it seems stupid that I think that a bag of M&M's might say so much. After all, handing someone a few bucks for snacks doesn't really mean anything, right?"

Aubrey thought of how Nick had handled her birthday. "No, I understand. Sometimes the thought *does* count. And, sometimes … it's just nice to feel like you're still a little important to someone."

"I guess. You know, I've been staring out of this dark window for a while now. Even if I squint, I can't see anything out there in the distance. It's pitch black. Like my future. It's some big dark mystery. Each time I'm here, I literally have no idea on earth what I am working towards. No inkling as to what I'm looking forward to. I honestly can't remember the last time I had a dream for myself." Cindy rested her chin on her knees that she'd pulled to her chest and wrapped her arms around her legs.

Aubrey felt her eyes burn with tears that wanted to fall. "Oh, Cindy. Just believe that you truly deserve to dream, and then the dreams will come. You're young. You're here. You're alive. You have so many opportunities available to you. Happiness comes in the form of sobriety. You just have to decide you want it."

A voice cut through the silence behind them. "Oh, here you are! Cindy, it's past *lights out*. Time to get back to your room." Aubrey looked over and recognized Pauline, an overnight nurse on the unit, and waved at her.

Cindy stood up. "Well, it's back to room three-thirty-three I go. Goodnight, Aubrey. It's good to see you again and thanks for always being so nice to me."

"Goodnight, Cindy. Think about what I said." Aubrey watched as Cindy weakly nodded, stood up, gathered the blanket around herself, and joined Pauline to head down the hall.

Once again, Aubrey began to make her way to the time clock and once again, she took pause, before turning around. She squinted when she entered the short corridor with the machine's lights glowing loudly in the night.

When Aubrey reentered the hallway in the crisis unit, all was quiet. Just past the deserted nurse's station, Aubrey slipped into room number three-thirty-three. The bed was empty, and the bathroom door was closed, bright white light was shining from beneath it. Aubrey quietly tip-toed over to Cindy's bed and gently placed a bag of M & M's on the nightstand next to it, before silently slipping back out of the room.

Chapter Seven

After leaving the hospital, driving home, Aubrey was bleary-eyed. It was nearly midnight, since her scheduled twelve-hour shift from 11:00 A.M. to 11:00 P.M had become a thirteen-hour shift instead. She was glad she was almost home.

When she pulled the car into the driveway, Aubrey was a little surprised when she noticed all the lights were turned on upstairs. Her house looked like a spooky Halloween decoration, glowing against the canvas of the dark, black sky. The kitchen and great rooms were lit up as though it were daytime.

By now, especially on a school night, the kids should undoubtedly be sound asleep. Even for Nick, this was pretty late. It occurred to Aubrey that he may have failed to turn the lights out and lock up for the night since she was the one who usually took care of those things.

When she tried turning the front doorknob, it was locked. Aubrey mumbled *one out of two isn't bad* before putting her key in and unlocking the door.

She paused and raised an ear toward the upper staircase when she entered the foyer and thought she heard pans clanging around in the kitchen. Activity up there was confirmed when Aubrey recognized the distinct sound of the mixer whirring away, interrupting the night silence.

The sounds beckoned her to the kitchen. She paused in the living room when she spotted Nick, standing at the kitchen island, mixing something in a large bowl. He was scrumptious in jeans that fit just right, and a stonewashed denim button-down shirt, which he'd left completely unbuttoned, exposing his perfect abs—and proof of his gym membership. His hair was a tousled, sexy mess.

Aubrey could see a carton of eggs and the bottle of cooking oil on the counter next to the bowl. She couldn't imagine what Nick was up to.

Moving tentatively toward the kitchen, Aubrey felt her heart begin to beat faster as she got close enough to see his glistening eyes shimmering like sea glass.

Nick must have caught sight of her out of the corner of his eye because he jerked his head up and turned off the mixer. The glimmer in his smile would put a string of expensive pearls to shame. "Hey, baby!"

Feeling like she might melt right where she stood, she tried to quickly assess if he was possibly drunk, on drugs, or something else. Glancing around at the countertops, there wasn't so much as a wine glass or a beer bottle sitting out.

One thing Aubrey was sure of … this was definitely her Nicky—the guy from the other night—in the flesh and apparently here for an encore. She'd known it when he called her *baby*. It sounded so loving, so warm, and so … real.

With her lips nearly glued together, Aubrey asked, "What's going on, Nick? What are you up to here?"

Still grinning, Nick circled the counter to where she stood. "I've been waiting for you to get home. I missed you." He wrapped his arms around Aubrey, but she tried to push him away.

"Nick, we really need to talk." Aubrey wriggled out of his grip and stepped back a few feet.

Reaching out and grabbing her by the hand, Nick pulled her back toward him. "We can talk. But for now, I just want to hold you. I told you, I *missed* you." Wrapping his arms around her again, Nick held her tight and whispered into her ear. "For some reason, it feels like you were gone forever … as though I haven't held you in a really, really long time." Nick released his embrace and leaned back. He gripped her upper arms with his hands and looked into her eyes. "Isn't that crazy?"

Aubrey was incredibly tempted to play along. But, clearly, this wasn't the Nick she'd been living with recently. She looked into his eyes. They were so glassy, the blue seemed brighter. Was it possible that Nick was on some kind of drugs, could she be that completely off base? Aubrey usually prided herself on her ability to make a first glance diagnosis.

Right now, in the condition he appeared to be in, Aubrey wasn't sure if he would even understand the truth about their marriage. About them. Deciding she should at least try to explain, Aubrey started, "Well, Nick, actually you're right. It *is* a little crazy. You see, these days you usually don't hold ..."

He didn't let her finish before swinging his index finger into the air in front of Aubrey's face. "Oops! Hold that thought." Nick turned on his heel and sort of half-tiptoed, half-scooted over to the stove. If he were in a Broadway musical, his gait would have been perfect. But, he wasn't, and Aubrey couldn't help but absorb how this whole scenario was getting crazier by the minute.

Nick leaned sideways, stretching over the shiny cooktop as he reached for the control panel on the back of the stove, pressed *bake*, and began to tap the *up* arrow key. "Sorry, it's just that I almost forgot to preheat the oven." Turning away from her, Nick stopped pressing buttons when the display read *3-7-5*.

Moving swiftly back over to where Aubrey stood, Nick tried to wrap his arms around her again. Although she felt weak in the knees and wanted so desperately to respond to all of Nick's advances, Aubrey pushed him away again and, feeling a sense of urgency, raised her voice. "Nick!" Realizing she'd nearly shouted and witnessing Nick's eyes widen, Aubrey lowered her tone. "Nick, we really need to talk right now—"

Once again, Nick interrupted. "Wow. Aub, you sounded so strong just now. You've always been the strong one in this family. We're so lucky … me, the kids ..."

It was Aubrey's turn to interrupt. "Nick, I am trying t—"

"And, you're always so humble. Just listen to you." Nick's gaze shifted to stare at a wall over her shoulder. Nick started speaking in a dreamy sort of way. Slow. Calculated. "Do you remember the time Teddy fell down the stairs? Right over there. He must have been … what? Three years old?"

Aubrey nodded. "Yes. He was three." She'd remembered it like it was yesterday.

Nick acted as though he didn't hear her … like she hadn't answered him at all. "He was. Yes. Teddy was three years old. Gosh, there was blood everywhere … all over his face … on the step. I froze right there in place at the top of the stairs. I couldn't move." He raised his eyebrows and shook his head. "But not you, Aubrey. You were so strong. You moved so fast. You scooped him right up and whisked him off to the kitchen. He was bleeding all over you, the floor, everywhere … but you didn't waiver."

Aubrey waited, studying Nick's every move. Hanging onto his every word.

Nick actually returned his stare back toward her, enough that it felt as though he really was talking *to* her, now. "It wasn't until you started cleaning him up that we realized most of the blood was coming from his nose. The rest was from a small bite on his tongue. And, other than the knot on his head, that was it. But, you? Your hands didn't even shake … before we even knew what we were dealing with

… you were so brave—for Teddy and … for me. You didn't get mad at me, and you never made me feel weak or like I was a bad dad for freezing up like I did that day. You never even mentioned it." When he finished speaking, Nick actually had tears in eyes that otherwise showed no emotion.

Nick nodded in silence and patted Aubrey on the shoulder before returning to the counter and beginning to prep cake pans, for what appeared to be freshly whipped cake batter in the bowl next to the mixer.

It may have looked as though Nick was actually talking to Aubrey, but she knew better. Whatever was going on—drugs or otherwise—Nick couldn't be further away from this room if he were speaking to her from the face of the moon. Aubrey would have loved for him to *mean* all of the words he was saying. And, God knew how much she needed him to *feel* the way he appeared to feel tonight. As much as she adored these glimpses of her old Nick, she wholly understood that the newer version of Nick would surely return in the morning. Just like the last time. She had to stop this right now … whatever *this* was.

Aubrey crossed the room. Nick was putting two round cake pans into the oven. He closed the door and reached to the back of the stove to set the timer. When he turned to face Aubrey, Nick was smiling. She wanted to fall into his arms right then and there. It was so hard to do the right thing.

Before Nick could speak, Aubrey lowered her chin, raised her hand to rest it on Nick's arm and began rubbing up and down. It was as though each stroke served to fuel her courage. Right or wrong,

Aubrey honestly didn't want to do it, but she forged forward with the truth. "Nicky, we really need to talk. You have to understand, this isn't how you usually treat—"

Nick placed his index finger across Aubrey's lips. "Shhh. It's alright, baby."

Whatever Nick had been drinking or was taking seemed to make him continuously interupt Aubrey's attempts to reveal the truth about their situation. Their situation. Nick had constantly shut her down tonight. It was almost as though Nick actually understood this was a fantasy world, and he didn't want to let it go anymore than Aubrey did.

So, when she finally stopped protesting, Nick moved in, cupped her face in his hands, pulled her closer to him, and closed his eyes, before delivering a long, soft kiss.

Still cradling Aubrey's face, Nick opened his eyes and looked deep into Aubrey's. "There's nothing to talk about here. It's your fortieth birthday, Aubrey … I'm just baking you a cake."

Chapter Eight

Libby placed a cup of coffee on the table in front of where Aubrey sat, before grabbing her own cup and sitting down. Ordinarily, Libby wouldn't have even been on the island on a Monday. Usually, she would have gone back to the city Sunday night, but Austin had picked up the kids, and that warranted a day off for Libby to recover from Brody's party. Libby had been staring wide-eyed ever since Aubrey walked through her front door and began telling her what had happened last night.

Holding up her index finger, Libby shook her head. "So, wait. You got home from work and Nick was baking a cake … for your birthday? The birthday he barely acknowledged when it really *was* your birthday?"

Aubrey was nodding. "Yes. And he kissed me again. And, heaven help me, I liked it … again."

"Well, what happened after that? I mean was he nice to you today?"

"No, he was aloof and distant again. That's the thing. He's only doing this stuff at night. And he clearly has no idea the next morning. Like this morning, he walked into the kitchen, and I heard him ask Peyton who baked the cake."

In hindsight, Aubrey wished she had thought to take a video of Nick so she could show it to Libby. His behavior and demeanor were just too hard to explain. She described to Libby how she'd studied him last night as he floured two eight-inch pans, poured batter in each one, and put them in the oven. He set the timer for twenty-five minutes. And, how, while they'd waited, he'd spent the time professing his undying love for Aubrey.

As a substance abuse and mental health nurse, Aubrey was pretty sure her assessment of Nick really seemed to suggest that he was under the influence of drugs or alcohol. But, in complete contrast, there'd been no hint of slurred words. He didn't stumble around. Nick had been as steady as a hundred-year-old redwood. So, it didn't add up.

If anything, the thing that stood out to Aubrey was Nick's stare. It seemed as though he wasn't blinking enough. Also, at times, it looked as though he would drift off in a daydream—staring into space for long periods and then snapping back, seemingly present. Which led her to believe there was possibly something psychiatric going on. But, even that seemed like a longshot.

Libby narrowed her eyes, clearly still attempting to imagine the scenario. "So, he bakes this cake … did he put the icing on it, too?"

"Yup." Aubrey's voice sounded incredulous. She wasn't even trying to pretend she understood any of this.

"… and … what? Did Nick sing *Happy Birthday*… cut you a slice?"

"No. Actually, he transferred the whole thing onto a cake plate and put the lid over it. After that, Nick kind of looked around the room, almost as though he forgot where he was. Then, he smiled and said he'd be right back." Aubrey took a sip of her coffee. "I assumed he'd gone to the bathroom. So, I cleaned up the dishes, turned off the oven, and put the mixer away. When I finished, Nick still hadn't come back. I went to look for him and found him sound asleep, passed out in our bed."

Libby sunk back in her chair and folded her arms. She shook her head and furrowed her brow when she spoke. "You know how crazy this sounds, right? I mean, if you told me he was drunk, we could blame it on a blackout."

Leaning in, Aubrey rested her elbows on the table. She folded her hands and tucked them under her chin. Locking her eyes on Libby, she said, "I'm fairly certain Nick wasn't drunk. I'm no doctor, but I do think I might know what's happening." Aubrey hesitated before continuing, unsure if Libby would believe what she was about to share. "Once Nick went to sleep, I couldn't turn my brain off. "And, I'm not positive, by any means, but I think I might know what's wrong with Nick."

"You do?" Libby sat forward. "Well, tell me. Because, short of being a drug addict or a black-out drunk, all of this is as bizarre as anything I've ever heard."

"Back in college, for one of my psychology courses, I did a paper on a class of sleep disorders called parasomnias."

Libby jiggled her head. "Para-what?"

"Parasomnias. There are several different kinds. I read a bunch of articles about it back then ... one example is somnambulism. You know, sleepwalking. People actually do crazy things while sleeping, but they appear awake. Afterward, they have no memory of it."

Half-laughing, Libby said, "You're kidding me."

Aubrey raised her eyebrows."No. No, I'm not. People with parasomnia will do things like binge eat, cook, clean, iron, have sex, and there have been some incidences where people have driven a car."

Libby threw her hands in the air. "Do you think he has a brain tumor or something? I mean, what *causes* that?"

"Well, it's funny you should ask because anxiety is a big trigger and this started on the same day he saw that divorce attorney." Aubrey, fiddling as she always did when she was uncomfortable, played with her wedding ring, spinning it around in circles on her finger.

"Wow. So! When are you going to tell Nick about what's going on?"

"Tell Nick? Oh, no. I'm not telling him. Libby. I'm not even sure that I'm right. And, the jury is still out on whether he's drinking, drugging, or God knows what." Aubrey picked her mug up. "Besides, last night I tried to tell him that something was off about him. He didn't want me to. He wouldn't *let* me tell him." Aubrey took a sip of coffee and put her cup down. "Now? I may finally have *my* husband back. He's attentive warm and loving. Even if it's in the middle of the night … even if it's weird." She shook her head. "No. Just no. I'm not doing anything about this yet. So far, his interactions are only with me. Nick may love me by night, but he *hates* me by day, so he'd never listen to me anyway. I want to wait to see where this is going."

Unable to believe her ears, Libby's voice pitched high. "He's attentive, warm, and loving? Aubrey! You believe that there's a possibility he's actually asleep!" Then, seeming to soften and reaching across the table, Libby squeezed Aubrey's forearm. "Oh, honey, you have to tell him. It's the right thing to do. I mean look at it from a safety issue. What if he got injured?" Libby was nodding. "I know how hard this has been for you. Believe me, I do. But, this isn't a good way to get what you need."

Aubrey put her hand on top of Libby's. "I've heard everything you said. But, this means everything to me. It might even be a chance to save my marriage. If it continues, and it can't be blamed on alcohol or drugs, I'll give serious consideration to telling Nick my suspicions. But, it won't be today. I can't. I need more time."

"More time?"

Aubrey shook her head. "More time to get him to fall back in love with me … in the daytime. You know, like … for real."

Silent, Libby raised her eyebrows. Aubrey understood, there was just nothing for her friend to say to that comment.

Aubrey finished her coffee and thanked Libby for her ear. As she was leaving, she turned back to hug Libby. "I promise. If this continues and there's no other explanation except for parasomnia, I'll tell Nick he needs to see a doctor, Lib."

Still, even though being so dishonest—even if only by omission—with Nick was wrong, considering all Aubrey had at stake, they both pretty much understood … she was probably lying.

Chapter Nine

Dreaming of the first time they'd taken the kids to Disney World, Aubrey was suddenly feeling as though someone was pushing her from behind as they waited in line for Space Mountain. Until she stirred, realizing it wasn't part of her dream. It was real.

Nick was in bed behind Aubrey, pressed up against her, grasping her shoulder, and shaking her awake. His voice was low and raspy. "Come on, Aubrey. Wake up. Let's have a little fun before the sun comes up."

Once Aubrey's eyes were open, Nick released his hand from her shoulder and instead slid it underneath her tank top. The delicate touch of his fingers gliding across her stomach tickled Aubrey, and she was instantly covered in goosebumps. Feeling powerless against the strength of her own needs, Aubrey tried to fight the urge to respond to Nick. He began to kiss her shoulder, then moved on to nuzzle her neck. Feeling dizzy, Aubrey struggled with what to do. Nick's breath was hot on her cheek, as he dusted a kiss there, in one swift motion. He rolled her over toward him.

Aubrey came face to face with Nick. She felt as though she were being pulled underwater and held there, and her breath caught. Nick put his lips on hers, and Aubrey responded in kind. Nick released her and tucked his arm around her. She didn't resist. When Nick began to gently stroke her hair, allowing individual strands to fall back onto the pillow, Aubrey shuddered.

"Ummm," he purred. "Sorry to wake you up. I just really needed to hold you."

After a few minutes of silence passed, resting in the crook of Nick's arm, Aubrey tipped her chin up to look into Nick's eyes, but they were closed. She had no idea what time it was. The clock was on the nightstand behind her, but Aubrey was afraid to move in case Nick had nodded out again. It was still fairly dark in the room. She figured she probably had a few hours before the alarm would go off. Aubrey closed her eyes, waiting for Nick's measured, paced breathing to cue her that it was time to move back to her side of the bed.

Nick jolted. "Remember when we used to talk about hiking the Appalachian Trail? What is it? Twenty-two hundred miles or so? Gosh, we had big plans, didn't we, Aubrey?" Nick bent his arm and pulled her in tighter, almost as if to hug her.

"I do remember. That was a really long time ago." Aubrey smiled at the thought.

"I guess we never meant to get so busy so fast. I mean, once we had the first house and grown up jobs, the kids just naturally followed. I guess I miss the times when it was just the two of us."

Nick lifted his head off the pillow. "Don't get me wrong. I love the kids. I just really miss us as a couple." He put his head back down.

"I think we need to get better at being a couple, Nick. We should have established date nights. I don't know, maybe we should take a few trips a year without the kids. It's not too late, you know." Aubrey found herself wondering, once again, if she was crazy. Nick sounded so coherent.

"You're right. I think we should get a few books on hiking and start training. I know there are different sections of the trail you can do as day trips, weekend trips, or weeklong trips. How about if we create an Appalachian Trail bucket list of all the trails we want to hike? We can cross them off as we complete each one. It would be fun. Don't you think?"

Aubrey could see it in her mind. Nick and her spending days at a time out in the woods, cooking over an open fire, hiking in the bright sunshine, and falling in love all over again. While Aubrey had her doubts, she couldn't help but hope that this moment was real. That Nick was really awake, and sober, and talking about a future together. "I think that's a great idea, Nicky. We could do some research and plan trips from Georgia to Maine, spread over the next several years."

Nick pulled his arm from under Aubrey and shifted onto his side, propping himself up with his elbow. Aubrey settled her head onto the pillow and Nick leaned over her. "You know, if we plan this right, we could be ready to hike on *Naked Hiking Day*. I think that would be a great start to our hiking adventures." Nick growled when he spoke the word *great*.

Aubrey giggled. "Naked Hiking Day? I think you've made that up."

Nick raised the hand that had been resting on his hip up into the air. "Scouts honor. I'm not making it up. *Naked Hiking Day* is on the summer solstice, June twenty-first. Hikers go out wearing their boots, their backpacks, and a smile … nothing else." Nick lowered his hand onto Aubrey's belly.

She was grinning ear to ear. "Is that right? Well, we'll see." Aubrey playfully tapped his bare chest with her index finger. "I think the *let's do the Appalachian Trail* thing was a set-up. I think you're in this exclusively for the naked hiking."

Sheepishly grinning, Nick shook his head. "No, really. I think creating a bucket list of hikes would be really fun. I mean it. Well, I guess as long as the solstice hike is on it, that is." He quickly tickled her, before falling back onto his pillow, laughing.

"Twenty-two hundred miles of trails is going to make for a pretty long bucket list, Nick. We'll need a whole notebook and a whole lot of time to plan these trips, you know."

Nick turned and grabbed both of her hands in his. "We have the rest of our whole lives, a little over two thousand miles is nothing, baby." He kissed her hands and settled back onto his side of the bed. Within seconds, Nick's breaths ebbed and flowed like the ocean's waves.

Her heart sank. Aubrey knew her Nicky was gone again. And, in just a few hours, the Nick that refused counseling—the one who wanted to divorce her—would be waking up.

Aubrey's stomach twisted into knots as she desperately tried to figure out how she could possibly enlighten Nick as to exactly why they didn't *need* a divorce at all. Aubrey wondered how she might even convince Nick, that deep down inside he actually really loved her … without giving this secret away?

Chapter Ten

When *Libby White* flashed on the screen of her ringing cell phone, Aubrey hesitated to answer. It'd been three weeks since she'd promised Libby she would tell Nick if she indeed concluded he probably suffered from parasomnia. Now, even though Aubrey was pretty convinced that's what was going on with Nick, she hadn't told him yet. It was odd for Libby to call on a Friday night, so on the fourth ring, Aubrey relented and answered.

"Hello?"

Libby didn't beat around the bush. "Okay, I know you're avoiding me because you didn't tell Nick. But that's not what I'm calling about. I need your help."

Aubrey felt panicked. "Oh, no. Is everything okay?"

After a pause, Libby answered, "I'm not sure. I need you to go on a stakeout in Philly with me. Can you come over to my place? I'm in Mystic."

Relieved, because Libby wasn't calling about Nick and it didn't sound like something was terribly wrong, Aubrey promised, "I'm on my way."

"That's perfect." Libby's voice was low. "Listen, I have to go. I'll see you soon."

Libby opened the front door before Aubrey even had a chance to knock. She glanced over one of Aubrey's shoulders, then the other, before grabbing her arm and pulling her in the front door and closing it.

Her behavior was so bizarre, it made Aubrey wonder if Libby was in some kind of legal trouble. She quickly discarded the thought.

Aubrey raised an eyebrow. "What's going on, Lib? You're kind of scaring me."

Libby put her index finger to her lips and waved her hand in a motion that told Aubrey to just follow her. Once they were in the kitchen, Libby explained that the kids were upstairs sleeping and she didn't want them to hear her.

It turned out Libby's new guy, Jed, had been acting pretty shady. This weekend he was supposed to come to Mystic with Libby, but at the last minute canceled. It wasn't the first time. Libby was worried because she realized that, after several months of dating, Jed had never invited her into his home. They'd always met at restaurants, or he'd come to her house. While Libby knew where he lived, they just never hung out at his place. Jed had casually mentioned how it was easier to hang out at Libby's house since she had the kids there. Libby had never questioned it. Until now.

Now, with the last minute cancellations and the realization she'd never even been inside his townhome, all of a sudden it was as though a light went on, and Libby feared she was quite possibly dating a married man.

Libby told Aubrey that Jed said he was working tomorrow. In all the time Libby had been dating Jed, he had never worked on a Saturday. For that reason, and because Aubrey was her best friend and she knew she'd go along with it, Libby wanted to tail him tomorrow. Since Jed knew her car, she needed Aubrey—and her car—to chauffeur her.

This wasn't their first spy mission. They'd pulled this *Thelma and Louise* routine before. When Austin had suddenly wanted a divorce and refused to go to counseling, Libby was sure he was having an affair. So, she and Aubrey staked out the extended stay hotel where Austin was living to see if it was true. They'd even gone so far as to rent a room in the place. After a week, no mistress surfaced, and Libby was finally convinced there wasn't one. Aubrey always felt that it would have been easier on Libby if there had been another woman. It would have been better than Libby having to accept that, to Austin, she simply wasn't lovable enough.

Aubrey agreed to the mission. Doing so, partly because she wanted to help Libby get to the truth, but more importantly, because she was grateful this wasn't about Nick.

These last weeks with Nick had been heavenly. Aubrey was living her old life. She lit candles again, put a vase of fresh flowers in the kitchen and another in their bedroom. Aubrey had even bought the chocolates Nick was crazy about from his favorite candy store, *Aunt Charlotte's*, in downtown Merchantville. She hid them in her nightstand. On the nights when her *Nicky* would show up … she'd bring them out. She'd also figured out that *Nicky* was more likely to show up if Nick had a glass of wine. Subsequently, she made sure they were never out of his favorite red.

Since the night they'd talked about their hiking plans, their night *dates,* which—in her own head—is what Aubrey considered them to be, were beginning to last a little longer. What started out with Nick interacting with her for fifteen to twenty-minute intervals, had graduated to forty-five minutes and on one occasion over an hour. And, it was the same theme every time. Nick would shower her with affection and attention. He'd tell her she was amazing and he'd go on and on about how she was the absolute love of his life. With every *date*, Aubrey found herself more and more in love with her husband.

By day, Aubrey knew Nick looked exhausted. His poor sleeping patterns were taking a toll on him. She was equally exhausted and looked the part, as well. But, God help her, she just couldn't give him up. Her promise to Teddy was never far from her heart either. Aubrey knew it was risky, but she continued to justify it as something that could ultimately save their marriage. To some degree, it was true.

Their daytime relationship had slowly begun to get better. They were actually *talking* to one another again.

Earlier in the week, Aubrey saw the ticket for Nick's dry cleaning that he'd left on top of his dresser. It'd been ages since she'd relinquished the chore of picking up his clothes for him. On a whim, she'd grabbed the ticket and had run to the cleaners to collect his suits and shirts, hanging everything up on his side of the closet when she'd returned home.

Later that night, she was reading a book in the living room, when Nick came looking for her. He'd glanced at her—frowning—and asked if she'd picked up his dry cleaning. When she told him she had, he tilted his head, and tentatively thanked her. For a minute, Aubrey worried she might have taken random acts of kindness a little too far.

After all, she had to keep reminding herself … she was the only one in their relationship who understood they still even *had* a relationship.

Chapter Eleven

As planned, early Saturday morning, Aubrey pulled her SUV into Libby's driveway and texted her to let her know she'd arrived. They'd agreed it was best that she not knock on the door or beep the horn. Libby hoped to escape the house without waking her kids.

Aubrey had to laugh as she watched Libby tiptoeing down the steps and across the driveway to the car.

When Libby open the passenger side door, Aubrey raised her eyebrows. "Did you really think the kids were going to hear you once you were *outside* of the house?"

"I wasn't taking any chances." Libby hopped up on the seat and fastened her seatbelt. She had two Phillies hats in her hand. She tossed one at Aubrey. "Here, put this on."

Aubrey scrunched her mouth to the side, her eyes narrowing. "Seriously? Disguises? You've gotta be kidding me."

"No, I'm not kidding." Libby grabbed the cap by the brim and plopped it onto her own head. "We can't get caught, Aubrey. I'm sorry to drag you into this at all. But, I just can't be blindsided again. It was too painful. I won't make it through that again." Libby, seeming to shake off the sentiment, took a deep breath and returned to giving out orders. "Jed can't see us. Wear the hat."

Grabbing the cap from her lap, Aubrey tossed it onto the middle of the dashboard. "Well, these bright red hats sure look discreet. Nevermind the fact, I just did my hair." She put the car in reverse and backed out of the gravel driveway. "We have at least an hour long drive to get to Philly. I don't have to wear that silly thing now. Besides, you forgot the sunglasses." Aubrey giggled.

Reaching into her Michael Kohrs Jet-Set Travel Bag, Libby shook her head. "Oh, no, I didn't." And, true to her word, she pulled out two pairs of glasses and waved them in the air. "I forgot nothing, my friend." She grinned like she was auditioning to be one of the Three Stooges.

Aubrey shook her head and rolled her eyes. "I'm afraid to ask what else you have in that bag."

Libby peered into her purse. "Well, let's see, I have bottles of water, granola bars, peanut butter and jelly sandwiches, pretzels, gum … you name it."

"Dear God, how long do you think we are going to be at this? Are we spending the night? Because if we are, I forgot to bring a change of underwear." Aubrey glanced at Libby and smiled, before turning her attention back to the highway.

"Speaking of spending the night … how's Nick?" Libby crinkled her nose, smirking.

The question hung in the air. Aubrey had been dreading this drive to Philly because she realized it would lend itself to a question and answer session. She just wasn't prepared to tell Nick about what was happening when he was sleeping, and she wasn't about to allow herself to be coerced into doing so. Aubrey didn't want to have this conversation with Libby, but she answered anyway. "Nick is fine." She shook her head. "Look, Lib, I do think he's a parasomniac. And, with that in mind, I know you don't agree with what I am doing, but you're going to have to trust me on this. It will all work out okay."

Libby winced. "I figured as much when I didn't hear from you. I know that you think what you're doing is a *means to an end* thing … but have you thought about this from Nick's side? Like, he must be exhausted, and he has no idea why. Maybe he's worried about it. What if Nick thinks he's legit sick or something?"

"I didn't really think about that, you're right. Nick wouldn't necessarily be sharing those concerns with me these days. But, in all fairness about what I'm doing, *he* does benefit if this actually saves our relationship. This isn't a zero-sum game for Nick. Our family is his investment, too. Also, just so you know, when he's sleepwalking—I know it seems crazy to call it that when he's not *actually* walking, but they do—he's never out of my sight. Outside of the *cake baking* night, Nick has never even left our bed, and he always goes back into a deep sleep, long before I'm able to fall asleep again." Aubrey half held her breath waiting for Libby's response.

Sighing, Libby reached over and patted Aubrey's shoulder. "I just hope you know what you're doing." She'd let it go, and the remainder of the ride into the city was filled with small talk.

They were approaching the Walt Whitman Bridge. "Lib, once we're over the Walt you'll have to tell me where we're going."

Libby nodded. "Just get us in the area of Christ Church Cemetery, I'll direct you from there. His place is only a few streets over at that point." She leaned forward to retrieve the baseball cap and put it on Aubrey's lap. "Now, put that on, would ya?"

Before too long, Aubrey frowned and rolled her eyes as she put the hat on her head. "We're coming up on the cemetery. Where to now?"

Pointing at the windshield, Libby said, "Make this right. Then, two streets up make a left. As soon as you make the left, pull over and park wherever you can.

When Aubrey made the left, there was an open parking space, so she began to parallel park when Libby shouted like a maniac. "Oh, no! That's him! You can't park here."

Before Aubrey could process what was happening, Libby grabbed the wheel. In a knee-jerk reaction, Aubrey pulled the steering wheel back, in essence, overcompensating and swinging the car too far to the right. They were still moving, and heard a loud thud, as they were jolted forward. Libby tossed her seatbelt off and hit the floor.

Crouched in front of her seat, she whispered, "Can you see him? Is he looking over here?"

Aubrey craned her neck, "Was he the guy wearing a yellow jacket and jeans?"

"Yes. Yes, he was. Oh, God, did he see us?"

"No. He just turned the corner. And, you *do* realize, we just hit a car, right?"

There was panic in Libby's voice. "Follow him! We can't lose him!"

Aubrey's mouth dropped open. "Libby! That's leaving the scene of an accident. We have to find out who this car we hit belongs to."

"We'll come back. Just go. You have to go, or we'll lose Jed."

Knowing she'd lost her mind, Aubrey did as Libby said, and turned the wheel, and gunned it. She got to the edge of the street just in time to see the yellow jacket getting into a car and pulling out onto the main drag. Libby remained crouched on the floor shooting off a million and one questions … *can you see him? … what's he doing? … is anyone with him? … where are we now?*

As they moved around the city, Aubrey repeatedly told Libby to get up and sit on her seat. Jed was several cars in front of them and would never be able to see her. She'd kept refusing.

"Why did you bring a hat if you were going to hide on the floor?" Aubrey made a right since she watched Jed go in that direction.

"Very funny. I didn't plan on being on the floor." Libby grabbed the brim and pulled the hat off her head and dropped it onto the seat. "How do we end up like this, Aubrey? Why am I all hunched on the floor, trying to see what yet another guy is—or is not—doing to me? Is someone really going to be giving my eulogy one day and say I was all these good things, but good ole Libby *was never lucky in love?*"

Aubrey felt bad. "I don't know, Libby. You sure deserve a good guy. You bring a lot to the table."

Sighing, Libby folded her arms on the seat and rested her head on them. "Thanks."

Aubrey glanced in her rearview mirror. "Oh, no!"

Libby's head popped up.

Grabbing Libby's head, Aubrey pushed it back down onto the seat. "Stay down. There's a cop behind me."

Ducking, Libby shifted her eyes to look up at Aubrey. "Stay cool. It's alright."

"Stay cool? I have you crouched on my floor and a brand new dent in my car. Oh, a new dent from the accident I just caused and failed to report. Oh, yeah, I'm totally cool."

"Can you still see Jed?"

Aubrey shot a dirty look at Libby. "Are you kidding me right now? My heart is in my throat. I'm sweating like a death row inmate on execution day, and *that's* what your concern is?"

Looking like a scolded child, Libby whispered, "Well, a little."

"Libby!"

Persistent, Libby begged, "Can you just tell me if you see him?"

Exasperated, Aubrey answered, "Yes. I see him. Okay?" She glanced in her rearview mirror, as she was crossing a large intersection, and heaved a sigh of relief when she watched the police car make a left turn. "The cop just turned off."

Looking ahead, she realized Jed turned his car into a parking garage. She pulled into an alley and stopped, putting her flashers on. She had a clear view of the exit of the garage. No one could come or go from that exit without her seeing them.

Libby perked up. What's going on? Why did you stop?"

Never taking her eye off the garage, Aubrey answered. "You can come out now. Jed drove into the parking garage across the street from where we're sitting. I'm waiting for him to come out."

Libby stretched her neck and looked around before rising and getting back onto her seat and buckling her seatbelt. No sooner had she situated herself, Jed exited the garage on foot. He made a right toward Seventh Street.

Giving him about a block and a half of leeway, Aubrey slowly crept out onto the street and proceeded to roll along, barely more than idling. Finally, Jed stopped at a storefront and grabbed the handle.

Libby started bouncing up and down in her seat and fanning herself with her hands. "Oh, my God. Oh, my God."

That's when Aubrey realized where they were, and her mouth dropped wide open.

Jed was entering a jewelry store. And, it wasn't just any jewelry store. The one he'd just walked into was widely known as the city of Philadelphia's biggest broker … of engagement rings.

Chapter Twelve

When Aubrey walked through the door at home, after dropping Libby off at her own house, Nick was waiting for her in the kitchen. She thought, *oh, no, here we go, he's going to pick now ... to tell me he wants a divorce.*

She put her purse and keys on the island counter, Nick was sitting on a bar stool there. Trying to be nonchalant, Aubrey turned to get a bottle of water from the fridge. With her back to him, she asked, "Where are the kids?"

Nick's voice was raspy. "Peyton is at a movie and Teddy's at a friend's—the new kid's house, a few doors down. Do you have a minute? I need to talk to you."

Twisting the cap off her water bottle, she realized his voice had a hint of anger in it. Her tongue was feeling so dry it was nearly plastered to the roof of her mouth. She turned toward Nick, sounding one thousand times more casual then she felt. "Sure. What's up?" Adrenaline raced through Aubrey's body. She tried to will her hands not to shake as she put her water down on the counter and scooted herself onto a bar stool, safely leaving an empty one between them.

Nick began, "I went to see our doctor this morning."

Their doctor of ten years was Doctor Jeff DiMarco. Aubrey had no idea Nick had made an appointment with Doctor Jeff.

Nick cleared his throat and continued. "I made a doctor appointment because I've been so exhausted …"

Wait, the doctor? He's not asking me for a divorce. Aubrey shook her head and blinked, her own thoughts blocking out what Nick was saying. She tried to catch up.

"… so, I was wondering if you know anything about that?" Nick cocked his head to the side.

Aubrey's mind raced, trying to recover what he'd said. She couldn't. She'd been too lost in her own head. "I … uh, wait … the doctor said what?"

Nick rolled his eyes and shook his head. "Aren't you even listening to me? The doctor said he believes it's possible I could be sleepwalking."

Aubrey widened her eyes, trying to look surprised. She worried her rusty acting skills—unused since high school—were failing her. "Oh, gosh. Well, that's strange." Aubrey felt dread threatening to weigh her down. *I can't tell him now. I'm almost there. Everything has been going so well.*

Raising one eyebrow, Nick looked Aubrey directly in the eye. "Doctor Jeff told me if I was sleepwalking, you, as my spouse, most likely would know about it. Especially since you come to bed later than me."

Hoping her face wasn't giving her away, Aubrey panicked, and so she shrugged her shoulders nonchalantly. "Actually, you've only recently been going to bed before me. Normally, I'm in bed first." Aubrey couldn't believe what she said next, but she'd heard her own voice in her head. "Either way, it's news to me. Maybe he's wrong." She knew she just took this whole thing to another level. Aubrey was cringing inside.

"Well, he's ordered an EEG. He's even suggested I get one of those watches that track steps. They zero out at midnight, so he said it should always be zero when I wake up in the morning." Nick seemed to be studying Aubrey's face.

Shifting in her chair, Aubrey silently hoped the anxiety she felt inside wasn't palpable. She enjoyed her nights with Nick. Aubrey felt bad that he was tired, but it had been so incredible to have glimpses of her husband back. More importantly, it really was having a positive impact on their waking relationship. But, that wouldn't matter if Nick found out what she'd been up to now. If he did, he'd surely divorce her.

Still, she rationalized, Nick's sleepwalking wasn't her fault. It was no one's fault. She tried not to think about whose fault it was that she knew and wasn't telling him. Aubrey couldn't quite sort that part out.

Aubrey reached back and rubbed the back of her neck. "Why does Doctor Jeff think it's sleepwalking? A lot of people wake up exhausted for a whole bunch of different reasons. It could be hormones, mid-life changes, or even restless-leg syndrome. It seems to me, it's a little premature to just throw a random diagnosis at a little tiredness." Aubrey knew she'd just stooped to a whole new low.

She followed her swamp dive by immediately promising herself that she'd allow just one more week of this so she could work on Nick in the daytime. Then, that was it. Aubrey vowed to tell him.

"Well, it's not just tiredness … it's exhaustion." Nick looked annoyed that Aubrey had downplayed it. "He asked me several questions. When I answered him and was reflecting back, I realized that things have been moved from where I've placed them before bed. For instance, when I've been certain that I'd left my keys on top of my dresser, I've found them in my top drawer in the morning."

Nick paused and scratched the top of his head, before going on. "My briefcase has been moved from where I've left it. And, just the other day, there was a candy wrapper on my nightstand when I woke up. I've even found my slippers in the kitchen when I definitely remembered taking them off and sliding them under my side of the bed." Nick gazed off into the distance, as though he were trying to recall it.

When Nick returned his gaze to Aubrey, he nearly shocked her. "Oh, and there was one morning a while back, near your birthday, I woke up with chocolate under my fingernails. When I went downstairs, there was a cake on the counter." He furrowed his brow. "It was *you* who baked the cake, right? Aubrey?"

Feeling as though Nick's eyes were looking right through her, Aubrey looked up at the ceiling and back down again. "A cake?" She tapped her fingers on the counter and tried to look thoughtful. "Oh, wait … yes. A while back, I do remember baking a cake. Gosh, I hadn't baked one in so long." The lie hung—screaming—in the air.

Nick shook his head. "Well, I must have gone down there at some point to have ended up with icing under my nails."

Aubrey ignored his statement as she scolded herself. *What was I thinking? Paying attention to things like that should have been vitally important to me.* She should have noticed if Nick had moved anything from where it was before he went to sleep. All of that must have happened the night he'd baked the cake. What she'd told Libby was the truth. Every encounter after that was strictly in bed. Nick never got up and moved around.

Making a mental note not to be so sloppy in the future, Aubrey did take a moment to remind herself she'd never had a secret affair with her own husband before. She couldn't really have been expected to know such things.

Standing up, Aubrey headed to the recycle bin with her water bottle. "When is your test?"

"First thing Monday morning. I have bloodwork Doctor Jeff ordered, too." Nick leaned back in his chair, laced his fingers together, and rested them on top of his head.

Tossing the bottle into the can, Aubrey turned back. "Well, make sure you let me know how it turns out. Was there anything else you need to talk to me about?" She nearly held her breath waiting for his answer. The only thing she wanted was to get out of this room and out of this conversation.

"No." Nick's eyes narrowed. "Aubrey? You would tell me if I were sleepwalking?" He paused and leaned forward. "Wouldn't you? I mean, you wouldn't keep it from me … right?"

Drums were thumping in Aubrey's chest. She could feel the heat rise up to her face. *Just keep your cool,* she warned herself. Grateful that liars pants really don't catch on fire, she shook her head. "Nick, of course, I would tell you. Why wouldn't I? What would I have to gain?" *Just one more week,* Aubrey reminded herself. *This is the only chance you have to save your marriage.*

Nick lowered his chin. "You're right. You're right. Of course, you would tell me. I'm just so exhausted." As if to prove he was telling the truth, Nick dropped his hands to his face and rubbed his eyes. "Doctor Jeff's preliminary diagnosis and his explanation for it just seemed to make sense. All the pieces seemed to be fitting together. Well, all the pieces except for the one that would include you being a definite witness to my sleepwalking. I'll get the testing done, and hopefully, Doctor Jeff can find the missing puzzle piece."

Aubrey didn't care for puzzle building. But, on the few occasions when she participated in putting them together with Nick and the kids, it would drive her crazy when they'd get to the very end of the puzzle, only to have them discover a piece was missing.

Regarding the puzzle surrounding Nick's exhaustion, she secretly hoped—at least for now—the last missing piece was one her husband would never be able to find.

Chapter Thirteen

On Sunday, as soon as Nick finished breakfast, he told Aubrey he was leaving to go to the electronics store to buy one of those step counting watches. She'd suggested he just use the app for step counting on his phone. But the doctor wanted the watch because it recorded the length and quality of sleep, as well.

Aubrey realized this would create a huge hurdle in her plans. She'd hoped Nick wouldn't follow through on the watch. While she realized it might seem ridiculous, she'd hoped he'd forgotten all about it. But, needless to say, apparently he hadn't.

The thought of losing their night *dates* made Aubrey feel unbelievably miserable. As soon as the step counter served to prove Nick was indeed sleepwalking, she knew right well he'd be prescribed medication, which would end it. All of it. Thus, terminating their romantic evening rendezvous.

Just considering that reality instantly made her feel as though she were losing Nick all over again. Before all this, Aubrey had gotten used to being alone. But now, having had Nick back, she felt like she appreciated him so much more. Aubrey enjoyed his company … his presence. The feelings were so much like those she'd felt before life began to weigh them both down. Before they'd lost their way.

While Nick was gone, Aubrey ran the kids around for their usual weekend stuff. One stop was at the office supply store to buy poster board for Teddy for a school project, another was a stop at the local pharmacy so Peyton could buy mascara, and finally, they ended up at the grocery store. After almost three hundred dollars spent on weekly dinners, stuff for lunches, and restock on shampoos and paper products, they were on their way home.

As Aubrey, Peyton, and Teddy unloaded groceries, Nick arrived home and walked into the kitchen holding his cell phone in his hand.

Aubrey smiled. "Hey! Did you get what you need?"

Still looking somewhat suspicious at her overly friendly gestures, Nick nodded. "I did. I got a watch that syncs with my phone so I can see the quality of my sleep, steps walked, and hours slept. It's pretty cool." He held his phone up in the air. "All of it will show up right here, each morning."

Aubrey felt as though concrete had been poured down her esophagus and been left there to dry. She quickly managed to shake it off and, once again, she called upon her acting skills. "That's great. Hopefully, Doctor Jeff will get to the bottom of this for you." Aubrey took a breath and without thinking any further, motioned to a bag on the counter. "The grocery store had those sweet rolls that you like on sale, so I got you some."

Raising an eyebrow, Nick walked over to where the bag was and peeked into it. "Uh, thanks, Aub, but you didn't have to do that."

Shrugging, and continuing to put the groceries away, Aubrey said, "It was no big deal. I saw them and thought you'd like them."

She'd failed to notice Nick's suspicious glance.

Later that evening and for the first time in ages, Aubrey cooked a big family dinner. It was like the old days … Mexican flair: Chili, nachos, tacos, and her own unique three-layer refried bean dip. Everyone seems so relaxed and happy. Even Nick.

At dinner, Aubrey noticed Nick was now wearing his brand-new fitness watch. So, she knew, in the unlikely event Nick was to get up out of their bed tonight, steps would be logged, and ultimately his diagnosis would be confirmed. Any chance Aubrey had of saving their marriage would be over.

One more week. That's all she was asking for. Aubrey hoped that was all she needed. She'd really have to get a little more aggressive about their daytime relationship, if Aubrey wanted this to work. After all, she'd come this far.

The fact that she was getting a little too good at lies and deception wasn't lost on Aubrey. She equated it to being stranded on an island … desperate people do desperate things. Her marriage and the happiness of her children was at stake. Survival of the fittest at its best.

Enjoying the evening, Nick had indulged in two glasses of wine. Aubrey knew what that meant. This had been going on long enough now, she'd memorized the routine.

Within the first hour, after Nick retired for the night, he was sure to awaken. Well, technically, not exactly *awaken*. Aubrey was never sure what to call it. Nick did *look* awake.

Sure enough, Aubrey climbed into bed, switched off the light on her nightstand, and settled in, facing the outside of the bed. After a few minutes passed, Nick stirred.

Suddenly, she'd felt one of his arms cross over her, pulling her into him. And just like so many times before, her body became his wonderland. Aubrey purred at his touch. Most of their nights together were merely filled with sweet nothings, heavy petting, and some good old-fashioned making out. Nick hadn't taken intimacy any further than that and Aubrey was afraid to push it, not knowing what might serve to wake him up. So, she'd always surrendered to his lead.

Nick whispered all the things Aubrey had grown to love to hear him say again. "You're beautiful, I love you, all these years later and I still can't believe you're mine."

Aubrey put her hand on Nick's forearm and rubbed it. Before she could completely melt into him, her hand came in contact with that watch. Like an alarm, it reminded her of what she couldn't get away with any longer.

In spite of everything Aubrey wanted right now, she somehow found the restraint to say, "I love you, too, Nick, but I'm just feeling a little tired tonight."

She wanted to just sit up and take that stupid watch off of his arm. Aubrey knew she needed to figure out a way to do a factory reset on that thing so she'd be able to erase it every night for the next week. But, she also realized—for tonight—patience was her best friend.

So, in spite of everything she needed and craved from Nick, she lay there restrained—wanting him so badly, but waiting until the stillness that fell over him, confirmed … he was fast asleep once again.

Chapter Fourteen

On Tuesday, Aubrey had arrived home from another hell-driven overnight shift at the hospital. Nasty batches of fentanyl-laced heroin were taking young people out in staggering numbers, and she was finding herself, more often than not, right in the center of the war zone.

Nick told her he'd had his testing done yesterday and, to Aubrey, the idea of his results possibly coming in today remained unnerving to her.

As was their family routine, when she worked overnight shifts at the hospital, Aubrey came home and, before going to bed, would get the kids off to school. Once that was accomplished, she would go get the rest she desperately needed.

Waking around two in the afternoon, Aubrey checked her phone. Nothing from Nick. She sighed with relief. He mustn't have heard anything from Doctor Jeff, or he would've surely called Aubrey. No news was good news.

Peyton and Teddy had scheduled afternoon activities at school. Aubrey took advantage of the time. It was in between visits from her housekeeper, so she took the opportunity to wipe down the kitchen and bathrooms, mop some floors, and she sorted through some unopened mail, before settling at the computer and paying bills.

So much of her time lately had been dedicated to the craziness that had become their life, Aubrey was sincerely grateful for a day that actually felt more routine and normal.

Honestly? Aubrey had felt as though the word *normal* had exited her vocabulary for good. She'd been going through the motions for so long, in survival mode, she wasn't exactly sure she remembered what her idea of normal was anymore. But Aubrey certainly realized she could get used to this old routine again.

Aubrey secretly prayed this wasn't the calm before the storm. After all, Nick had test results out there waiting to be delivered to him. Aubrey worried they might expose her for what she'd become. She tried to be honest with herself. Expose her for what? Aubrey knew it would expose her for all the unpleasant adjectives that might describe her behavior these last months. Adjectives she couldn't live with … but, had surely earned nonetheless.

As far as how the days were playing out in their house lately, today had been a good one. When the kids came home, Aubrey prepared meatloaf and mashed potatoes for dinner, and Nick strolled in at what now was his new regular time. A second night of having dinner as a family was on the books. Each positive thing that transpired between them was a reassurance to Aubrey that her plan was working. With Nick refusing to go to counseling, she just didn't know what else to do. Until these past few days, Nick wasn't even speaking to her more than to say hello or goodbye. Now, they were having dinners together.

After dinner, Aubrey had to rush out for a mandatory staff meeting at the hospital. By the time she returned, the kids were in bed. Nick was, too.

Tiptoeing around, Aubrey took care of some dishes that were in the sink. She turned out lights and locked up before heading upstairs to bed herself. It was early, but Aubrey was always a little more tired after coming off an overnight shift. She welcomed the extra sleep, and it would've been great had there actually been any.

She no sooner tucked her self under the blankets when Nick stirred. Aubrey froze. She wanted Nick in more ways than she cared to admit, but there was that watch. Spying on them like a battery operated *Big Brother*.

Just as so many of their recent encounters began, Nick snuggled in against Aubrey's back. His words soothed her. "Hey beautiful, you're late. I've been missing you." Nick's hands roamed where they wanted to, and as usual, Aubrey definitely didn't object.

Aubrey looked more forward to the words Nick spoke than she did to the actual physical contact. While she loved Nick's touch, it was his kindness, love, and appreciation she'd missed the most. His words had been so cruel for so long.

Inevitably, Aubrey came in contact with the snitch attached to his wrist. She took her chances, turning toward him, she lamented, "Nicky, your watch has scratched me twice. How about if we take it off and put it on the nightstand?"

Nick shot straight up.

Aubrey thought for sure she was caught.

She exhaled when in the kindest voice he could muster, Nick said, "Of course, of course. I'm sorry, Aubrey, let me take this off." Aubrey ignored how his voice sounded just a little too robotic.

Relieved, she held out her hand and took the watch from Nick. Aubrey put it on the nightstand, insisting to herself that she must remember to get it back on his wrist before he woke up without it in the morning.

No sooner had Aubrey placed the watch on the nightstand, Nick said, "Dance with me, baby, I can't remember the last time you danced with me."

With that, Nick dragged Aubrey out of bed and then, in that dark room, with only the slightest hint of light from a streetlamp, they danced. The only music was that reverberating from the rhythm of their hearts and the sounds of their breath getting tangled up in one another's.

Nick dragged his lips, followed by his warm whispers, over Aubrey's neck. Chills ran up her spine.

As one thing led to another—and before Aubrey could decide if she should object, or even consider stopping what happened next—it came so naturally, Nick lowered her back onto the edge of the bed and made love to her. It took Aubrey's breath away, and tears weren't far behind. She'd really had no idea just how much she'd missed, no ... longed for ... Nick's love.

Afterward, as she lay in the stillness of complete satisfaction, Nick turned away and scooted back up the bed to put his head on his pillow. Aubrey's eyes popped open. As panic set in, her thoughts raced ... *Nick couldn't go back to sleep, his watch was still on the nightstand, the smell of her ... of what they'd done ... surely was all over him ...*

If Nick had already fallen asleep, she'd risk waking him as she'd try to return things to the way they were before he'd fallen asleep... to *normal.*

Aubrey crawled to the top of the bed and was relieved when he smiled at her. She reached for the watch. "Here, don't forget this," she mumbled as she fastened it back onto his wrist, glad she'd remembered to put it on the same wrist from which he'd taken it off.

Once the watch was secure, nearly running to the bathroom and back, she'd grabbed a wet washcloth and washed any signs they'd been intimate away from Nick's body. As she'd bathed him, he'd even laughed—teasing Aubrey—saying it was really okay ... he was pretty sure his wife would be okay with what they'd just done.

Aubrey coerced him back into his discarded pajama pants he'd left on the floor at the foot of the bed. Her actions had been just in time. When Aubrey returned from tossing the washcloth into their hamper in the bathroom, Nick was curled on his side, already sound asleep.

Aubrey was faced with the truth. Nick always reverted to a deep sleep. Just like all those other nights. She was sure, in the morning, he'd have no idea what transpired between them. But, typically, lovemaking wasn't in the equation. Tonight it had been, leaving Aubrey to wonder what all this *really* had meant, to both of them, particularly if Nick wasn't *actually* awake.

Could his advances tonight be considered advances at all? Could someone who was medically deemed to be asleep, give consent to intimacy … even if they'd been the party who'd initiated it?

And, if the truthful answer was that a sleeping person couldn't consent … no matter who instigated the act … Aubrey wondered exactly who she was … who'd she'd become … and exactly what major moral lines she'd really permitted herself to cross tonight.

Chapter Fifteen

The three rings it took before Libby finally answered the phone felt like an eternity to Aubrey. She'd just taken the kids to school and called her best friend's cell phone the second they'd exited the car. "Lib? You have to come down to the Island today!"

"Aubrey?" Libby's voice sounded tired. "Gosh, is everything alright? What's going on?"

"You won't believe what's happened. I need your help. Holy cow. I'm in some deep water. You have to come down here. I really need you!"

"Are the kids okay? What'd you do?" Libby's voice suddenly sounded more awake and definitely concerned.

Aubrey took a deep breath in and blew it out. "Last night, when Nick was sleepwalking, we danced." She paused and closed her eyes. "And, that led to us having sex."

Libby practically shouted. "Led to *wh-at*?"

"I know, Libby. I know, okay?" That wasn't even the worst of it as far as Aubrey was concerned. "You can lecture me later about how my morals are in the toilet on this one. But, there's more ... that's why I need you here!"

Libby's voice sounded exasperated. "I can't imagine how much worse it could get."

Aubrey felt like she could vomit. "Nick recorded it."

"Aubrey! How could you let him record it? You knew ..."

"Oh, my God. I didn't let him! I didn't notice his laptop was even in our room!" While last night's actions weren't defensible, Aubrey really had no idea, and certainly didn't consent to, the recording.

She went on to explain to Libby how Nick stopped in the kitchen this morning, while Aubrey was having her coffee, and told her not to let Teddy mess with his laptop today. He was leaving it behind because he had a meeting in the city and didn't want to cart it around, nor did he want to leave it in the car to be stolen.

Because of Nick's increasing tiredness—this morning had been no exception—last night he'd left his laptop on his dresser in video recording mode so he could determine if he was indeed sleepwalking. Therefore, their charades would no doubt be on there in living color. Thankfully, he'd been running late and didn't have time to check what he'd captured before leaving.

The second he'd pulled out of the driveway, Aubrey ran downstairs and grabbed the laptop, sat down on her bed, and typed in the password. Except, it wasn't the right password. Nick must've changed it. She guessed twenty different passwords she'd known Nick to use. None of them would allow her access.

Libby remained silent on the other end of the phone.

Aubrey was near tears. "I don't know what to do."

Libby shot off a few ideas. "We could take the laptop on the Cape May ferry and toss it overboard in the middle of the ocean. No one would be on those outer decks in this cold weather. It could work. You could let Nick believe it was stolen.

"He'd report it to the police. And, possibly to our homeowner's insurance. Then, I could add filing a false police report and insurance fraud to last Saturday's leaving the scene of an accident." When they'd circled back to the car they'd hit in Philly, it was gone. Aubrey could hear the panic in her own voice. She could feel it in her throat.

Apparently, Libby heard it, too. "I'll be there. I have a couple of meetings this morning that I have to get to, but I'll be there."

Aubrey flung open the door before Libby made it to the top step. Hugging the laptop to her chest with one arm, she used her free arm to hug her friend. "Thank you so much for coming."

Leading the way upstairs to the kitchen, Aubrey placed the laptop onto the counter in front of one of the empty stools.

She motioned toward the seat. "Libby, you can sit down and try anything you think Nick could possibly have used as a password.

I've easily made a hundred attempts to get into that thing. Luckily, it's not like email or a website. I'd have been locked out long ago."

Libby tried everything she could think of … from the obvious *p-a-s-s-w-o-r-d* to the kid's names, the dog's name, the name of their street, and she even tried Aubrey's name … all to no avail.

Aubrey poured two cups of coffee and placed them on the counter. She put cream, sugar, and a spoon next to the laptop, in front of Libby.

As she sat back down, Aubrey watched as Libby made one unsuccessful attempt after another. If Nick saw that video of what they … she … did, Aubrey knew it would be the last straw. "What am I going to do?"

Libby suddenly sat up straight and raised her eyebrows. "Hey, I have an idea. You could tell Nick you loaned me his laptop. I was down here on the island and got into a jam with work and had forgotten my computer in the city. I could take this with me, and you could call him saying the password you gave me wouldn't work. That way, you can get the new password from him. You could come to my house later, under the premise of picking up the laptop, erase all the evidence of the crime, and bring it back here." Libby looked proud of herself, as she nodded her head and smiled.

Aubrey thought that that sounded like a great idea. She was so grateful to have Libby as her best friend. Even though Libby didn't agree with what she'd been doing, she was still trying to keep Aubrey from ruining her whole life while she figured out what to do next—how to make this right.

She was about to agree to the plan, but then a thought popped into Aubrey's head. "Oh, wait. Why wouldn't I have loaned you *my* computer? Computers are so personal. It wouldn't make sense that I loaned you Nick's …"

Shrugging, Libby scrunched her nose. "Your computer's broken?"

"No, I was using it this morning when he left for work." Aubrey dropped her chin as she realized they were back to square one again.

Libby heard the sound of someone barreling through the front door followed by the sound of someone running up the steps, Aubrey turned to Libby and answered the unasked question. "It's just Teddy. He's home from school."

Libby's eyes brightened, and seconds before Teddy charged into the room, she whispered, "I have an idea."

As Teddy appeared, Aubrey nonchalantly pushed the laptop into the center of the island. "Hey, buddy, how was school?"

Delightful as always, Teddy hugged his mother. "It was good. Can I get a snack?" He let go. "Hi, Aunt Libby. Is Brody here?"

Aubrey answered for her. "No, honey. Brody's not here. You can get a snack."

"Hey, big guy. I'll bring Brody next time." Libby tousled Teddy's hair as he walked by.

When he was far enough away, speaking out of the side of her mouth, Aubrey leaned in toward Libby. "What idea?"

Libby shifted her eyes to Teddy and back again. "If Nick warned you to keep Teddy away from the laptop, then Teddy knows the password!"

It was true. If Aubrey was at work and Teddy was bored, he often played games on the laptop in Nick's office. She wondered why she hadn't thought of that herself.

Teddy was heading back toward them with a package of peanut butter crackers in his hand. He tore the wrapper open, climbed up onto one of the barstools, pulled a cracker from the pack and took a bite.

Libby wagged her eyebrows at Aubrey and bobbed her chin toward Teddy. Aubrey knew Libby wanted her to ask him for the password. But, Aubrey subtly shook her head no.

There was no way she could just *ask* Teddy for it. He would surely tell Nick. Aubrey had no idea how she might secretly obtain it from him and was instantly grateful for Libby's quick thinking when she spoke up.

"Hey, Teddy, your mom was telling me you've gotten pretty good at that video game you play online. Think you could show me what it's all about?" Libby pushed the laptop down the counter in front of Teddy. "Here. You can show me on your dad's laptop."

Glancing first at the laptop and then, at Libby, Teddy shrugged. "It's better on the big monitor in the living room. Do you want to watch there?" He took another bite of the cracker.

Almost without missing a beat, Libby stood up. "You know what? I think I'm going to have a snack, too. So, how about if you just show me here. When we're done with our snacks, we can go out, and you can show me on the desktop." Libby walked toward the pantry.

Aubrey released the breath she was holding as she watched Teddy comply.

Libby was so clever. She never even said the word *password* to Teddy. He opened the laptop and begin to type using only his index finger. Aubrey leaned slightly as she strained to see which keys Teddy tapped. T–S–U–G–U-A.

It took Aubrey a minute … TSUGUA? It blew her mind when she realized it was Nick's birth month—August—spelled backward. He really didn't want to take a chance that Aubrey would be able to access his laptop. She'd tried the word *August* earlier. It would never have occurred to her to spell it backward. Aubrey wondered what he was hiding.

She exchanged glances with Libby across the room, and Aubrey nodded as she saw Nick's homepage load. Barely able to contain herself, Aubrey wanted to throw her arms around Teddy and yelp for joy. Instead, she began cracking her knuckles, wondering what Libby was going to do next. As usual, Libby was quick on her feet and didn't let Aubrey down.

Smiling, Libby walked back over with her own package of peanut butter crackers. "Hey, you know what, Ted? Let's go ahead and go into the other room. I didn't realize how late it was getting. I'll just have you show me your game on the bigger screen, now, before I have to go home."

Unfazed, Teddy raised one shoulder, shrugged, and dropped it. "Okay." He began to close the lid on the computer, but Aubrey intercepted it.

"I've got this, buddy. You go ahead with Aunt Libby." Aubrey smiled.

As soon as they rounded the corner, Aubrey grabbed the open laptop and made a mad dash for her bedroom. She feared running into Peyton as she arrived home from school. But, Aubrey quickly realized, it wouldn't matter if her daughter saw her with Nick's laptop. It looked identical to her own.

Aubrey heard Peyton coming into the house, as soon as she shut the door to her bedroom, so she paused, locking it.

Sitting cross-legged on her bed, she located and opened the video from last night. Sure enough, there Nick and she were ... in bed. Aubrey watched as Nick slowly rolled over to her side of the bed and put his arm around her. When she witnessed her own manipulation as she convinced him to remove his watch, she shuddered. The truth was worse in living color. As the video went on, Aubrey couldn't help but watch. Her favorite was the part when they'd danced—sans music.

Aubrey even wanted to witness their lovemaking but was surprised to find she couldn't. As soon as that part of the video began, she turned it off. She started to feel nauseous. Something inside of her knew to make love with Nick while he was sleepwalking simply wasn't right. But, it had felt so right at the moment. We *are* married. Aubrey justified it again ... *Nicky was the one who initiated it*. That meant it was okay. Granted it was a little weird, but okay. *Right*?

Unable to allow herself to think about it any longer, Aubrey deleted the video. Before placing the laptop back where Nick had left it on the dresser, she's grabbed a hand towel and wiped any evidence of herself from his computer, as though Nick was going to have it dusted for fingerprints or something.

As almost an afterthought, Aubrey decided to take a look at one more thing. It was really bothering her that Nick had not only changed his password, but he also went so far as to make it something un-discoverable to her. Aubrey needed to know why.

Opening the lid, she typed in the password. Clicking on Nick's email, Aubrey's heart sunk when she saw the name, *John Jackson,* the attorney Nick had gone to see, in an email at the top of Nick's *inbox.* The email was from late yesterday afternoon, and it was evident that Nick had already read it. Aubrey opened it:

Dear Nick,
I've prepared your divorce papers. They are ready to
be signed by you and sent to your wife.
As per our conversation, let me know when you
are ready to pull the trigger on this. I know you wanted
a chance to talk to Aubrey before we serve her.
As discussed, I'll wait to hear from you.
Sincerely,
John Jackson

JACKSON, KENT, AND MARSHALL, ATTORNEY'S AT LAW

Aubrey's hands were shaking, and her heart thumped in her throat. Tears streamed down her face as she clicked on Nick's *sent mail* tab to see if he'd responded to that email. He had. She pulled up the response and closed her eyes for a moment before opening it to read it. Nick's response to John Jackson's email was brief:

Hi, John,
Surprisingly enough, things have been a little better at home.
Because of that, I'm going to hold off on filing for divorce for a bit.
I'll be in touch.

Nick

There's an old saying credited to the ancient Greek physician, Hippocrates: *desperate times call for desperate measures*. Aubrey *was* desperate. The email was tangible proof that her plan was working. Nick was rushing to divorce her, and now, he wasn't.

And, God help her … no matter what, Aubrey knew what she had to do.

Chapter Sixteen

Libby was long gone by the time Nick came home from work, but she'd been shocked when Aubrey shared the news about the emails she'd found on his computer.

When Aubrey told Libby she didn't know what she'd say when Nick discovered the video was missing, Libby had suggested Aubrey tell Nick that the computer had likely timed out and just gone into sleep mode. Nick was no techie, so they'd both decided there was a decent chance he just might buy it.

Hoping for a lovely evening, Aubrey had prepared another big dinner. While it was a rare event these days, it actually used to be an everyday occurrence. Since Teddy had been born and she'd cut her working hours back to only a few twelve-hour shifts a week at the hospital, Aubrey had cooked nearly every night. It'd continued that way until her marriage had hit a brick wall. Then, one day at a time, just like all the other things they'd shared as a family, dinners gathered around the table nearly ended.

She'd deliberately made Nick's favorite, spaghetti and meatballs, in her own homemade sauce. A look that couldn't be described as anything other than surprise had come over Nick's face when Aubrey announced dinner was ready. He'd even smiled at her when they all sat down at the table. It was beginning to seem just like old times.

Watching the kids happily chatter back and forth without a hint of tension in the room warmed Aubrey's heart. She couldn't remember the last time they'd all been so comfortable together. Until recently, Aubrey had been throwing food in front of the kids as they sat at the table. Most nights found Aubrey doing the dishes, after eating her own cold meal while hunched over the kitchen counter.

For as long as she could remember, what Nick ate for dinner had been a mystery, as more often than not, he'd retreat to his office and she wouldn't see him again until the following morning.

Today, things were definitely looking up.

Teddy asked for more milk. When Aubrey got up to fill his glass, she nonchalantly asked over her shoulder, "Nick, more wine?" Aubrey was looking for a replay of last night. It was odd to feel shame and desire almost simultaneously. But, Aubrey reasoned, she had a job to do, and she was running out of time.

Nick's voice was tentative. "Uh, sure. That'd be great. Thanks." Aubrey was more than aware, even though Nick was playing along nicely, he remained suspicious. It was more than a little weird that they didn't talk about it ... that he never even asked. Maybe, or at least Aubrey hoped, Nick was afraid to break the spell, too.

Aubrey placed Teddy's glass in front of him and casually walked over and poured a generous helping of red wine into Nick's glass. When he smiled at her, she nearly melted. He was as breathtaking to her as he'd ever been. During all those awful months of tension, Aubrey couldn't believe how much she'd failed to notice. The visuals of last night were still fresh in her mind. It'd been ages since she'd seen him in the buff and Aubrey had forgotten what a fantastic sight she'd been missing. Nick was delicious.

Snowball was curled up on the floor at Nick's feet. Even the dog seemed to tune in to the improved vibration in the air these days.

As Peyton, and then Teddy, asked to be excused from the table, Aubrey's heart sank. She wished she could make this time last forever. Well, at least until bedtime, when the plans Aubrey had for Nick could unfold.

The kids had gone off to do homework, text, facetime, and whatever else kids did when their parents weren't looking. Tonight, Aubrey didn't care. She didn't even care if Teddy played video games. Nick was quiet as he finished his wine.

Aubrey perked up. "Oh, I almost forgot! Libby came to visit today, so I had her pick up that pound cake you like from Stocks in Philly on the way. Would you like some?"

Nick's eyes narrowed and then softened. Aubrey realized she was probably trying a little too hard and moving way too fast. As of right now, knowing what had happened between them last night, she knew her own feelings were running stadium fields ahead of Nick's.

She couldn't afford to be sloppy. Aubrey held her breath—something she did an awful lot these days—until Nick flashed a crooked smile at her. "I'd love some."

As she walked over to get Nick a slice of cake, Aubrey tried to act as though she'd been doing this all along. They both knew it had been a thing of the past for quite some time. Cutting a piece of cake, Aubrey plopped it onto a plate and retrieved a fork from the drawer for Nick.

When she set it down in front of him, he said, "This feels like my birthday. My favorite dinner, my favorite wine, and now, my favorite dessert. I hope I haven't forgotten a special occasion."

Aubrey shrugged as she returned to her chair. "No. Just a coincidence." Even to her own ears, it sounded less than genuine.

Clearing the table, Aubrey could feel Nick's eyes on her. She knew he was trying to figure out what was going on without asking her. As she loaded plates into the dishwasher, Aubrey was sad when he took the last sip of wine and brought the glass over and placed it on the counter next to the sink. Aubrey knew Nick's next move was that he'd retire to his office, and she cringed at the thought that he'd check his computer for that video now.

She heard Nick's footsteps as he was leaving the room. Aubrey turned to confirm it, just in time to catch Nick as he grabbed ahold of the door jam, rocked back on his heels, and turned back toward her. "Thanks for dinner, Aubrey. This was really nice."

Raising her eyebrows and smiling, Aubrey said, "I'm glad you liked it."

Nick nodded and, looking almost reluctant, left the room.

As she finished cleaning up the kitchen, Aubrey felt nervous about what Nick was doing downstairs. She didn't know what to think when he hadn't returned, demanding to know who'd erased his video. Aubrey realized that she'd be low on the list of suspects since Nick believed she didn't have his password.

Trying to take her mind off things, Aubrey caught up on a few of her shows on Netflix. She stopped in Peyton's room and then in Teddy's to kiss them goodnight. When Aubrey entered her own room, once again, Nick was in bed sleeping. Noticing his laptop was precisely where she'd left it, Aubrey was pretty sure he hadn't checked for the video at all. While he was no doubt curious, she knew it was likely the combination of wine and exhaustion had won out.

Aubrey was feeling just the slightest ping of guilt for giving him the extra wine in hopes it would be the recipe she needed to have a repeat of last night.

Aubrey tried to forgive herself by likening it to the sleep lost by parents when caring for a newborn … sometimes people had to do what was necessary in the name of love. After all, it wasn't like she was getting any more sleep than Nick was … in fact, Aubrey was getting less.

Slipping into the bathroom, Aubrey washed her face and brushed her teeth. She stripped out of her clothes and tossed them into the hamper.

Naked, and walking across the bedroom as though she were traveling upon a cloud, Aubrey pulled her pajama drawer open. When she reached for a tank top and bed pants, she thought better of it and grabbed a silk nightgown instead.

When she slipped it on, it felt amazing as it glided over her skin. Aubrey hadn't worn anything so soft or felt this sensual in a really long time. Too long. She slid into bed next to Nick, but her hopes tanked when she heard his breathing remain slow and steady. Wanting to jiggle the bed, Aubrey knew better, understanding that would only serve to actually wake him up. And what she wanted was a sleeping Nick. The Nick who still needed and desired her.

As she began to doze off with her back to him, Aubrey felt Nick's arm suddenly drop across her. He grabbed her breast and moaned. As she snuggled back against him, he nuzzled her neck. Aubrey was so happy this was happening again. Their dinnertime interaction earlier was proof that something more substantial was surely returning between them. Aubrey knew, subconsciously, these encounters only served to add more strength to their relationship. As a side benefit, Aubrey's breath caught as she imagined how incredible it would feel to have Nick make love to her again so soon.

His pelvis ground against her. His voice was raspy. "You feel amazing, Aubrey. I need you so bad."

Exercising absolutely no restraint, Aubrey rolled to face him. "Then take me."

Nick closed his eyes. "Umm-hmm. I'm going to ..."

As Aubrey moved in closer to place her lips on his, she paused midway as the tell-all sound of Nick's even breaths meant he'd drifted back into the real world of genuine slumber again.

Too much wine. Aubrey scolded herself as she turned away in disappointment and resigned herself to a night of loveless sleep.

Chapter Seventeen

Aubrey spent the whole morning feeling completely frustrated about last night. She knew it was ridiculous to hinge her happiness on her husbands sleepwalking episodes. Still, the disappointment caused her to feel miserable as she went through the motions of their regular morning routine.

After everyone had left the house, Aubrey wondered why she was living this insanity anyway. It only continued to force her into a complicated web of lies and omissions … all behaviors revealing someone Aubrey didn't even recognize.

Unable to fully understand why the *day-to-day Nick* was treading so cautiously, Aubrey kept reminding herself, she obviously had the inside track on the value of their relationship, which Nick wasn't privy to.

For months now, Aubrey had been perfectly willing to put all their differences aside and just start over ... to let bygones be bygones. But, until these night dates began, Nick hadn't arrived at that point. Instead, all appearances indicated, he seemed to want to firmly hold onto the resentment and anger of their past rather than embrace the future. In some ways, it'd routinely felt as though he was deliberately resisting progress. Since Nick refused to go to counseling, they never talked about it, so there was no way for her to know for sure. In fact, Nick and Aubrey no longer talked about much of anything.

To be fair, Aubrey hadn't been open to the rekindling of a relationship that she thought was dead either. Their *dates* had allowed Aubrey to rediscover her own elusive, deep-rooted love for Nick, once he'd begun expressing—albeit unwittingly— his love for her.

So, the question remained: could his *love* truly be *love*, if he had no clue it existed once he'd awakened each morning? Or, had parasomnia come along and acted like a truth serum, extracting Nick's most genuine feelings from a place he didn't even seem to know existed? Either way, Aubrey knew her love was real.

At least she'd thought so. Over these past months, Aubrey recognized that her dishonesty was causing her to lose track of what her own truth was. This craziness had been going on for long enough, she'd begun to fear that *night date* Nick and *day-to-day* Nick might never merge. That realization felt like a turning point to her. Aubrey decided she didn't want to continue to spend her time and energy with her overnight *pretend* husband anymore. She wanted the real deal. The guy she'd married. She wanted Nick back.

Until now, Aubrey had felt she'd had no choice but to continue to go through with these exhausting night charades. But, in spite of believing her reasons were valid, their encounters had graduated to levels of deception which were proving to be impossible for Aubrey to live with. On those nights when Nick had stayed in a deep sleep, Aubrey remained awake, staring at the ceiling in the dark, sorting through the loads of guilt she'd been accumulating.

Promising Teddy—and herself—that she wouldn't allow their family to be broken apart by divorce, Aubrey never imagined it would all go this far and feel this wrong.

Lately, things had been going pretty well between them when Nick was awake. Consequently, Aubrey made the decision to tell Nick they needed to go back to counseling, to make this work. She'd talk to him after dinner tonight. And, knowing she might be giving up everything, Aubrey decided to tell him the truth about his parasomnia so he could get proper treatment. If Aubrey were to avoid blowing all their progress, she'd have to lie just one more time and tell Nick it'd happened only once. But, she'd do so knowing that was all it would take for Nick to finally get the treatment he needed. No matter what the outcome, in its irony, it would be Aubrey's honesty that would finally get them off this crazy merry go round they'd been riding.

Aubrey was only a little bit surprised at the overwhelming sense of relief she felt as she went about her day and, later, waited for Nick to come home.

Nick arrived from work at his regular time. Aubrey had made a pot of chili and homemade cornbread for dinner. It was the quickest meal she could think of serving. When they finished eating, the kids dispersed as usual.

When Nick predictably poured a glass of wine preparing to retire to his office, Aubrey poured a glass of her own and asked him if he'd join her in the living room to talk. Nick raised an eyebrow but followed her into the other room nonetheless.

Aubrey felt an immediate change in his demeanor as he sat down on a chair across from the couch. His frame was stiff. Nick didn't rest back onto the cushion. Instead, he remained perched on the edge of the chair as though he might flee at any minute.

Trying not to be intimidated by Nick's body language, which was absolutely screaming at her, Aubrey began speaking slowly. "I have a few things I wanted to talk to you about. They're important." She shifted in her chair and placed her glass on the end table. "I know that you'd indicated that you didn't want to go back to counseling ..." Aubrey ignored Nick's narrowed eyes as he took a sip of his wine. "... but, I was thinking, since things seemed a little better between us, maybe you'd reconsider and give it another try. Maybe a different counselor? I heard about this place ..."

Anymore, Nick was always wound up and ready to explode with anger. The least of things could set him off. Tonight was no different. He shot to his feet, his wine threatening to splash over the rim of the glass. "Just stop it, Au-brey!" He walked across the room to the couch, stood over Aubrey, pointing at her. "You can't leave well enough alone. Can you?" Nick began pacing back and forth, up and down, in the aisle between where she sat on the sofa and the coffee table that held their wedding album. "You can't just allow things to rest and allow us to have a few weeks like a normal couple."

Aubrey blinked in shock, surprised at what felt like a complete overreaction on Nick's part. It revealed more layers of bitterness than she'd expected. "Nick. We're not a normal couple. Nothing has been normal for a very long time. I was just trying …"

He was in front of her again and finished her sentence sarcastically. "… to control me. To control everything. That's what you're *trying* to do. Because that's what you do, Au-brey." Nick paced in the other direction. "You can't just sit back to see where things will go. You're always pushing me to do what you need."

Control issues had been a common theme in their counseling. Nick would accuse Aubrey of being controlling, and she'd argue that it was by default, based on the things Nick failed to take care of, which forced her to take charge all the time.

Aubrey eyes burned with the warmth of the tears she couldn't stop. "But, you need it, too, Nick. *We* need it. Deep down inside, I promise you. You want this, too." Aubrey, with her stomach in knots, leaned forward, balancing her bent elbows on her knees and resting her chin on top of her folded hands.

At the far end of the couch, Nick spun around. "What I need …" He forcefully jammed his finger up and down toward the floor. "… is *not* to be here dealing with this crap. You have no idea what I think about or worry about. You're clueless."

"But, I do." Aubrey gathered her courage. "If you'd just listen to me. You've told me …"

"Aubrey! Stop!" Nick shook his head. "You're relentless. And, I'm done with this conversation." He turned and walked toward the staircase leading downstairs.

Scrambling to her feet, Aubrey's voice broke. "Nick, that wasn't all I needed …"

As he started down the steps, Nick disregarded her words, never even looking back over his shoulder. "Good night, Au-brey."

Feeling defeated since this conversation had just ended the same as so many others over the last few years, Aubrey sighed, picked up her glass, and brought it to her lips. The secret she'd been trying to share remained as it had been … tucked safely between the sheets in their bedroom downstairs.

Chapter Eighteen

By the time April rolled around, things had settled down again. There hadn't been any further attempts by Aubrey—or Nick—to talk about their marriage. No longer pushing for counseling, Aubrey had learned her lesson after approaching Nick a while back.

After that time, it'd taken nearly a week before Nick joined them for dinner again and, even longer for him to return to being nice to Aubrey on a daily basis. Understanding she had to back off on the things she was trying to do in their waking hours, Aubrey took it slowly again. However, in doing so, she felt she had no choice but to allow their night *dates* to continue or Aubrey would stand to lose the progress they'd made. Or, the progress she'd thought they'd made. Aubrey really didn't know anymore.

Ultimately, it left her on her own to experience months of special times with Nick. Aubrey was feeling a little more like her old self … a content, happily married woman. It was so contradictory, though. Daily, she'd wished Nick understood how happy they were, or at least could be.

Their pontoon boat was back in the water, and thanks to a mild spring, they'd been out on it several times. Nick seemed to grow a little more loving toward her. But, it was baby steps with him. They *were* spending more family time together, too.

Some months back, after realizing there wasn't a video recorded on his laptop, Nick didn't appear totally convinced when Aubrey had suggested his computer had probably entered sleep mode and failed to record anything. Still, after that, Nick had never mentioned it again, and Aubrey wasn't crazy enough to bring it back up. The good news was that Nick hadn't brought the laptop back into their bedroom again. It'd remained in Nick's office, right where it belonged.

These days, the only thing she had to keep careful track of was that darned watch. It was exhausting, always trying to beat the clock and get it fastened onto Nick's wrist before he'd fall asleep and she'd risk waking him for real.

While Aubrey was enjoying the family dinners and barbeques, she hated that something was still amiss between her and Nick. In spite of their relationship being markedly improved, they were still not being intimate. Something was still holding him back. Well, that was … only when Nick was awake.

Otherwise, in spite of Libby's dismay and frequent objections, Aubrey had often failed to resist if Nick tried to make love to her. It only rarely even happened. The truth was, more often than not, when Nick *woke up*, they talked or—more accurately— they dreamed. Just like they used to.

Aubrey suspected Nick's failure to initiate intimacy was likely due to when Doctor Jeff formally diagnosed him, months ago—after all the testing was done—with parasomnia. To this day, the doctor continued to insist he didn't understand why Aubrey didn't know something more, allowing her to come forward to confirm his diagnosis.

At the time Aubrey had denied any knowledge of Nick's disorder, she'd believed the lie would only need to linger for another week. Aubrey had been trying to buy herself just a mere seven days. After Aubrey had sealed the deal on their daytime relationship, she'd planned to tell Nick something along the lines of finally having witnessed him sitting up and sleep talking. It was *just* a week. Aubrey never believed that big blowout in their living room would happen and cause the fib to grow legs, landing her in the twist of lies she found herself caught up in, now.

On Nick's part, there was apparently enough uncertainty between what the doctor claimed and what she'd denied, it'd left an unspoken barrier of untrustworthiness between them. Needless to say, Aubrey had no room to blame Nick for his feelings of doubt.

Wearing down, Aubrey didn't know how much more she could take of Nick's inquisitions each time he'd return from Doctor Jeff's office … *Are you sure? … You've never, ever see me wandering*

*around? Do you even see me get up and go to the bathroom? …
Anything?* It wasn't like she was a natural at lying, though if you asked her now, Aubrey would hate to admit that she'd become far too good at it. That had never been her intention. It was an inconvenient side effect of her attempt to save her family. To save *them.*

In her subsequent denials, when backed into a corner enough, Aubrey even dragged the children into the whole mess by pointing out that Peyton and Teddy had never seen their father sleepwalking either. But, since she and Nick shared a room—and a bed—the doctor continued to question Nick, and he'd continued to interrogate Aubrey. Of course, each time, as exhausted as it made her, Aubrey knew all too well, it wasn't exactly as though he were out of line in doing so. Anytime the thought entered Aubrey's mind to just tell Nick about the parasomnia, Aubrey reminded herself about the last time she'd tried to talk to him. The memory was always enough to warn her to keep her mouth shut.

With that in mind, Aubrey stuck to her story that there'd been no sightings of his sleepwalking, which was enough evidence for Nick to continue to question the accuracy of his diagnosis in the first place. Therefore, he'd declined to take the medications Doctor Jeff offered. Nick told the doctor he'd reconsider if Aubrey or the kids *witnessed* him actually sleepwalking.

For Aubrey, hiding Nick's disorder had nearly become a full-time job. On some nights, Nick wouldn't even acknowledge Aubrey was in the room. Rather, he'd make his way to the kitchen to prepare a sandwich, a glass of wine, or whatever else struck his fancy. Aubrey would have to stay awake until Nick settled back into bed so she could make sure he was safe and clear away the evidence.

Some nights, Nick insisted they shower together after lovemaking. While it spared her from the crazy routine of sponge bathing him, on those occasions, Aubrey would insist on blow drying his hair so his pillow wouldn't be soaking wet in the morning. She'd hesitated at first, but remembered the night he'd used the mixer to bake her a cake. If that didn't wake him, nothing would. The longer he stayed awake, the more elaborate and over the top her efforts had become.

It was always her job to stay one step ahead … to make sure everything returned to how it was before they'd gone to sleep. But, even having a one-sided relationship with her husband was enough for Aubrey right now and it was worth all the shenanigans to her. Mostly, all that happened between them at night continued to give her hope for their future.

Libby had scolded Aubrey too many times to count. She really struggled with the moral side of what Aubrey had been up to. On one occasion, they'd even argued about it—something they never did. That time, Libby had compared Aubrey's calculated acts of serving Nick wine, knowing it would increase her chances of their making love, to someone slipping another person a rufie with the express purpose of taking advantage of them without their knowledge.

To say Aubrey was offended would be an understatement. She'd argued that they were married and they'd had consensual intercourse for years. Nick wasn't a stranger. They'd shared a bed every night for God's sake.

But, Libby stuck to her guns and wouldn't back down on the accusation. It was an exchange that might have ended a weaker friendship. But, deep down inside, Aubrey realized it was more close to the truth than she was comfortable with believing.

Continuing on her lone journey to save her marriage, Aubrey repeatedly provided updates to Libby on how improved her relationship with Nick had become in their waking hours and how much happier the kids were, too. She'd directly credited what was happening overnight. Ultimately, to preserve their relationship, Aubrey and Libby had agreed to disagree.

But, after that discussion, whenever Aubrey and Nick made love, she would have been lying if she'd have said the comparison didn't serve to haunt her. Every. Single. Time.

Chapter Nineteen

The May sun rose early, but today was overcast. Aubrey was dancing around the dimly lit kitchen when Peyton walked into the room. Not realizing her daughter had come in, Aubrey continued to embrace her coffee cup, while gliding around the floor in her socks. An upbeat country song played quietly in the background.

Aubrey spun around and caught sight of Peyton, who immediately rolled her eyes. "Nobody should have that kind of energy at six thirty in the morning, Mom."

Playfully bopping toward her daughter, tongue in cheek, Aubrey rocked her head back and forth. "It's my jam, Peyton, I couldn't help it." She sipped her coffee and continued to dance around.

"Mom! You are too old to use *it's my jam*. Oh, my God."

"You can only be too young for things … you can never be too old for anything." Aubrey smiled.

Peyton shook her head and added another roll of her eyes. "I just can't …"

Not willing to engage, Aubrey ignored her daughter's negativity. She put her cup on the counter. "Do you want pancakes?"

"You realize this is Thursday, right? You never cook breakfast on school days." Based on her tone of voice, Peyton might as well have begun the sentence with *yo, stupid*.

Aubrey pulled the griddle from the cabinet, placed it on the island counter, and plugged it in. "I don't on most school days. I'll give you that, but I have in the past. Do you want pancakes or not?" She wished she didn't sound as impatient as she felt. Peyton could exhaust Aubrey in only a few sentences these days. Her daughter was always so combative.

"Sure, I'll have pancakes." Peyton grabbed a magazine on the way to the table and quickly buried her face in it. Her message to her mother was clear: *I don't want to talk to you*.

Aubrey whisked the batter. She decided she wasn't allowing Peyton to ruin this amazing morning for her. Last night, Nick had been fabulous. They reminisced about their dating years, laughing at how daring they'd been. When Nick made love to her, he stared closely into Aubrey's eyes, never once looking away. Even as she remembered it, Aubrey could feel the intensity. Her thoughts were interrupted when Nick and Teddy walked into the kitchen.

As she turned the pancakes over, Aubrey said, "Teddy, honey, I'm making you pancakes. Get a glass of juice and sit down. They'll be ready in a few minutes."

Teddy licked his lips. "Oh, yum." He headed for the fridge.

Nick pushed a barstool aside and leaned onto the counter, coming to rest on his elbows and forearms. "Any chance you have an extra pancake or two on there for me?" He flashed her that million dollar smile.

She nodded. "Sure. Sure, I do." Aubrey couldn't believe her ears. Nick was actually going to sit down and eat breakfast with them today. She was grateful she'd made extra pancakes with the intention of freezing them for the kids to eat later. Unable to believe how badly she wanted to stretch across the counter to kiss him—and fearing she might—Aubrey used the spatula to point at the table. "Go ahead and sit down. These are almost done."

Grinning and dazzling her one more time, Nick tapped on the counter twice and stood up. "Perfect. That's perfect. Thanks, Aubrey."

Having turned away to retrieve a fourth plate from the cabinet, adding it to the pile of three sitting next to the griddle, Aubrey spun back around to glance at Nick. He'd turned away, his back to her now. She closed her eyes for a moment and smiled. For the first time in forever, Nick was wide awake and spoke her name like an old, familiar song.

Aubrey, Nick, and Teddy settled into their seats at Peyton's spring choir concert. This morning, at breakfast, Aubrey could hardly believe it when Nick said he'd get home from work early so they could all attend together. It had further shocked her when, on the way out the door this morning, Nick had kissed her on the cheek and thanked her for breakfast.

Since Aubrey hadn't expected the kiss, when Nick leaned in, they each did an awkward bob before he landed his lips on her cheek and almost whispered when he'd said *the pancakes were delicious, thanks, Aub.*

Aubrey couldn't wait to update Libby, hoping her friend would rethink the judgment she'd passed on her once she learned how well things were going between Nick and her. She still wasn't over having to listen to those harsh words from Libby … *like slipping someone a rufie.*

The show was great, and Peyton did a good job on the solo she'd been assigned. She sang an Adele song that Aubrey had heard her practice over the last several weeks. Her delivery was flawless, and her parents beamed with pride.

On the way home, Nick even stopped off to treat everyone to ice cream. As they were all seated on the benches outside of the ice cream shop, Aubrey had looked around, wanting to pinch herself to be sure this was all really happening, and she wasn't dreaming.

When the kids retired to their respective bedrooms, Aubrey watched Nick pour a glass of wine. She felt sad that the night was ending. It'd been so perfect. In recent months, Nick having alcohol would have offered her hope for their overnight time. Not anymore.

Aubrey was exhausted. Nick was, too. No, she craved an *awake life* with her husband, just like it used to be.

Nick surprised her when he raised the bottle of wine in the air with one hand and pointed at his glass with the other. "Hey, Aub, you want a glass?"

She smiled at him. "I'd love one." Aubrey watched as he grabbed another glass and poured wine into it.

When Nick handed her the glass, he suggested they sit on the deck outside of their bedroom. Aubrey agreed. She had no idea what he had in mind, but she was hoping this was the night he was going to resume their waking physical relationship so she could finally put an end to their sleeping one. It would also be the night she could claim to have witnessed him sleepwalking so Nick could finally get the help, and the sleep, he desperately needed.

They sat on the fire-engine-red Adirondack chairs outside of their room. The cloud cover from this morning had cleared, making way for a beautiful star-filled and moonlit sky. It was breathtaking.

Aubrey and Nick chatted easily about Peyton's performance, how good the ice cream had tasted, and preparing themselves for the rush of Shoebies coming into town for the summer season. What they didn't talk about—avoided even—was anything about their relationship with one another.

Having finished her wine first, Aubrey was already feeling a nice buzz. She was grateful for it as she knew it would help her to sleep.

It wasn't too long before Aubrey's hopes, about Nick taking this to a whole new level, were smashed. He took a final sip of his wine, turned to her and said, "Today was really nice. I'm really tired, so I'm going to turn in now. Are you?"

Before she could answer, Nick was already standing. Aubrey shook her head. "Yeah, it's been a long day. I'm heading in, too."

They went through their usual bedtime routines, staying out of each other's way. Their empty glasses were sitting side-by-side on Aubrey's dresser … like a souvenir reminder to prove this day had really happened.

Nick was in bed when Aubrey finished up in the bathroom. She walked over to her side of the bed. Nick's back was to her. Softly sighing, Aubrey lifted the blanket and slid in under the covers. She adjusted her pillows and settled in. Mercifully, sleep came quickly.

Not knowing how long she'd been sleeping, Aubrey was surprised to wake to Nick tugging at her nightgown. She was thrilled when he slid his hands behind her back and pulled the gown up over her head before tossing it onto the floor. Nick was passionate, and she felt like she couldn't get enough of him. Aubrey decided, the only thing better than this would be if Nick were actually awake and wanting her like he did now. His glazed eyes gave away the truth, though. Aubrey could tell … even when he stared directly into her eyes … Nick definitely remained fast asleep.

Nick had moved on top of Aubrey—his head buried into her neck—making love to her. And, as if the sleepwalking Gods heard her exact thoughts from a few moments before, all of a sudden Nick startled her when he jolted upright and bolted across the bed to sit where he'd been sleeping earlier.

Looking around wide-eyed, Nick narrowed his brow. "What's going on here? What's happening?" He leaned in closer to her. "Aubrey?"

"Uh, what do you mean?" Unsure if he'd hurt himself or something, Aubrey scrambled to sit up and face him. She pulled the top sheet to her neck, staring at Nick, who was frantically shifting his eyes around the room, trying to take things in. Aubrey froze as understanding choked her. He was awake. Nick had woken up, and now she didn't know what to do.

"What do I mean? Aubrey, I wake up, and we are in the middle of having sex! How did this happen?" Nick's voice sounded panicked.

Trying to sound confused, Aubrey said, "You woke me, Nick. You pulled off my gown. You appeared to be awake. We had a nice day. I thought you …"

"I didn't … anything. I literally just woke up! Has this ever happened before? This is the stuff Doctor Jeff asked about … I *must* be sleep *walking*." Nick ran his fingers through his hair.

Aubrey realized the watch wasn't on his wrist. In a panic, she went for vagueness. "I mean, no, this hasn't happened before. You certainly seemed awake to me. We'd had wine. Today had gone well …" Her voice trailed off, she couldn't decide if he believed her or not.

Nick pressed further. "Aubrey, the last time I remember making love with you was easily a year ago. Have. We. Had. Sex. Recently?"

She swallowed hard before answering. "No. No, we haven't. Not before tonight. It's been a really long time." Aubrey stopped in fear her tongue would shrivel up and fall right out of her mouth onto the bed before bouncing onto the floor.

Releasing an audible sigh, Nick's voice was calmer now. "Good." Reaching over, Nick put his hand on Aubrey's shoulder. "Look, I'm sorry. I had no idea what I was doing here. I'll call the doctor tomorrow. I know things have been better between us, but I'm just not ready for this step yet. I'm not comfortable enough with where we are and, when I am, I want it to be special." Nick reached for his nylon shorts which he'd discarded on the floor earlier. "My watch!"

Aubrey's heart nearly stopped. She froze and closed her eyes, waiting for it.

Nick reached over and retrieved his watch from the nightstand. "I guess this is useless if I'm taking it off in my sleep anyway."

Opening her eyes, Aubrey was relieved when she realized Nick thought he'd removed the watch himself. With Nick still turned away from her, Aubrey took the opportunity to ditch the sheet to grab her nightgown and pull it over her head. By the time Nick turned around, she was slipping back underneath of the covers.

As Nick climbed into bed, he shook his head. "It's really hard to believe my body did all that without my consent. It's disturbing." He settled his head onto his pillows, with his back to Aubrey once again. "I'm sorry, Aubrey. Night."

"Night, Nick." Aubrey was frozen, wide-eyed, and sick to her stomach, Nick's words rapping over and over in her head … *without my consent, without my consent, without my consent.*

Chapter Twenty

First thing Saturday morning, Aubrey's phone rang. When she answered it, Libby's voice sounded excited. "Guess what happened last night?"

Aubrey wanted to say... *no, YOU guess what happened Thursday night* ... but, she didn't. Instead, she took the bait. "Did Jed pop the question?" For the life of her, Aubrey couldn't get the Beverly Hillbillies theme song out of her head every time she said Jed's name ... ♫ *Next thing you know ole Jed's a millionaire* ... ♪

Libby sounded like she might burst. "He did. It was so romantic. Wait until you see my ring, it's beautiful!"

"That's awesome news, Lib. Congratulations. I can't wait to see it." Aubrey tried hard to make her voice sound happy. "How about if I come up to the city today? We can have a few drinks and celebrate.

I'll come in the late afternoon. Let's do happy hour on the Wheelhouse Deck."

The Wheelhouse Deck was on the Moshulu, a three-hundred-fifty-nine-foot long ship which had been turned into a landmark restaurant. It was a tall ship, built in the early 1900s, with bragging rights to cameos in the movies Rocky, Godfather II, and Blow Out. It was located on the Philadelphia waterfront. The end of May's mild temperatures made it a great time to go there.

"That sounds great. What time?" Libby's delight was palpable.

With the school year winding down, the kids didn't need much. So, Aubrey's day was pretty open. "Does four work?"

"Four is perfect. I'll see you there." Libby paused. "Oh, and Aubrey? Bring sunglasses. This ring will blind you." Libby giggled.

Aubrey laughed. "I can't wait to see it. I'll see you at four."

Just as they hung up, Nick came in to see if Aubrey wanted to go out on the boat with him that afternoon. She shared Libby's good news and told him that she was going to Philly to celebrate. Aubrey promised to be home by seven if Nick wanted to take her out then. He agreed and also suggested they bring a bottle of wine to enjoy during the sunset on the bay. This was actually their first date in almost a year. Aubrey was looking forward to it.

Aubrey arrived at the Wheelhouse Deck and spotted Libby immediately. She was seated at one of the many wicker tables on the deck and already had some sort of fancy drink in front of her. As soon as Libby saw Aubrey, she jumped from her chair, almost running across the deck with her left hand held out in front of her, her ring sparkling in the beautiful sunshine.

Libby was overflowing with joy. It was almost contagious. "Oh, my God. Can you believe this? I'm engaged!" Her smiled shined as bright as the ring.

Grabbing her hand, Aubrey said, "It's beautiful, Libby. I am so, so happy for you." And, she was. Her best friend was finally being lifted up in love again. Libby had been through so much and had remained so strong and stable for her kids. Aubrey couldn't help but be happy for her.

Once they were seated, Aubrey ordered a drink and, after it arrived, made a toast to Libby's happiness. It was odd that Aubrey hadn't even met Jed yet, but the craziness that was Aubrey's life hadn't really allowed for it. She hoped, now that things were getting better between her and Nick, that she might have a chance to arrange a dinner for the four of them during Libby's extended stays in Mystic this summer.

Acoustic music serenaded them from the speakers. The sun was peeking in and out from behind clouds, so the eighty-degree day and the light breeze coming off the Delaware River made for perfect conditions aboard the tall ship. It seemed there was no better time than now to be celebrating a whole new beginning for Libby. Actually, Aubrey couldn't help but feel this was a whole new beginning for both of them.

They ordered some jumbo shrimp, buffalo wings, and another round of drinks. While they waited, Aubrey asked, "So, how did Jed do it? What happened?"

Libby's eyes lit up, and she raised her eyebrows. "He called me yesterday around lunchtime and told me he was sorry, but he wouldn't be able to see me last night. He had this boring cocktail party he had to attend for work. Then, he kind of paused and said *unless you want to go with me*." Libby was nodding.

She told Aubrey she didn't have the kids, they were with Austin, so Libby said she'd figured, *why not*? Obviously, in hindsight, Jed had rested his hopes on Libby feeling as though nothing was holding her back, so she'd go with him. Lucky for Jed, he knew her well, and she'd agreed.

"He took me to the Skygarten in Philly. You know, it's that German Biergarten on the fifty-first floor, with amazing views, that opened to the public a few years ago? Oh, my God. It was fabulous."

Aubrey nodded. She had seen something about that restaurant on one of the *Visit Philly* websites. "Yes. I read about that place."

Libby leaned in. "We got there, and he led me over to a table by the window. I looked out the window, and the views took my breath away. The sun was setting in the distance. Aubrey, it was so perfect. Then, I turned back to ask Jed where his co-workers were, and he was down on one knee."

Trying to swallow the lump in her throat, Aubrey reached across the table and squeezed Libby's arm. "I am really happy for you, Lib. How perfect."

"Oh, Aubrey. I love him. I really, really do." Libby's eyes looked dreamy. "You should have been there. People were clapping, I was crying … it was one of the most incredible moments of my life."

Aubrey was so happy for her friend. She understood the high of being in love. And, she more than understood what lengths one would and could go to protect or save *real* love.

As though Libby was trying to defend their brief courtship, she added, "He's so good to me. And he's really good to the kids, too."

"I'm so glad you said *yes*. I think you'll be very happy with Jed." Aubrey tried to offer the validation that she felt Libby needed, but her words were genuine. She'd never seen Libby this happy before. "Did Jed suspect you may have known about the ring?"

"No! Not a chance. With the way he surprised me, I had no problem looking shocked. Now, we can add that little *Thelma and Louise mission* to the burial casket full of stuff we're taking to our respective graves."

They both laughed out loud.

Their food was delivered to their table, along with their second round of drinks. Libby dipped a shrimp in cocktail sauce. "So, how are things going with you and Nick?"

Aubrey took a deep breath, exhaled, and looked away.

Picking right up on the sudden change in Aubrey's demeanor, Libby said, "Uh, oh."

Aubrey nodded. "*Uh, oh* is an understatement. You were so right, Lib. I should never have been doing the things I've been doing." Her eyes dropped down to her drink in front of her.

Libby fell into best friend mode. "Oh, sweetie, I didn't want to be right. I wanted things to be okay for you. What happened?"

With a grateful heart, Aubrey pressed on. "Oh, Libby, things have been getting better and better. We had such a great day on Thursday. Nick had breakfast with us in the morning. We went to Peyton's concert as a family. When we got home, Nick poured us some wine. We sat on the deck together. His idea. It was all so perfectly perfect." Aubrey looked off in the distance as a sailboat drifted by.

"But?" Libby clearly understood there was more to the story.

Aubrey started again. "Well, Nick didn't make any moves, so we climbed into bed. But … after we'd gone to sleep, I woke to Nick pulling my nightgown off. As usual, I went with it." Aubrey closed her eyes, before opening them and locking them on Libby's curious gaze. "After fifteen minutes or so, Nick woke up. He woke up right in the middle of making love."

Libby's mouth dropped wide open. "What did you do?"

"At first I wasn't sure what was going on. But, before long I realized Nick was actually awake. I was terrified." Aubrey looked away. The truth was about to pass over her lips, and she hated it.

Libby's eyes were wide. "I mean, what did you say? What did he do?"

Aubrey put her hands over her face and then dropped them to grasp the end of the table. She gently rocked in her seat. "He said he'd woken up to find himself on top of me. He had no recollection of anything before that. He was sure he'd been sleeping and felt disturbed that his body had been doing that without his consent."

Shrinking back in her chair, Libby winced. "What did you say to that?"

"Nothing." Aubrey shook her head. " I just tried to glaze over it. I felt so ashamed. I realized you'd been totally right. Nick looked so … so … violated." She massaged the back of her neck.

"Look. I've known you for forever." Libby held one finger in the air. "I know that you have truly believed what you've been doing was serving the greater good and it was okay because you were married. There was no malice here. You've argued that with me all along."

Putting her elbows on the table, Aubrey rested her chin on her hands. "But, you were right, Lib. I should have listened to you. It wasn't consensual sex. Oh, God, what does that make me?"

"Someone who was trying to do the best she could to save her marriage. That's what this makes you." Libby leaned in. "That's all you were trying to do. Look, I know better than anyone. You're no monster. You were desperate. And, you never meant for it to go on like this."

Aubrey hesitated. "He asked me how many times it'd happened. How many times his body had been having sex without his consent."

Libby cringed. "He really said *without his consent*? Ouch. And you said?"

Aubrey looked down at her plate. "That's exactly what he said, and I said what I had to say. There was only one correct answer. I told him it was the first time. I told him it was the first time he'd touched me in a year. God, help me. What choice did I have? We've come so far. I had to lie."

Libby sat straight mouthed, across the table without comment.

Lacing her fingers and pressing her index fingers across her lips like a steeple, almost as if to quiet the words that were coming next, with tears in her eyes, Aubrey freed her mouth for a moment to ask, "Libby, dear God, who have I become? Am I a predator because it suited me? I've violated my husband. What does that really *say* about the person I am? What have I done?"

Aubrey knew the greatest gift Libby could have ever given her right now, was the silence that existed—frantically waving its arms in the air—between them.

Chapter Twenty~One

It'd been weeks since the Saturday Nick had taken Aubrey out on the boat. They'd shared a bottle of wine and watched the sunset on the bay. Nick had even put his hand on the small of Aubrey's back while they'd watched the sun appear to sink into the water and again when she'd climbed out of the boat and up onto the dock.

That following Monday, Nick had seen Doctor Jeff and—after telling him what had happened—began to take the medication that would squash his sleepwalking. Much to Aubrey's disappointment, Nick hadn't had an episode of sleepwalking since that day. Aubrey knew it was best that way. She always worried about what went on with Nick on the few nights a week when she would work, so there was some relief that came with Nick's treatment. Selfishly, Aubrey still missed the nights when Nicky would show up.

On the bright side, ever since the *pancake day*, Nick had been joining Aubrey and the kids for breakfasts and dinners. He also had been hanging out in the living room, talking or watching movies with Aubrey after dinner. They'd gone out on the boat a few times alone, and their relationship was certainly warming up. So much so, Nick had resumed pecking Aubrey on the cheek when he left for the office and kissing her hello when he got home. But, it was always benign, and that was about the extent of physical contact that existed between them. Aubrey was terrified to push it after what had happened. No, anything physical would have to be all on Nick's terms, he'd already made it clear that he wasn't ready for that step. Aubrey could only continue to wish that would change.

Since they were becoming closer in their waking hours, Aubrey was trying to be happy for Nick. He looked more rested, which only served to make her feel even more guilty. She'd ignored the fact she'd been robbing him of sleep by keeping his parasomnia a secret.

Now, it was Aubrey who looked tired all the time. Often, when they'd climbed into their four-poster bed, she'd lie enveloped in darkness for hours feeling utterly starved for attention. For touch. The truth was she'd missed Nick like crazy over these last weeks. Aubrey literally craved their romantic encounters, and she'd longed for Nick to move his hands over her body and hold her with all the passion he'd been showering on her before he'd begun the medication.

Aubrey wouldn't even think of admitting any of this to anyone other than Libby, who'd continuously had been reminding her it was best this way. Even knowing what they both knew, Aubrey thought it was easy for Libby to say since she'd had someone holding her each night. And, for that matter, any other time she desired.

After working an overnight shift at the hospital, Aubrey got home this morning and asked Nick to drop Teddy at Libby's house for the day, on his way to work. Libby and her kids were spending this week on the island. Shift work always felt easier when the kids were on summer break from school, and she didn't have to run back out as soon as she got home. Aubrey had slept all day. Now, at four o'clock in the afternoon, she found herself alone. It was a rare occurrence.

Peyton had left to go water skiing with a friend and her family. Afterward, she was having dinner at their house and spending the night. Teddy had called a while ago and asked if he could have dinner with Brody tonight. After giving him permission, Aubrey realized, this would be the first evening in a very long time where both kids were gone, leaving Nick and her alone for dinner. She really didn't know what to expect.

Knowing they'd be alone, Aubrey had showered, shaved all the parts that mattered, and slipped into a white, strapless sundress. She was so tan already, she'd only needed to put on some light makeup today.

After reapplying a coat of pale pink lipstick, Aubrey was at the stove tossing the ingredients for dinner into a pan when Nick got home from work. He strolled into the kitchen and pecked her on her cheek. "Smells good." Nick rubbed his hand on Aubrey's arm.

That small amount of skin-to-skin contact actually gave her chills. "It's for chicken quesadillas. They'll be ready in about twenty minutes." Aubrey would give anything for the moment they were in right now to actually be the *old times* it was pretending to be.

"That sounds great." Nick raised an eyebrow. "It's pretty quiet. Where are the kids?"

Aubrey stirred the chicken and peppers with a wooden spoon before turning to face him. "Oh, Peyton's water skiing with the Johansons and Teddy's at Libby's until after dinner."

Nick tipped his head to the side. "So … it's just you …" He paused. "Um … and me?"

Aubrey knew she hadn't made dinner for just the two of them in more than a year. Trying her best to act more nonchalant than she felt, Aubrey crossed the room to the refrigerator and grabbed the shredded cheese and a head of lettuce—one in each hand. Her answer sounded too high-pitched. "Uh-huh." When her breath caught in her throat, Aubrey swallowed hard. With her face still in the fridge, she frowned and scolded herself … *relax.*

Adjusting her expression and closing the refrigerator door, Aubrey exhaled. *Just keep your head*, she reminded herself. She turned and emptied the contents in her hands onto the counter.

Nick pointed at the doorway. "Wow, um, okay. I'm going to go and change into some shorts."

"Okay. Take your time." Aubrey smiled.

As soon as Nick was out of sight, Aubrey smacked her palm against her forehead reprimanding herself for nearly losing her cool. She grabbed her phone and quickly dialed Libby's number. No sooner had her friend said *hello*, Aubrey blurted out, "I don't have time for questions. In fifteen minutes I need you to call me and ask if Teddy can stay the night. Tell me he can use a pair of Brody's pajamas. Teddy can stay, right?"

It was no surprise to Aubrey when Libby sounded hesitant. "Yes, he can, but Aubrey, what's going on? You're not planning …"

She could hear Nick's footsteps returning up the staircase from their bedroom below. "Darn it, Lib, I told you, I don't have time to answer questions. You don't have to worry."

Libby was whispering as though she were standing next to Aubrey, right there in the house. "Just promise me you're not …"

Aubrey heard Nick getting closer, so she hung up on Libby, placed her phone back onto the counter, and counted on her best friend to do what she always did … what they both always did … cover her butt without question.

When Nick walked in, Aubrey was casually placing the quesadilla shells into the tortilla warmer.

Smiling, Nick tipped his nose up in the air. "It smells so delicious."

When Aubrey glanced up, the sight of him nearly left her breathless. He was wearing a white tank top and khaki shorts. His skin was every bit as bronze as Aubrey's, he looked incredible. She wanted *him* for dinner.

Aubrey returned the grin. "Your timing is perfect. Dinner is ready."

Nick moved in closer. Seconds, which felt like minutes, ticked by. Aubrey was nearly holding her breath. It'd been forever since he'd lingered in her social space for this long. "Do we have the ingredients for margaritas? If we do, I could whip up a few for us."

Wide-eyed, Aubrey said, "Yes, actually I think we do." She squatted down and opened the cabinet under the middle island. "We're in luck. She pulled a bottle of Triple Sec from the shelf and reached up, handing it to Nick. Still crouching down, she grabbed a bottle of Margarita mix in one hand and a bottle of Tequila in the other.

Aubrey stood up. She held the bottles in the air. "Ta-da!"

Having already placed the first bottle on the counter, Nick grabbed the other two from Aubrey. "Perfect. While you set the table, I'll fill the blender with ice and whip us up a few frozen sides." He playfully wagged his eyebrows up and down, but all Aubrey could see was his captivating smile.

Smoothing her dress, Aubrey nodded. "Deal." She tried to hide the first date giddiness she was feeling inside. She motioned to the counter behind them. "I have some limes cut up for the quesadillas over there. Use what you need for our drinks, there's plenty."

The blender whirred as she grabbed plates and silverware before arranging two place settings on the table. Aubrey nearly forgot the wheels she'd set in motion only moments before, when Nick turned off the blender and announced, "I think your phone is ringing."

The next ring confirmed he was correct. Aubrey crossed over and picked up her phone. Feigning surprise, she held up an index finger and announced, "It's Libby. Since Teddy is there, I better answer."

Nick nodded, before turning away to get two margarita glasses from the cabinet behind him.

Aubrey tapped the green button on her phone. "Oh, hey, Libby … is everything okay?"

As ordered, Libby asked if Teddy could sleep over. When Aubrey pretended to object because Teddy didn't have an overnight bag, Libby—on script—offered a pair of Brody's pajamas. Aubrey couldn't afford for this to sound pre-planned so after a few convincing *are you sure?* challenges, Aubrey pretended to give in and agreed to allow Teddy to stay, promising to be there first thing tomorrow morning with doughnuts, bagels, and a cup of coffee for her friend. As they hung up, Aubrey remembered to silently thank her lucky stars for a friendship as loyal as Libby's.

Nick placed the glasses on the counter next to the blender. "Everything okay with Libby?"

Aubrey quickly turned her back to Nick and faced the stove. She grabbed the pan of chicken, onions, and peppers to transfer into the bowl she'd left resting on the counter. "Yup. Teddy and Brody just wanted to have a sleepover tonight, so Libby was checking in with me to make sure it was okay."

"From this end, it sounded like you said it was alright?"

Aubrey could almost feel his stare boring into the back of her head. She picked up the bowl holding the chicken mixture in one hand, and the quesadilla warmer in the other, grateful Nick couldn't see her deceitful eyes. "Yes. He's going to use a pair of Brody's P.J.'s. I'm off tomorrow. I'll just run over to pick him up in the morning." As she made her way to the table, Aubrey was grateful when the whir of the blender drowned out yet another one of her fibs.

Chapter Twenty~Two

At seven-thirty in the morning, Aubrey called Libby, and she answered on the first ring. Her voice was soft and tentative. "Uh, hello?"

Aubrey had a vision in her head of Libby raising her shoulders and cringing when she answered. "Oh, my God, Lib. Your voice sounds like you're guilty of helping me commit a crime last night. You didn't. Nick is alive and well. Everything that happened last night was consensual."

"I didn't mean to doubt you. It's just, well, I know how much you've been missing Nick. I was just afraid ... "

Knowing Libby only had her best interests at heart, Aubrey interrupted, "I know Lib. Thanks for the *Teddy save*. It totally paid off.

We did end up making love, but last night was all Nick's doing. He was wide awake, and it was amazing."

And … it had been.

Last night, after Aubrey and Libby's little phone skit had ended, Nick finished making their frozen drinks. Even that part of the evening had been memorable. Aubrey had nearly drooled as she'd watched the muscles in Nick's arms naturally flexing and relaxing again as he moved around the kitchen.

At one point, Nick had even caught her watching him as he was sliding a lime wedge around the tops of each of their glasses before turning one, and then the other, upside down and holding them by the stem to dip and twirl each glass in the kosher salt he'd spread across a saucer. Realizing she'd been caught staring, Aubrey immediately blushed. Nick had noticed and simply smiled—his beautiful eyes followed suit.

Their dinner conversation had been light. Nick shared stuff about work, something he hadn't done in, well, nearly forever. Aubrey shared her woes about Peyton's teen years. Nick had said he hadn't really noticed much of a change in their daughter over this past school year. That was hardly a surprise to Aubrey since Peyton always saved her best face for her father.

The quesadillas were perfect, and they both had seconds on the margaritas. Nick always made them exactly the way Aubrey liked them, a little on the stiff side but not so strong as to incapacitate her.

After they'd finished eating, Nick carried their second drinks over to the table. He'd held them in the air, grinned and teased, "Dessert's ready!" As Nick started to place the glasses onto the table, he appeared to change his mind. "Let's take these out onto the deck. We can enjoy them on the swing.

Aubrey thought it was a great idea and had turned on some light jazz on their indoor-outdoor music system.

If Aubrey were to close her eyes right now, she was certain she could still feel the way last evening's breeze had felt as it caressed her face. The sun had set shortly before she and Nick walked out onto the deck. The two of them had curled up on the aquamarine cushion resting on the porch swing. It'd been a quiet night on the lagoon, especially considering it was summertime and most of the houses surrounding theirs were occupied. Jazz played softly in the background. Nick and Aubrey had sat silently in the twilight of the day, drinking margaritas, and gently rocking to and fro to the rhythm of the water lapping at the dock below.

It had startled Aubrey when Nick reached over and brushed his fingers across her cheek. "You look beautiful tonight. This has been nice."

Surprised, and somewhat caught off guard, Aubrey lowered her chin and raised her eyes up to meet Nick's. "Thanks, Nicky. And, you're right, this has been really enjoyable. We couldn't have ordered more perfect weather than this."

On the swing, they'd gently drifted back and forth until what was left of the day had turned into night, and their glasses were empty. When Nick suggested they go inside and clean up the kitchen, Aubrey had felt deflated. With the kids out of the house, she'd really hoped this would be the night that Nick decided he wanted her again … wanted *them* again.

Once inside, they'd cleared the table together. Aubrey was rinsing dishes and loading the dishwasher while Nick put the alcohol back into the cabinet and the open bottle of margarita mix into the refrigerator, and returned the base of the blender to its place on the shelf in the pantry.

Before Aubrey knew what was happening, Nick had snuck up behind her and wrapped his arms around her. He buried his face in her hair as he moved his hands wherever he desired. He'd mumbled, as he used his chin to brush her hair back so he could kiss her neck. "I've missed you so much. I've missed *us* so much."

With the water still running, Aubrey had turned to face him— in disbelief this was actually happening. Nick was here. Awake. Wanting her. Before she could speak, Nick cupped a hand on each side of her face, pulling Aubrey toward him. Tipping his head to the side, he kissed her lips before kissing her long and deep … exactly like he used to. Aubrey wrapped her arms around his strong shoulders, pressing against him, and allowing his hands to do whatever they wanted to do and roam wherever they wanted to roam.

After they'd come up for air, Nick had reached behind Aubrey and turned the water off. He'd never taken his eyes off hers when he'd reached for Aubrey's hand and led her downstairs to their bedroom where he made passionate love to her as though it were their very first time.

Momentarily lost in the bittersweet memory, Aubrey had nearly forgotten why she'd called Libby in the first place. "Oh! I thought since I'm off today, do you want to hang out on the dock and catch up? I can come over there since the boys are there already."

A more relieved-sounding Libby responded, "I'd love that. Jed's up in the city, and you know our boys. They were up half the night playing video games. They'll sleep most of the day away anyway."

Aubrey walked over to the window and admired the beautiful blue sky. On the lagoon below, one of their neighbors was maneuvering his boat through the no-wake zone presumably on the way to the bay's choppy, fish-filled waters. She recognized a few of his kids, as they were kneeling on the rear seats, watching the small wake the vessel created behind the boat. "Okay. I'm going to take a quick shower, and then I'll be over." She smiled at the sweet serenity on the water.

Libby quickly added, "Oh, and don't worry about the doughnuts. I have plenty of milk and cereal for the kids and some fresh fruit here for us. I'll put on a pot of coffee in thirty minutes or so. See you soon."

"Sounds perfect. See you in a little bit." Aubrey hung up and sighed.

As the boat she'd had her eyes fixed on faded into the distance, Aubrey couldn't stop herself from drifting back to the part of the memory she didn't share with Libby … when shame had overwhelmed her once Nick's breathing had finally hummed deep and steady beside her last night.

Chapter Twenty~Three

Just before nine o'clock in the morning, Aubrey watched as Libby placed a tray of croissants and fruit on a side table between the cedar Adirondack chairs situated on the dock facing the water. She'd carried down each of their cups filled with coffee and handed Libby's off to her before sitting down.

They'd been enjoying a spell of great weather and today was no exception. They'd no sooner gotten settled when three ducks swam over to where they were sitting. Aubrey balanced her mug on the arm of the chair, reached over to pluck a croissant from the tray, and broke it into halves. She left one half on the tray and tore the other into tiny pieces before tossing them into the water. Between quacks and splashes, the grateful ducks devoured the bits she'd shared with them. A man and a woman, each on a wave-runner, waved as they'd idled by on the way to the open bay. It was a beautiful, albeit typical summer morning on the lagoon.

While they sipped coffee and nibbled on fruit, Libby gave Aubrey the rundown of all the things Brody and Teddy did yesterday. When she'd finished, she filled Aubrey in on all the improvements Jed was going to be working on for the rest of the summer. The biggest improvement was to screen in one of their porches. Aubrey tried to stay present but realized she apparently hadn't done the best job of doing so, when Libby paused abruptly and placed her coffee on the arm of the chair. She leaned forward and raised an eyebrow. "Wait. What's going on here? You're being w-a-ay too quiet."

Aubrey closed her eyes and took in a deep, cleansing breath before letting it go.

Libby laced her fingers together. "Oh, my God. What happened last night?"

Aubrey opened her eyes. "It was almost perfect, really."

Tipping her head to the side, Libby asked, "Almost?"

Aubrey went on to explain what had transpired after their phone call. Aubrey described how Nick had made incredible margaritas to have with dinner. She elaborated on how scrumptious the quesadillas tasted. Aubrey left no part out when she'd shared the details of their time on the swing with their second round of drinks. She spilled the beans on all the steps that led up to their beautiful lovemaking. When she was finished speaking, Aubrey reached over and grabbed a grape, popping it into her mouth.

After leaning against the back of her chair, Libby raised her hands in the air, palms up. "I don't get it. All of that sounds wonderful.

It sounds like a fantastic night, and it feels like you got everything you've been wanting. Everything you hoped for. No?

It was true. All Aubrey had been wanting was to have consensual sex with her husband. To be intimate with Nick, like it used to be. Before she had time to answer, Brody and Teddy came running down the steps and over to where they sat, each yelling *mom, mom* the whole way down.

Brody, sporting a comic-perfect bed-head, addressed Libby first. "Hey, Mom! Can you take us to the movies this afternoon? That new movie I told you about is in theaters today!"

Libby laughed. "It's only ten thirty in the morning. I can't even believe you two are awake."

Ignoring that comment, Teddy tried to strengthen the request and turned to Aubrey. "Yeah, Mom, please, can we?"

Not waiting for Libby's response, Aubrey's eyes were locked on Teddy's. She gently explained that she'd scheduled a hair appointment for late this afternoon and told him another day would probably work better. Ultimately, with a little more pleading from Brody, Libby had ultimately agreed to take both boys to the matinee.

Once that was decided, Aubrey and Libby light-heartedly chased the boys away to get their breakfast. Afterward, they had instructions for the two of them to walk over to Aubrey's house so Teddy could retrieve clothes and his toothbrush.

As soon as their sons climbed the steps and were out of earshot, Libby asked, "So, your night sounds terrific ... what's the *almost* about?"

Quickly glancing at the upper deck to verify the boys had gone inside and once satisfied they had, Aubrey sat forward and leaned in toward Libby. "It was fabulous. It's what happened after the fact that has me so disturbed, Libby." Aubrey paused and gazed out over the lagoon as the memory played back in full color for her as she shared all the gory details out loud.

After their lovemaking, Nick flopped back on the bed, a hint of perspiration collected on his brow. Aside from the few quick showers they'd taken together when he'd been sleepwalking, it was often too dark for Aubrey to see Nick naked like this. The last time had been when he was sleeping. And, just as it had that night, the sight of him took her breath away.

Aubrey scootched up next to him and turned onto her side. Nick reached out an arm, so she snuggled in and put her head across the top of his chest and shoulder. His heart thumped beautiful calming noise into her ear. She ran her fingers over his stomach. The nice thing about this being the real deal was that Aubrey didn't have those feeling of racing against the clock … to grab a washcloth, get the watch back onto his arm to beat the actual moment when Nick would fall back into a real sleep.

Nick pulled at loose strands of her hair and smiled. "You really are amazing. Tonight was off the charts. I don't know what caused us to get so off track, but how you felt tonight was worth the wait for all these months." He kissed the top of her head. "I know we have some work to do. I'm just so glad we're here … in this moment."

Aubrey kissed his chest. "Me, too. We'll figure all the rest out." She hoped Nick would just drift off to sleep, so they didn't have to talk anymore. She didn't want to tell any more lies. But, karma had been keeping score and wasn't letting her off that easy.

Nick shifted and rolled toward Aubrey, pulling his arm back enough that she'd naturally slid into the crook of his elbow. "I mean, you felt it, right? There was an electricity to tonight … like when we were young." It was more of a question than a statement. Nick's eyes bore into Aubrey's.

At least she could be truthful, tonight had been great. "It was like that for me, too, Nicky. Just like that."

Nick leaned in and kissed her soft and slow before turning back to lay his head on his pillow. "This is exactly why I wanted to wait. I wanted it to be special. When things began to get better between us, I needed all those ill feelings to be long gone. I wanted the first time we made love again to be memorable and important. Do you know what I mean, Aubrey?"

She clenched her jaw, begging her lips not to tell another lie, yet knowing she couldn't blow it at this late date. Aubrey was grateful Nick wasn't looking directly at her when she answered, "I do, Nick. I know exactly what you mean."

Aubrey got out of bed and turned off the light. A few minutes after she slid back under the covers, Nick's breathing told her he was sound asleep. As she tried to join him, she was kept wide awake by the deceitfulness that threatened to haunt her forever.

When Aubrey stopped talking, Libby's eyes were wide. "Holy cow, Aubrey! I can't imagine …"

Shaking her head, Aubrey moved her coffee cup from the arm of the chair to the tray resting on the table. "It's my life … I have a front row seat to this show, and I can hardly believe this is even real. If I could turn back time …"

"You need to forgive yourself, Aubrey. You did what you thought was right and chances are you'd have already been served with divorce papers and divorced months ago if you didn't do what you've done."

Aubrey squinted. "Lib, do you know I actually don't even understand why I was mad at Nick all the time. I mean … this is the same *Nick*. It's all so crazy. I just want to fast forward a few months to when intimacy isn't so new, and Nick won't be analyzing it anymore."

"You'll get there, and before you know it, this will all just be a bad memory." Libby smiled.

It was getting close to noon, so Libby stood up and picked up the tray. "I need to get ready to go to the movies. What are you going to do now?" She started for the walkway.

Aubrey stood up and followed. "I'm going to just keep going. Time is my best friend right now." She audibly sighed. "And, I'll just have to keep on praying. Nick never finds out what a liar he married."

Chapter Twenty~Four

Aubrey was surprised to see Nick's car when she got home from Libby's house. Knowing the kids were still out, she hoped Nick had bagged work and come home for an encore. Aubrey quickly reasoned—it would have been one tryst closer to not having to discuss their sex life anymore ... one step closer to leaving all this deception behind. She parked the car and hurried to get inside.

Tilting her head toward her shoulder, Aubrey listened as one of the island stools screeched across the floor upstairs in the kitchen. She tossed her keys into a decorative tray resting on the blue-green table in the foyer before heading up the steps.

Jogging up the stairs, Aubrey made her way into the kitchen. Nick's back was to her. He was staring out of the far window when she placed her hand on his shoulder. "Hey, babe! What a surpr ..."

Her words were interrupted when Nick smacked her hand away before spinning to face her. "How dare you touch me!"

Adrenaline rushed through Aubrey's body. Nick's face was so red, it was as though he'd been holding his breath and finally was able to release it. Before she could formulate a question, a thought, or even figure out what was going on, Nick stood up from the chair—he and his anger towered over her so threateningly she wanted to cower to the floor. She could never recall being afraid of him. Until now.

Her mind raced. Aubrey frantically wondered if Nick hadn't really been awake last night and was now as mad as a hornet before rapidly chalking it off as a ridiculous thought. She quickly reasoned … they'd come in from the deck together, cleaned the kitchen together, and had gone to bed together. No, she concluded, Nick was definitely awake.

Aubrey's voice shook when she spoke. "Nick, what's the matter? I mean, what did I do?"

"What DID you do, Aubrey?" he spat. "I can't believe how pitiful you are! How … how … disgusting you are!" Nick's voice barreled across the room and bounced off the walls. There was fire in his eyes.

Feeling like she might throw up, Aubrey tried to make the connection as to what Nick had become so enraged about. Her thoughts raced as she wondered if he'd somehow figured out what she'd done. But how? The only living soul who knew how low Aubrey had stooped was Libby, and there was no way her best friend would ever have sold her out. Aubrey knew she may have just as well confessed her sins to a door for all the information anyone would ever get out of Libby.

"Nick, everything was fine. I don't know what's going on here. Last night …"

"Last night!" Nick raged. "Last night? You mean the first night we'd made love in what? Months? Almost a year? THAT last night, Au-brey?" The caustic echo of turpentine returned when her name rolled off his tongue.

"I …" Aubrey felt the room spin as Nick cut her off again.

He violently wrung his hands together and then, pointing at Aubrey, jutting his arm back and forth. "Do you know what happens when you delete a video from a computer, Au-brey?" Nick stepped closer. "Do you?"

Feeling like she'd just been punched in the stomach, Aubrey reached for the edge of the island to steady herself, as she vividly recalled the video she'd deleted all those months ago. In an instant, she realized the mistake she'd made, Aubrey knew what he was going to say before he said it. "Nick, I …"

Nick answered his own question. "It's moved into your trash. So, if you really didn't want someone to find it, you'd have had to delete it from there, too!" Nick's nostrils flared.

Aubrey searched for words. "I can explain …" She reached her hand out toward him, only to have him swat it away again.

Nick furrowed his brow. "Explain? Explain? Let me explain something to you. I was counting on you to tell me the truth about what was going on with my health. The doctor was counting on you, to tell the truth about what was going on with my health. Do you have any idea what it was like to wake up in the morning and find myself in different underwear than what I'd remembered wearing to bed? I was questioning my own sanity, for God's sake! Do you understand, on several occasions I found the seat in my car reclined and thought I'd been hitting the button when I was getting out of the car? I was getting into my car at night, Aubrey. Asleep! Who knows where I went … what I did? I could have killed someone!" Now, Nick was pacing and waving his hands frantically in the air. "Nevermind the fact that I was utterly exhausted."

Believing she'd kept careful watch over Nick so he wouldn't get hurt or injure anyone else, it'd never occurred to Aubrey that Nick might have woken and done other things after she'd fallen asleep each night. Aubrey shuddered before stepping towards him. She tried to grab his arm, but Nick roughly shrugged her off.

"Please, Nicky."

Turning to face her, the veins in Nick's neck throbbed as he narrowed his eyes. "Sex? Was this about sex?" His hands were balled up into fists. "Do you know how violated I feel? I mean … that video … I look like a zombie! What could you possibly have gotten out of it? Oh, my God! I threw up after I watched you …"

Aubrey pressed her hands together as though she were praying. "Nick, please, just listen to me. It wasn't about sex. It was your words, the kindness, the way it was bringing us back together."

Nick was still pacing, his back was to Aubrey.

"Nicky, I swear, you initiated …"

Nick spun around. Spit flew from his lips as he screamed at Aubrey. "Initiated? I initiated? I was *sleeping*!" His eyes were wild.

He pointed at her again. "You are one sick human being. I … I don't even know who you are."

The hate in Nick's voice overwhelmed Aubrey to the point she could barely think to defend herself.

Nick walked over and stood in front of her, his eyes boring into her. "How many times, Aubrey? How many times did my body have sex with you while I was sleeping?"

"Nick, it wasn't like that. We were doing better. Things were getting better. We fell back in love again. I just thought if I could …"

Grabbing her shoulder, Nick screamed. "Tell me!"

Aubrey cried out. "I don't know!" Tears streamed down her cheeks. "Many." She turned away.

"Many? How often is *many*?" Nick grabbed her chin and pulled Aubrey to face him. He spoke through clenched teeth. "How often is *many*?"

Aubrey grabbed Nick's wrist to pull his hand from her face. He was hurting her. "It was a few times a week." She dropped her eyes to the floor.

"A few … ?" Nick stepped away from her, throwing both hands up in the air. "You know what? I'm not doing this. How dare you."

For the first time, Aubrey noticed the black suitcase Nick had tucked under the island countertop. In one swift move, Nick bent over, grabbed the flight bag, and headed for the staircase leading to the front door.

Aubrey was on his heels. "Nicky, please. You have to realize I didn't know what else to do. I was losing you. We were losing *us*. I'm not saying I was right. I'm saying I was desperate … desperate to save our marriage." She stopped at the top of the steps and watched Nick jog down to the landing and grab hold of the front doorknob. Aubrey choked. "Please. What would you have done, Nick? If this were in reverse … really … wouldn't you have done what I did? To save us? Our family?"

Nick's shoulders dropped, and he turned back to glance up at Aubrey. His eyes were filled to the brim, and they were sad. "You'll hear from my attorney."

And, without saying another word, Nick opened the door and stepped out before slamming it behind himself.

Chapter Twenty~Five

After receiving Aubrey's S.O.S. text, Libby left Brody and Teddy in the theater and rushed into the ladies' room. With the phone held to her right ear and her index finger jammed in her left ear, Libby's words echoed off of the tiled bathroom walls and through the phone. "Nick did what?"

Aubrey raised her voice while trying, once again, to stifle her crying. "He left me, Libby."

"No. What? Why? Aubrey, I just talked to you a few hours ago, and everything was perfect! What on earth happened?"

Aubrey began to sob again. "He … he found the video. Oh, my gosh, Libby. When I deleted it, I didn't delete it from his trash file. He must have gone to empty the trash on his computer and saw it there. Libby, he hates me."

"No, he doesn't, Aubrey. He's just mad. He'll come around."

"Lib, he was so angry. I thought he was going to hit me. You were right. I should have listened to you. Everything I've been doing has been so wrong. Oh, my God, why didn't I just listen to you?" Aubrey put her phone on speaker and placed it on the kitchen counter, grabbed a tissue from the box of Kleenex, and blew her nose.

Libby sounded sad. "Oh, Aubrey, there was no way of knowing who was right. As of this morning, it looked as though your instincts were correct. It really seemed as though you'd single-handedly saved your marriage."

Aubrey leaned her elbows on the counter and hovered over her phone. "Nick made me feel like a predator … or worse … It was so ugly." Tears chased their way down her cheeks again.

After giving Libby the blow by blow of everything that had happened between her and Nick, Aubrey was exhausted. It all felt incredibly surreal, and she still couldn't believe that she'd completely forgotten to remove the video from Nick's computer trash file. How stupid of her.

Before they hung up, Libby told Aubrey after the movie was over, she'd pick up Peyton and keep her and Teddy for the night. Aubrey knew she was in no shape to talk to her children about what had happened, so she was grateful for the delay. Libby told her, once the kids were all fed their dinner and settled at her house, she would leave and come over to hang out with Aubrey for a while.

Libby's sigh seemed to hang heavy over the lagoon's still surface. It appeared as though someone drained the water and replaced it with solid glass. "Aubrey, I don't know what to say. I was so hopeful that the whole divorce thing was behind you. It really felt like you'd pulled this off. There's no shame in trying to save your marriage."

Aubrey reached over and squeezed her friend's hand. "Thanks, Lib, but we both know ... you've been trying to tell me all along exactly how wrong I was ... and, you were so right. There *is* shame in taking advantage of another person. We simply can't live based on the *any means to an end* theory. We just can't." She pulled her hand back and took a sip of her wine. "In hindsight, I don't even know what I was thinking. How crazy was I?" Aubrey pressed her bare foot against the decking and pushed, effectively setting the porch swing in motion again.

"You can't live there, Aubrey. Look, I've been on this whole ride with you. I know in my heart of hearts you believed you were doing the right thing. It's hard to make good decisions when you're the one who is living in the thick of things. It just is." Libby nodded, as though she was trying to get Aubrey to mimic her agreement.

"In my own defense, I sincerely meant what I kept saying to you. I saw what I was doing as something between a married couple. And, Nick *was* the one who was initiating everything. To me, my agreeing would never be viewed as a violation. I mean, there were times after talking to you when I'd questioned it, but I was always able to justify what I was doing. Except, not now, after I saw nothing but betrayal all over Nick's face. He was so hurt, Libby. Hurt isn't even the right word. He was insanely offended." A tear ran down Aubrey's face. "And, seeing myself through his eyes, I've never felt so wickedly gross in my whole life."

It was dark outside. As always, after the sun went down in Mystic, the island would begin to live up to its name. In the evening, everything always looked a little more magical. Windows on the houses up and down the lagoon would illuminate in shades of white and yellow light. Accent lights, water features, and underwater swimming pool lights all began to glow, adding to the sparkling show. Those which were situated close enough to the water reflected off its surface. During the Christmas holiday season—now, not so far away—some residents placed lit and decorated trees out on their docks, each used the water's reflection as a mirror to appear as though a million twinkling stars had simply fallen from the sky.

Aubrey couldn't believe, only twenty-four hours ago, that she and Nick had been sitting in this very spot, enjoying the best evening they'd shared together in more than a year. Now, Nick was gone, her marriage was over, and she had to live with the shame of what she'd done and how ridiculously far she'd taken things to get what she wanted. She consoled herself with one thought about last night's lovemaking—no matter what anyone wanted to think about what she'd done—Nick *was* indeed wide awake, and he'd proven to Aubrey... it'd been exactly what he'd been wanting, too. She silently scolded herself for even keeping the smallest bit of hope that he'd realize that fact and eventually find a way to forgive her.

Libby broke the silence. "Listen, Aubrey, you just have to pray for the best, but surrender to the worst possible outcome. There's nothing else you can do. There was no real predicting how this would turn out. Oh, honey, there just wasn't."

Aubrey stopped the swing and stood up. She didn't even try to hide the defeat in her voice. "We've easily beaten this horse dead ten times over in these last months. Go on home. Get back to the kids. Thanks for keeping them. Explaining what's going on to Peyton and Teddy is going to happen way sooner than I'm ready as it is. I'm grateful for the postponement. We both know … I deserve what's coming to me."

Libby stood up and hugged her without disagreeing. Nick's reaction offered finite proof, there was no more to argue about. Intentions didn't matter, wrong was wrong. Plain and simple.

Now, Aubrey would have to pay the price for her deeds, and she was all too aware—it was going to be a steep one.

Chapter Twenty-Six

Aubrey was shocked the next morning when she walked into the kitchen to get a cup of coffee to find Nick sitting on a stool at the island. He looked awful. She knew it was too much to hope he'd somehow changed his mind. She hesitated. "I didn't expect to find you here. What's going on, Nick?"

He didn't look up from the coffee cup he was spinning around in circles. "I came so we could talk to the kids when they get up. Both of their rooms are empty. Where are they?"

As her heart sank at the realization Nick not only hadn't changed his mind and he wasn't here for her, but rushed back first thing this morning to share the news with their kids. Aubrey walked to the cabinet to fetch a mug. "They're at Libby's. They'll be home in a little while."

Hearing the stool scrape across the floor behind her, Aubrey glanced over her shoulder and watched as Nick stood up, collected his cup, and headed toward the sliding glass doors. Without looking back, he mumbled, "I'll be outside."

Once her coffee was ready, Aubrey walked outside to sit on the swing. Nick wasn't there. She glanced over the railing and spotted him on the dock below. Standing there, with a blank expression on his face, Nick gazed off into the distance. Aubrey considered the staircase leading down to the dock, but thought better of it and instead sat down on the swing as she'd planned. She wondered what he could be thinking and then shivered at the torturous thoughts that followed.

Aubrey turned her eyes away when Nick began to walk back toward the steps. As she listened to his footsteps ascending the stairs, her heart raced in her chest so fast Aubrey could feel it in her throat, as it had done so often lately. She understood it was an unrealistic hope, but she prayed Nick was returning to accept her heartfelt apology … to say he understood and somehow would find a way to forgive her.

When Nick got back on the deck, he stood in front of Aubrey. She slid to the side, looked up at him, and patted the cushion next to her. "Do you want to sit down?"

Nick stepped back to lean against the railing behind him. He closed his eyes and paused, ignoring the invitation. His voice was strained when he spoke. "I want to discuss what it is we're going to tell the kids before they get here."

Feeling as though she'd start crying any minute, Aubrey stopped the swing and leaned over to put her mug on the side table.

Clasping her hands together she began to plead, "Please, Nick, just let me ..."

Holding his hand up in front of her, Nick shook his head. "I'm sorry. I didn't mean to say discuss. I'm not discussing anything with you."

Unable to stop the tears, Aubrey choked, "But, Nick ..."

No longer able to contain himself, Nick shouted, "Aubrey!" He took a deep breath, his hostility was palpable. "Nothing is up for negotiation here. We are doing this my way."

With tears falling like rain, Aubrey dropped her chin. Holding her breath, she spun her wedding rings in circles on her finger.

Seeming to pause long enough to confirm Aubrey was no longer arguing, Nick went on. "Since I can't even fathom telling them anything near the truth, we're telling the kids we grew apart. We tried counseling, and it just didn't work out."

Knowing there wasn't a chance Nick was going to hear her out, a defeated Aubrey just nodded and looked away. A ship's bell rang in the distance. Children could be heard laughing on neighboring decks and docks as the houses on the lagoon came alive. Everything coming to life only served to make Aubrey further wish she were dead.

A huge seagull landed on the flagpole in the yard next door. Even the bird gawked at her, unblinking, as though it knew Aubrey's secret and she'd disappointed the bird, too.

Their neighbor's boat motor began to hum, causing Nick to glance over and render a half-hearted wave. Looking back at Aubrey, he motioned toward her phone that she'd placed on the side table.

"Call Libby and tell her I'm on my way to pick up the kids." Without waiting for her response, Nick walked back into the house.

When Aubrey heard the sliding door close, she picked up the phone and began to type. *Nick showed up this morning to talk to the kids. He's on his way to your place to pick them up. I'll touch base after he leaves.* Aubrey hit *send.*

Before she even had time to put the phone down, it pinged notification of Libby's response. *Ugh. Sorry, friend.*

While Nick was gone, Aubrey went downstairs to get dressed. She was just finishing sweeping her hair back into a ponytail when she heard Nick and the kids as they came through the front door and headed upstairs. Aubrey's stomach felt as though she'd unwittingly boarded a rollercoaster. She placed the brush on the dresser and walked upstairs to face her dreaded reality.

When Nick caught sight of her, he asked the kids to sit down at the kitchen table. They did as their father asked and Aubrey followed suit.

Nick sat at the head of the table and cleared his throat before speaking. "Your mother and I need to talk to you."

Peyton and Teddy glanced from one parent to the other in unison. Peyton narrowed her eyes and spoke first. "What's going on, Dad?"

Clearly oblivious, Teddy sat, blinking, alongside his sister.

Leaning forward, Nick folded his hands and rested them on the table. "Well, your mom and I have been having some troubles. And, after a long discussion, we've decided that we're going to try living apart for a while."

Peyton sprung forward. "A divorce? You're getting a divorce?" She whirled around to face Aubrey. "This is *your* fault, isn't it, Mom? You're always mad at Dad. You …"

Nick interrupted as Aubrey failed to defend herself. "Peyton, honey, that's enough. Marriages don't fail due to just one person. We've been to counseling, and this is what we've decided is best for everyone."

Try as she might, Aubrey couldn't find her voice. Indeed Peyton was right in believing this was Aubrey's fault.

Peyton smacked her open hand onto the table. "I want to live with Dad." Her eyes bore holes through her mother. Aubrey looked down at her own lap.

Teddy, wide-eyed, swung his gaze from one end of the table to the other as though he were watching a tennis match. "Who am I going to live with? I don't want to have to pick."

"No one is picking anything, pal. You kids will live here with your mom. I'll live in the apartment behind my office until we sort this all out." Nick's voice was calm. "I'll still see you every day. For now, I'll pick you up a few weeknights for dinner, and you'll stay with me every other weekend. When school begins, I'll be picking both of you up every day. Depending on your schedules and your activities, a couple of those days we'll have dinner together before I bring you home. You'll see, this will all work out."

Peyton shot out of her chair. "This is so unfair! You've been tricking us all summer! Last school year it was clear that something was wrong. I prayed every night that things would get better. Then all summer long you pretended like we were a happy family again. When you were really seeing a counselor and deciding to get a divorce no matter how we felt. Right now, I hate you both!" She turned and charged toward the doorway.

Aubrey hollered after her, "Peyton!"

Holding his hand up, Nick shook his head. "Let her go." He turned his attention to Teddy. "Hey, buddy, why don't you go and play video games in your room. Your mom and I have some things to work out."

Teddy frowned and his lip quivered. "I just want to say I don't hate either of you. But I do feel really sad right now. I didn't want our family to get divorced." He stood up, and as he walked past her, Aubrey reached out and squeezed his arm before offering a weak smile and a nod.

Once Teddy was out of earshot, Nick told Aubrey he'd continue to pay the household bills through their divorce process. He also offered a generous, temporary child support sum that he'd be willing to pay until they could sort it out in court. Aubrey was almost shocked at how much he'd worked out in such a short period of time before she remembered Nick had seen an attorney months ago and these things were likely the recommendations his counsel had prepared for him way back then. Aubrey was beyond trying to argue with him, so she remained silent, occasionally nodding her head in agreement.

When Nick finished speaking his piece, he pushed his chair back and stood up to leave.

Blinking back tears, Aubrey rushed to stand and stammered, "Nick, couldn't we at least go back to the counselor and talk about all this?"

Before leaving the house, Nick, with his jaw clenched, locked his gaze on Aubrey's and offered only one word. "Never."

Chapter Twenty~Seven

Aubrey had cried buckets of tears in the more than eight weeks since Nick had left. Summer vacation ended and the school year had resumed. She could already feel fall laying its claim on Mystic. It was late September and seasons were changing. The days were growing as dark as Aubrey's mood.

In spite of Nick keeping his promise to pick Peyton and Teddy up from school, sharing a few dinners each week with them and every-other-weekend overnight visits with him, Nick hadn't spoken to Aubrey at all. He texted with the kids directly and never got out of the car when he dropped them off or picked them up.

One time, shortly after Nick left, Aubrey had run out to his car to attempt to speak to him. Before she could even get one sentence out, he'd threatened to pull away without the kids if she didn't step away and go back inside. Not wanting to make a scene in front of the neighbors and, more importantly, their children, Aubrey had returned to the house and never attempted to approach Nick again.

As he'd promised, she'd heard from Nick's attorney just days after he'd moved out. Aubrey had cringed on the day she'd read the paperwork. While they'd stopped short of saying the word *rape,* the papers stated that she'd *repeatedly engaged in sexual intercourse with the Plaintiff when he was in a state of unconsciousness in which he was unable to consent to said act.* Rape. The whole thing made Aubrey sick. Even to her own mind, her actions, which seemed so necessary at the time, were so utterly appalling now.

Today, she was finally meeting with an attorney—a guy someone at work had recommended. She only wished everything could be handled over the phone. It would be so much easier than facing a stranger who would inevitably read the words *repeatedly engaged in sexual intercourse with the Plaintiff when he was in a state of unconsciousness whereas he was unable to consent to said act* and then require Aubrey to explain it.

It actually reminded Aubrey a little of the time Peyton had ended up with a sprained neck. Aubrey would often hold her daughter by the ankles, upside down, and gently swing her back and forth while chanting the Mother Goose Rhyme *Hickory Dickory Dock.* Well, on one particular occasion, Peyton was wearing little pink stockings and a dress. Aubrey began to sway her back and forth. *Hickory Dickory dock, the mouse ran up the clock. The clock struck one, and down he run ...* Before Aubrey could finish the rhyme and quicker than she could process what was happening, she suddenly found herself only holding the empty feet of the stockings, twenty-month-old Peyton had slipped right out and landed flat on the top of her head, before rolling onto the floor coming to a stop on her back and wailing all the while. When they got to the hospital and Aubrey had to explain to the doctor why it seemed sensible, at the time, to hold a child upside down by their ankles and swing them back and forth, it'd sounded full-blown crazy to her own ears. So much so, she'd never done it again.

That's how this was ... a little. Well, now that she had to explain it. Except, in this case, something that didn't necessarily seem right, but had seemed justifiable, suddenly seemed so dark and downright indictable now. Aubrey could only hope that she'd be able to find someone willing to represent her in court. Oh, what on earth was the matter with her?

After she was done getting ready, Aubrey joined the kids in the kitchen. She would only have time to grab a quick cup of coffee before dropping each of them off at school. Then, she'd have to hurry to make it to her appointment with the attorney on time.

Not making it easy, as usual, Peyton shot hateful looks Aubrey's way. Teddy was his normal warm and loving self. Aubrey secretly worried about his ability to act as though nothing had happened in their family, as though everything seemed status quo. Once the divorce was settled, she had every intention of getting both kids into counseling.

Before long, she'd shuffled both kids into the car and dropped them each at school. She had butterflies in her stomach as she swung the car into the parking lot just in time for her appointment, coming to a stop in front of a sign that read MYSTIC ISLAND FAMILY LAW

PRACTICE. In smaller print underneath it read Ashton Rawlings, Esq. The butterflies instantly turned into a stampede of Clydesdales.

Aubrey checked in at the front desk and was told to have a seat and Mr. Rawlings would be with her shortly. She politely declined a cup of coffee because her stomach was a wreck. As she waited nervously, she kept rolling around in her mind all the ways she might try to explain herself when asked about the nonconsensual sex. Aubrey startled when the secretary announced, *Mr. Rawlings will see you now.* When she stood up to follow the voice that summoned her, Aubrey still had no clue as to how she would explain herself.

When the secretary introduced Aubrey to Ashton Rawlings, she was surprised. He was much older—nearing seventy, she guessed—than she'd expected. He had a head full of snow white hair and a contrasting golden tan. With a name like *Ashton* she somehow expected he'd be younger, like a fortysomething. It only made things harder because now Aubrey was going to have to explain to a man who was her father's age why on earth she thought it was acceptable to have nonconsensual sex with her sleeping husband. She wondered if it could get any more embarrassing, then pushed the question from her thoughts. Of course, it could. She could have to stand up and explain it before a judge. Perish the thought.

Handing him the stack of papers that she'd been served by Nick's attorney, she sat down on a crisp armchair across the desk from the gentleman and started fidgeting until they began.

Mr. Rawlings spent the first twenty minutes getting all the facts of the case together. Facts, meaning literally those things that weren't in dispute, such as Nick's birth date, Aubrey's birthdate, the date of their marriage, number of children, children's dates of birth, and how long they'd been having marital difficulties.

While Mr. Rawlings jotted down notes on a yellow lined legal tablet, Aubrey looked around the office. There were large bookcases behind Mr. Rawlings's desk. There was a scattering of what appeared to be family photos, several volumes of law books, and a brass replica of the scales of justice. There was another figurine of a lady in a blindfold, holding the scales of justice. Aubrey made a mental note to look up the meaning of that statue when she got home. A large, framed degree from Rutgers Law School hung on the side wall.

Aubrey was still taking it all in when she realized Mr. Rawlings had asked her something. She shook her head and blinked, "I'm sorry. What?"

Mr. Rawlings motioned to the stack of papers she'd handed him and furrowed his brow. "You're husband has filed for divorce based on mental cruelty and sexually deviant behavior. I'm trying to figure out why they moved in that direction, and I've found this paragraph where it reads you *repeatedly engaged in sexual intercourse with the Plaintiff when he was in a state of unconsciousness whereas he was unable to consent to said act.*" Mr. Rawlings peeked out over the top of his reading glasses, raised his eyebrows, and tipped his head to the side. "What exactly does that mean?"

Aubrey swallowed hard, twisting her hands, and trying to avoid eye contact with the elderly gentleman … *Hickory Dickory Dock.*

Chapter Twenty-Eight

Libby threw her head back and laughed. "Seriously? He just sat there staring at you? For? How long did you say? Like three minutes? Oh, my God. What did you do?" She laughed again, this time with such force, she snorted.

Aubrey glanced around the restaurant. They were at a spot the locals frequented, so she really hoped nobody had heard Libby carrying on like this. While she was grateful for the waterfront view and premium seating they'd scored, it was also the most crowded part of the restaurant. For the most part, no one seemed to be paying them any mind. It was still a little early for the lunch crowd. She leaned in and lowered her voice. "I can't believe you think this is that funny. You just snorted, for God's sake. You DO understand, this was like rendering true confessions about my sex life to a guy who reminded me of my father?" When Aubrey had agreed to meet Libby for lunch, after her morning appointment with the attorney, this was a far cry from what she'd expected from her friend.

Catching her breath, Libby held an open hand, with fingers spread wide apart, out in front of herself. "Wait. Wait. So, exactly what did you say to him?"

Aubrey rolled her eyes. "Well, in an effort to try to have everything make sense for him, I started by telling him Peyton's Hickory Dickory Dock stor ..."

She never even finished her sentence. Libby, who knew the whole story, slid down in her chair, dropping her head on the backrest, and howled. "Hick...? Hickory ...?" She could barely speak. Tears were rolling down her face, and she was wiping them away using both of her hands.

Beside herself, Aubrey lamented, "I seriously can't believe you're doing this. This is less than funny. Do you have any idea how embarrassed I was?"

Still hysterical, Libby was shaking her head. "I do. I do." She pushed herself back upright in her chair. She unraveled the cloth napkin on the table and used it to dab at her eyes. "I'm sorry, Aub. The visuals of how this unfolded are incredibly funny. It's just that I know how crazy the actual story is, to begin with. The fact that you added Hickory Dickory ..." Once again, Libby collapsed in a fit of laughter, prohibiting her from completing her thought.

Pulling the napkin from her lap, standing up, and tossing it onto the table, Aubrey said, "You need to pull yourself together. I'm going to the ladies room."

Libby's words chased after Aubrey. "Oh, Aubrey, don't be like that. Really, I think I'm just a little slaphappy. I haven't been sleeping well."

Without turning back, Aubrey half smiled in spite of herself and continued to head in the direction of the bathroom. By the time she'd returned to the table, Libby had, in fact, regrouped and was sipping a cup of tea. She'd ordered one for Aubrey as well.

When Aubrey sat down and dropped her napkin back into her lap, Libby began, "Aubrey, I'm sorry. I ..."

Aubrey held her hand up. "Really, Libby, it's alright. I get it. This whole thing is insane. You're my best friend, and you've loved me through this. Holy smokes, you'd even repeatedly warned me against it. I understand how weird everything must be for you to watch … nevermind to listen to."

"Still. I'm really sorry. I just didn't think about how it may have felt for you to be placed in the position of explaining—or trying to make sound reasonable—everything that's happened." Libby slid a small pitcher of milk across the table.

Pouring a splash of milk into her tea, Aubrey shook her head. "I really do understand. It's okay. Promise."

"So what happens now? Are you going to hire the guy?" Libby brought her cup to her lips.

"I did hire him this morning. I pretty much had to. I've put this off for so long. We have mediation next Friday." Aubrey's tone flipped to sound sarcastic. "To add to my joy, I had to write a check for thirty-five hundred dollars for his retainer. The attorney expects it to cost two to three times that, if we can't settle things fairly quickly." Aubrey sighed before sipping her tea and continuing on. "If I'm reasonable about a settlement, I can't imagine Nick delaying this at all. He really hates me, Libby. I'm certain all he wants to be … is rid of me."

Aubrey knew Libby probably considered protesting as she'd been doing since the day Nick confronted her in their kitchen, but the truth was, in the more than two months since then, he'd really seemed to have washed his hands of her. Libby's silence told Aubrey there would be no more objections.

Libby signaled their passing waitress and she and Aubrey each placed their usual orders. Aubrey picked up her phone to check the time and announced it was already twelve thirty, so both ladies added a glass of wine to their requested entrees.

Aubrey gazed out through the window at the water as it gently made its way out toward the open bay. It was calm today, totally contrasting with the chaos she was feeling inside. Her eyes filled to the brims. "Libby, the truth is … I would have been okay if Nick had left at the peak of our awful time. I thought I hated him, just like he believes he hates me. I'd have welcomed the divorce and my freedom, even though it meant the breakup of our family. I was just so over the loneliness. Now, the truth is, I know that I still love Nick, and the most frustrating part is knowing—in a place he's not even in touch with— he essentially still loves me. I wasn't wrong about that part."

Sympathetically, Libby reached across and grabbed Aubrey's hand. "I know you're right. You had that inside information. I'm sorry Nick found that video. I'm sorry you couldn't keep moving forward in the rekindling of your love and your marriage. I know how important it was to you. I know how much you believed in what you were trying to do. Even though I had trouble understanding how you were justifying it, there was no question in my mind that it was working. And, in the grand scheme of things, it was benefiting your kids as well."

Libby let go of Aubrey's hand when the waitress arrived with their food. They thanked her before she walked away.

Aubrey wrapped her arms around herself. "Forget the wine. I should have ordered a shot instead. This is all such a mess."

Drinking the last of her tea, Libby shoved the cup to the edge of the table. "I'm sorry this is all so hard. I guess my only hope for you now is for the divorce to be quick and not drag on and on."

Aubrey's eyes filled with tears. "… your lips to God's ears." While the prospect of being divorced was heartbreaking, the thought of the whole thing being dragged out over months, or even a year, made her sick. She glanced away as the waitress placed two glasses of wine on the table, pausing to collect their empty teacups before she walked away.

Libby raised her glass and held it hovering in the air midway across the table. "Here's to a brighter future, sanity, and your happiness."

Following suit, Aubrey raised her glass and tapped it against Libby's. "Let's hope so."

After taking a sip of her wine and placing her glass back onto the table, Libby sighed. "So, how are the kids holding up?"

Pausing to swallow, Aubrey shook her head. "Peyton is still blaming me. Every time she gets angry with me—which is often— she tells me I'm the reason her dad left and she doesn't want to live with me." Aubrey swiped her thumb over the condensation that had been accumulating on the side of her glass. "And Teddy? You know he's just as quiet and pleasant as always. I worry about him, though. You know he has to be hurt and angry, too. He's just not capable of being as mean as Peyton can be."

"I have the name of a good family counselor if you'd like. She actually lives just off the island. I can share her contact information with you." Libby gazed dolefully across the table.

"That'd be great. Thanks." Aubrey couldn't believe this was her reality. She couldn't even describe how badly she wished she could turn back time. She wondered if she'd still have taken the gamble and gone for saving her marriage. As it was, when this all began, the end of their marriage was imminent anyway ... albeit, back then it wouldn't have terminated with Aubrey going down in the thick fog of disgrace that surrounded her now. If only she'd have left things alone.

Libby, who'd been scrolling through her phone, placed it back on the table. "I just texted you the contact. You'll like her, and she'll be great with the kids."

Aubrey's smile was weak. "Thanks, Lib."

The waitress dropped the check. Libby insisted on paying, and Aubrey let her. She simply didn't have any fight left inside her. Besides, she was picking her battles these days.

The friends said their goodbyes at their respective cars, which were parked side by side. From there, Libby was headed inland … back to her house and back to her life with Jed and the kids. Aubrey was going back home to her empty house.

Once she arrived in her driveway, Aubrey considered taking a glass of wine out to the dock since it was sunny and there was only the slightest hint of a chill in the air. She knew her days of being able to sit out back were numbered now. Aubrey decided on a cup of coffee instead since it would soon be time to pick up the kids from school. It was Nick's night to have them for dinner, so she'd have plenty of time to drown herself in a bottle of wine later.

Once her coffee was brewed, Aubrey wrapped herself in a throw she retrieved from the oversized basket next to the fireplace in the living room. She made her way down to the dock and settled in on her rope rocker chair. It was her favorite seat. Aubrey had bought it in the Outer Banks while on vacation there a few years back.

The mooring whips danced in the wind, serving as an annoying reminder that summer was over and winter was well on its way. Normally, their boat would still be in the water to enjoy on a day like today, but soon after he'd left, Nick had it pulled from the lagoon, placed it on a trailer, parked it on the gravel in their front yard, and shrink-wrapped it for the winter. Nick hadn't even told her he was doing it. Aubrey just arrived home from work one day to find their boat sitting in the yard where they'd normally had it prepped and stored until the spring. She actually figured the boat was something she'd get in the divorce settlement. Nick wouldn't want to have anything to do with a boat named *Aubrey Lyn*. And, every boater knew … it was bad luck to rename a boat once it was christened.

When she'd considered objecting, Aubrey realized that would have been awfully audacious on her part. Complaining to Nick that he had no right to exclude her in the decision to pull the boat from the water early this year had no honorable comparison to her failure to include Nick in the decision to resume a sexual relationship with her. Had she even mustered up the gall to argue, Aubrey knew she'd have introduced a whole new low into their relationship. And, she was more than certain … the proverbial bar couldn't be reduced more than the depths she'd lowered it to already.

Chapter Twenty~Nine

Aubrey watched from the great room window as Peyton and Teddy climbed into Nick's car and continued to stare as they pulled away and disappeared from her view. It saddened her exactly how quickly this had become a way of life for them.

On those nights when she worked, Nick would pick them up for dinner and keep them overnight. The next morning, he'd drop them at school. If her shift happened to be on a Sunday night and it was Nick's scheduled weekend with the kids, Aubrey would not see them for four days in a row. It was hard.

Still only pulling a few shifts at the hospital each week, Aubrey had applied to human resources to move to day work and to increase her hours to full time. Once the divorce was final, she'd have to pay her own bills again, so she knew she'd be needing the money.

After pouring a glass of wine, Aubrey started to place the bottle back in the fridge. She hesitated and ultimately decided to bring the whole bottle into the living room. Sitting down on the couch, Aubrey picked up the remote and popped the television on. Snowball jumped up onto the couch and settled next to her. Aubrey ordinarily would chase him down, but she knew he must be confused about the new living arrangements. The first couple of times the kids left to spend the weekend with Nick, Snowball would lay on the landing near the front door. He was used to sleeping in Teddy's room but would sleep with Peyton if Teddy spent the night out with a friend. When the kids first began to spend weekends with Nick, he'd refused to sleep in Aubrey's room. Instead, he'd taken to objecting to their absence by staging a protest at the front door. Nowadays, he'd resigned himself to sleep in the master bedroom with Aubrey when they were gone. Even the family dog had become accustomed to the new routine.

Aubrey was channel surfing when she happened to look at the bottom shelf of the coffee table where a stack of photo books rested. She leaned down and grabbed a few of them, stacking them in her lap. Taking a sip of wine, she began paging through the extraordinary memories of her old life.

The first album she opened was full of pictures of their trip to Colorado. Nick had taught Aubrey to ski there. The memory almost stung, but Aubrey kept turning the pages. There were shots that Nick took of her as she wobbled along like a toddler learning to walk. She smiled when she noticed the death grip she had on the poles.

When she turned the page, she was gazing at the picture of all pictures. It was a selfie Nick took just after rescuing her from the side of the mountain. That's right … rescued. In the middle of one of the beginner slopes, Aubrey had told Nick she needed to use the ladies' room. So, he led her from the crowded slope through some trees and to a less traveled section of the trail. Or, so they'd thought. Their ignorance of the resort layout was about to teach them a lesson.

Unbeknownst to them, they'd made their way onto a double black diamond trail, meant for the best of skiing experts. As they started down, Nick was somewhat holding his own when Aubrey fell, losing her grip on her poles with her body still in motion. As she barreled forward, unable to stop herself, she slipped right off the side of the mountain. She'd had the wherewithal to grab at a dangling branch of a pine tree and held on for dear life until she saw Nick's face gazing down at her predicament.

Before Aubrey could say anything, Nick turned himself around, to lay on his belly, so his feet were facing Aubrey. He jammed each of his ski poles, shoulder width apart, into the snow. Then, holding on to each one, he warned Aubrey to *hold on tight*, and he aligned himself with the trunk of the tree growing out of the side of the mountain. Nick let go of the poles and simultaneously jammed his gloved fingers and the tips of his boots into the snow until he had *walked* his way down the steep incline to Aubrey. When his boot reached the base of the tree, he rolled over and allowed himself to slide down, spreading his legs and straddling the trunk of the tree. He reached his arms out and grabbed Aubrey's wrists, pulling her toward his perch. She'd wanted to cling to him for dear life, but Nick wouldn't let her.

Instead, he'd talked her into resting on her belly facing toward the top of the mountain, as he bellied up next to her. Nick never let go of Aubrey the entire time. He'd turned himself around and was using the base of the tree as his support. He pushed Aubrey by her boots as she clawed her way to the safety of the poles Nick had left for her to grab onto.

Aubrey turned and watched as Nick followed her trail. After they'd each settled down a bit, she told Nick he'd saved her life, and he would forever be her own personal hero. Afterward, Nick swore to Aubrey he'd never ever let her fall, no matter what happened in their lives. Nick pulled out the camera and snapped the selfie, forever freezing that moment in time. The moment when Nick loved Aubrey so much, he'd actually risked his life for her.

Chapter Thirty

Aubrey pulled into the Court House parking lot thirty minutes early and called Libby on her cell phone. "I feel like I'm having a heart attack." Her eyes darted around the parking lot as it filled with cars. She was looking for Nick. So far, there'd been no sign of him.

Libby sounded sympathetic. "Oh, sweetie, I know this is hard, but your attorney should be the one to do all the talking. The most you should have to do is be present."

She knew Libby was correct. Aubrey had met with her attorney the day before to prepare for mediation today. That didn't stop her from feeling as though she'd come down with the flu. Aubrey was sick to her stomach, felt dizzy, and all her muscles hurt from being so tensed up. "Lib, I know. But, I haven't been face-to-face with Nick in months. I just wish I didn't have to be here at all." Aubrey grabbed her water bottle from the cup holder in the console and took a sip.

"Aubrey, I feel so bad. I never should have listened to you. I should have taken the day off work and come with you to court today."

Shaking her head as if Libby could see her, Aubrey said, "No. No, it's okay. I told you, you wouldn't have been allowed in the mediation room anyway. It would have been pointless for you to use a vacation day to come down here and sit in a hallway alone. I'll be okay. I just needed someone to talk me off the ledge."

Libby sighed. "Well, I could have at least been there now and while you're waiting to go into mediation. I guess there's nothing we can do now. But, I'm not letting you talk me out of coming next time."

Aubrey didn't argue. She'd have been so relieved right now if Libby were sitting next to her. The distraction would have been helpful and more than welcome. "Well, water over the bridge or under the dam or whatever that saying is. Listen, I have to go. I have to get through security yet."

Libby converted into a cheerleader. "Aubrey, you've got this. Hold your head up. Go in strong. And, remember, right, wrong, or indifferent, you *were* trying to save your marriage. I was there. I'm your witness."

Reaching across to the passenger's seat, Aubrey grabbed her handbag and pulled it over to rest in her lap. "Thanks, friend. But I'm afraid you're the only person on the planet who feels that way. I'll call you when I'm done here. Love you."

"I'll be waiting on the edge of my seat. Love you, too."

Aubrey thought she heard Libby sigh before she hung up.

The lines for security and entrance into the building were long. Aubrey was afraid she'd spent too much time on the phone with Libby and was now late. She was grateful when the guards moved everyone through swiftly. Aubrey double-checked the floor number and conference room number, where she'd been ordered to appear, and headed for the elevators.

Having arrived on the third floor, Aubrey checked in with a receptionist and took a seat. Nervously gazing around, she didn't see Nick or her attorney. She pulled her phone from her purse and passed the time surfing the internet until Mr. Rawlings tapped her on the shoulder. He told her they would join Nick and his attorney in the conference room now. It seemed that they'd arrived early and were already seated behind the closed door.

That had certainly explained why Aubrey hadn't spotted Nick all morning. It seemed quite possible—if not probable—he'd been inside the courthouse long before she'd ever pulled into the parking lot this morning. Aubrey knew there was some lesson here about worrying about things that never happen, but she was too anxious to analyze all that right now.

Nick was sitting alongside his counsel on a highback chair with casters, tucked under a long, dark wood conference table. His attorney was introduced to her as John Jackson. Aubrey had remembered the name from the email she'd found on Nick's computer. Both Nick and his attorney had a laptop open on the table in front of each of their chairs. Aubrey wished she'd thought to bring something to hide behind, too.

Feeling as though she may just as well have been standing there naked, Aubrey watched as Mr. Jackson eyed her from head to toe and back up again. Aubrey knew it was not a compliment. She felt every one of his thoughts screaming at her. *So, this is the mastermind. The perverted rapist who assaulted my client.*

Aubrey purposely looked away and over to where Nick was sitting. He looked like a male fashion model in a dark suit with a deep burgundy shirt and matching tie. He was so incredibly handsome, she couldn't help but stare. Aubrey also couldn't help but notice he looked tired ... in fact, he looked aged. She felt so guilty knowing she owned that stress ... his decline. She lowered her eyes to the floor when Nick caught her checking him out.

Mr. Rawlings pulled out the chair situated directly across from Nick and motioned for Aubrey to sit down. Once she was seated, he took the seat next to her and directly across from Nick's attorney.

Now that they were set up as though this were a tennis match and the table served as the net, each attorney began to negotiate on behalf of their respective client.

Aubrey felt her face redden when Mr. Jackson announced that he and his client would not be very negotiable in their position considering the Defendant's (aka Aubrey's) behaviors, which were likely criminal, and they could pursue that with the prosecutor's office. He suggested if Aubrey were found guilty, it would leave her with nothing from Nick ... including custody of the kids.

One tear chased another down Aubrey's cheeks. She swatted them away.

Mr. Rawlings tossed back that Aubrey had no criminal intent. And he stated that her actions were solely in the interest of the family and, while perhaps seeming morally questionable, what she'd done had been working. He threatened they'd be able to prove that the marriage—which had been failing prior to *the middle of the night encounters*—began to thrive. Further, he said there were witnesses to the improvements of the marriage during that time ... including the couple's children. And, while they didn't want to drag the kids into court, they would if legal action were being threatened. Aubrey knew her attorney was bluffing, as she'd already advised him she would go to jail before bringing her children to court as witnesses on her behalf.

And the ball bounced back and forth over the net. She said ... he said ... she deserves nothing ... he owes this.

To Aubrey, it all began to sound like the Peanuts cartoon when Charlie Brown's mother, an invisible character, would speak ... *wah, wah, whant, wah, wah ...*

Aubrey wanted to act like a five-year-old and cover her ears. She didn't want this to be her story. But it was. And it was not only an upsetting tale, but it also had the worst ending possible.

You've got to be kidding ... you think your client deserves alimony? I don't care how long they've been married. She repeatedly assaulted my client. She placed him in grave physical danger, for God's sake.

My client wants the same custody and visitation that are in place now. It's been working for months. There is no need for Nick to change it now.

Your client's daughter doesn't even want to live with her.

The child support should remain as is. The children are used to a certain standard of living, and my client only works part-time as a nurse. They're used to having their mother home.

Are you kidding me? Your client should be in jail.

You know my client doesn't belong in jail. This is getting out of hand.

I'll say. We came in here willing to make some concessions. Yet, even with the poor judgment your client has demonstrated and the poor relationship she has with her daughter, you still arrived at this mediation in a position of greed.

Aubrey swiped her nose with the back of her hand before digging into her handbag to search for a tissue. Once she found one, she dabbed her cheeks and her nose before crumbling the Kleenex into a ball and clutching it in her closed fist.

The attorneys continued to bicker, taking jabs at each opposing client. Aubrey stole a glance at Nick and was surprised to find, his eyes were filled up with tears, too.

Charlie Brown's mother continued droning in the background … *wah, wah, wah …*

We'll contest the divorce. Your client withheld affection for a year before any of the medical issues ever happened.

Come on, Ashton. No one is going to care about that when they learn what she's done to him. Let's be real.

Maybe not, but it will cost your client a whole load of money for a contested divorce.

That's really low. I think a judge will see right through you.

Well, we've got all the time in the world. You and your client come up with a reasonable financial package to support my client and her children, or we're taking the long road here.

Nick closed his laptop, pushed it to the side, and leaned in, crossing his arms and resting them on the table. "The answer is *yes*."

Aubrey stared at the wall. She'd been so busy trying to tune out what the attorneys were saying, she didn't realize Nick had spoken to her.

He shifted in his chair and tried again. "Aubrey?"

Aubrey turned to him and furrowed her brow. "I'm sorry. Are you talking to me, Nick?"

Nick smiled and nodded. "I was trying to."

Mr. Jackson interrupted. "Nick, as your attorney, I don't recommend you speak directly with Mrs. Henson.

Nick placed his hand on his attorney's shoulder and shook his head. "Relax. I've got this."

Glancing back across the table at his wife, Nick wanted to be sure he had her attention. "Aubrey?"

Aubrey looked at her attorney, then over at her husband. She raised one eyebrow. "Nick?"

Closing his eyes, Nick breathed in deeply. He opened his eyes as he exhaled. "I said the answer is *yes*."

Aubrey narrowed her eyes and shrugged. "Yes, *what*? I don't understand."

Nick never broke eye contact. "That day ... the day I left, you asked me if this were in reverse would I have done what you did, to save us, to save our family?" He paused, lowered his eyes, and raised them again. "The answer is *yes*."

Mr. Jackson rolled his eyes and flung his pen onto the middle of the table. Mr. Rawlings leaned back in his chair, smiled, and allowed the rest to unfold.

Aubrey placed her hands over her face and sobbed. "I'm so sorry, Nicky. I …"

Nick didn't let her finish. He stood up and circled around the table to where she sat. When he got to Aubrey, he grabbed her by the arms and pulled her to her feet. He lifted her chin until her eyes met his. "I re-watched the video …"

Aubrey gasped. "Oh, God. Nicky, please forgive me. I …"

Shaking his head, Nick held his hand up and was unable to hold his tears back any longer. "Knowing we were coming here … that this was going to be so final, so forever … I decided to re-watch the video to see *your* face this time. When I initially saw the video, I only concentrated on me. How I looked. My reaction. Last night … I wanted to see *you* … try to understand your motives … figure out what you were possibly thinking. And, do you know what I saw, Aubrey? Do you?"

Slumping her shoulders, her voice came out so small and scared. "What?" She stopped breathing.

Nick choked. "I saw love. I saw *you*. The one who takes care of our family. The one who does what's best for everyone." Nick bit his lip. "I saw the woman who I married, who loves me … and would do anything to make sure that we make it. I saw you, Aubrey. Loving me … and trying desperately to save *us*."

Aubrey wrapped her arms around Nick. "I love you, Nicky. I love you so much."

"I love you, too, baby. I'm so sorry it took me so long to get this right. I love you, too." Nick released her embrace and put his arm around her waist. "Come on. Let's go home."

Epilogue

So, there you have it. My story. The way I see it is that Nicky and I probably overdid it by raising the sex bar pretty high early on in our relationship with our planes, trains, and automobile antics. It was a tough act to live up to once we'd married and had children. It was as though settling down into family life caused us to forget how to have any fun at all.

It wasn't just about sex, either. We forgot how to talk to each other. We forgot to share how we were feeling about things. About life. It really would have helped, if we'd communicated our growing sense of boredom with each other. Then, it would have been Nicky and me against boredom—not Nick and me against each other. We probably could have handled that.

And, for the record, I think that particular lesson can be applied to anything ... by anyone. As a couple, instead of fighting about something like money, it should always be the couple against the lack of money. You know, *united we stand, divided we fall,* and all that stuff. Call me crazy, but the idea isn't limited to serving as lyrics in a song.

It's scary for me to think about exactly how close Nicky and I came to actually getting a divorce. I am still left to wonder how many other couples divorced when they really shouldn't have. Parasomnia ended up being a gift, though I'm not sure Nick is quite ready to be one hundred percent on board with that sentiment yet.

Any way you look at it, Nick's disorder *did* permit me to glimpse at his core feelings, feelings about which even he had been completely oblivious. It did allow him to show me how he felt about me in a … well, completely uncensored fashion.

Parasomnia forced Nick to be vulnerable, and in doing so, allowed me to rediscover the man I fell in love with while he was sleeping. I'm totally confident Nick had no idea how he'd felt about me under all those layers of boredom, anger, resentment, and disappointment. Like an onion, parasomnia allowed those layers to be peeled back. The trickle-down effect was that I became vulnerable, too. How Nick was behaving toward me at night changed how I treated him during the day. Which, it's worth noting, ultimately caused Nick to alter how he was behaving towards me in the daytime. To further defend myself, I could go all *chicken and the egg* thing on you, but I won't.

Once all the negative emotions were removed, we found our love for each other again. I think couples who make it are probably the ones who truly learn to be one hundred percent vulnerable in front of each other. I mean, really, how else can you honestly tell how someone is feeling?

From individual people to giant corporate greeting card companies … just about everyone references *love* as being something that comes from the heart. Our hearts are our inner light. Since our hearts power our bodies, then, *love* is essentially energy, so it *can't* be destroyed. That means our love was *always* there. Nicky and me—well, we just had to find it again.

Before all this divorce stuff happened, we had a pretty good thing going on. Nick and I both had great jobs, a beautiful home, nice cars, and the proverbial *rich man's family.* You can even throw the dog and the white picket fence into the package. Ours was a great story. While I'm a little disappointed that we both scribbled on some of the pages, I guess it's something I'll just have to learn to live with. We both will.

Nick no longer sleepwalks. His parasomnia was likely caused by the stress and anxiety he'd felt about consulting with the attorney and the reality of being the one to file for divorce actually setting in.

Now, since we know Nick is prone to parasomnia when under stress, we've made a deal … if Nick should ever sleepwalk again, no sex allowed. I did promise, but, the truth is, I crossed my fingers (on both hands), and I crossed my legs. I even crossed my toes (yes, on both feet). But, really, knowing what I know now, how could I not? I'd have crossed my eyes if I didn't think Nick would have noticed.

Recently, Nicky woke me up in the middle of the night for a quickie. I refused because we'd both had wine and I was concerned as to whether or not he was actually awake. When he still remembered the next morning—and had given me a hard time about my having rejected him—that's when I'd finally become convinced he hadn't been sleepwalking. I guess it'll take a while before I really trust any middle of the night trysts again. *Go me,* for keeping my word. This time.

As for Libby, she married Jed. I was her maid of honor. It was a beautiful wedding. Now, having witnessed what happened in my life, she spends a great deal of time making sure to nurture all parts of her new marriage. No chance of her lady bits shriveling up.

So, if you want to ask me again if I would do what I did all over ... the answer remains a resounding *yes*. Judge me all you want. You know *they* say life isn't a dress rehearsal. I truly believe that. We each write our own story. Therefore, we are not completely powerless as to how it ends up. Many people surrender their power to fate. I think it's all about what you're willing to invest in getting to your desired ending.

Me? I was willing to go all in. It was a gamble, and I knew it could go either way. But it didn't. It went *my* way.

So, I did what I did, and at the end of the day, all I can really tell you about my story is ... Once upon a time, a girl named Aubrey married a guy named Nick, and, you know what happened? *They lived happily ever after.*

The End

Coming Christmas 2019

The First Noel

Virginia Hamilton is a successful lawyer who owns her own firm. Sadly, as a divorcée, with no children, she hasn't been as lucky in love as she has been with her career.

John Boone is an Afghanistan veteran suffering from PTSD and is living on the streets of Philadelphia. Like many of his Marine Corps brothers and sisters, he's finding it increasingly difficult to re-adapt to a civilian lifestyle.

The unlikely pair meet when Virginia must rely on John for directions.

Soon after, John must swallow his pride and force himself to ask Virginia for a favor.

The odd duo begins to develop a deeply meaningful friendship. But could it possibly turn into something more?

The First Noel is a touching novella that teaches a most valuable lesson …
our flaws are not our failures, and destruction can sometimes be the path to our redemption.

**READ ON FOR A SAMPLE CHAPTER OF
THE FIRST NOEL …**

Chapter One

Virginia

Taxi drivers leaned onto their horns, brakes squealed, and exhaust fumes threatened to choke Virginia Hamilton as she repeatedly paced up and down a full city block on Chestnut Street in downtown Center City, Philadelphia. She rubbed her left ear between her thumb and forefinger like she'd always done when she was nervous or upset. It was a comfort measure carried over from childhood.

Squinting to look up at the tops of entrance doors and moving her glance even further to the upper facades of the buildings, Virginia just couldn't locate the address she was looking for. As a prominent center city human rights attorney, it wasn't like her to be running late. A conference call regarding another client's matter, which was ready to settle, had delayed her. And, now here she was, marching up and down Chestnut Street—lost—with no time left to spare.

People were pushing and shoving their way past Virginia. It was the day before Thanksgiving and folks appeared to be hurriedly trying to get out of the city and back home—wherever that was. She silently cursed the opposing attorney for scheduling a deposition this late in the afternoon on the day before a holiday weekend.

Virginia's legs were cold, and she scolded herself for wearing a skirt today. Dressed in a gray wool suit, coordinating pumps, and an overcoat that stopped at mid-calf, was no match for the bitter bite in the air. Late November in Philly was always cold. The tall, grey buildings lining both sides of the street served as a makeshift wind tunnel for the nasty, damp air. What had she been thinking? Then, annoyed at her own interrogation, she answered herself; I was thinking *I wasn't going to be searching for this particular address for over twenty minutes.* Once again, she pulled the small piece of scrap paper from her coat pocket to glance at the address. Shaking her head, Virginia decided, in her haste, she must have written something wrong down and reluctantly pulled her cell phone from her purse to call and check the address with her opponent, who was surely waiting for her in the elusive conference room.

Before she had time to dial, a raspy voice rang out. "Excuse me, Miss?"

Virginia glanced around. Aside from the bustling, obnoxious crowds, the only person she saw was a homeless guy who was sitting on top of a suitcase with casters, an old beat-up looking black duffle back parked next to him. He was staring at her. Sadly, panhandlers were just about every street in the city. Virginia never gave money because she was afraid, she'd be contributing to a drug habit, but she'd always buy a sandwich or coffee for someone who'd approached her. Right now, she didn't have time for either.

She gazed back down at her phone, and Virginia heard, "Ma'am?"

Virginia cocked her head to the side and focused on the only human being who wasn't in motion—the homeless guy. She raised an eyebrow. "I'm sorry. Are you speaking to me?"

The man, with an overgrown, unruly beard and an overall tattered appearance, nodded. "Yes. Yes, ma'am, I am." He scrambled to his feet.

The street had emptied out. Virginia felt fear. She knew better than to ever behave as though she was lost or confused in the city. *Never, ever appear vulnerable, or you become a target*, she scolded herself. The man left his possessions on the sidewalk next to the building he'd been leaning against and walked closer. Virginia put her hand—fingers spread wide–out in front of herself. "I'm … I'm okay." She backed up nearly bumping into another woman who'd exited a nearby building and was passing behind her. "Really. I'm fine."

Appearing as though he were used to this, the man paused and took a step back. "I just wanted to ask you if needed help finding an address. You look a little lost, and I know this street pretty well."

At this point, Virginia was desperate, so she broke her own rule about not speaking to strangers. "Well, yes. Yes, I am." She extended a scrap of paper.

The man stepped forward and took the address from her hand. "Oh, yeah. I thought this might be the place. People are always pacing up and down, trying to find it. I end up showing a few people where this place is every day. It's right over this way." He turned his back and started to walk down the sidewalk, an apparent invitation for Virginia to follow.

Hesitating for a moment, Virginia swiftly decided that there were still a few people around in the event the stranger had ill intentions, so she began to follow the man who surely needed a bath. He walked in front of her for about half a block and came to a stop in front of a glass door. The door was void of an address or a company name. She waited to see what the man would do because there was no way Virginia was going to follow him into this building.

Her worries were rapidly put to rest when the man grabbed the handle of the door and opened it. "You should be fine now, ma'am, there's a directory inside. I have to get back to my stuff."

Virginia placed her hand on the inside of the door, taking the weight of it from the man who promptly released his grip on the handle. "Thank you so much. I would never have even thought to look inside this door. It's so vanilla. You think they'd have mentioned that little fact when providing me with the address."

For the first time, the man smiled. It wasn't an ordinary smile. Virginia noted how it reflected an odd contrast of a genuine grin coupled with a face that appeared as though he was cringing in pain as if it'd literally hurt for him to smile. "No problem. Happy Thanksgiving, Ma'am."

Feeling sad, Virginia nodded her head. "Thank you again." She immediately realized wishing him a *Happy Thanksgiving* would likely have been a redundant sentiment. Passing through the door, she sighed. As an afterthought, she quickly turned back, flung the door open, and shouted after the man. "U-m-m-m, excuse me!"

The man turned around and tipped his head to the side. "Ma'am?"

Virginia squinted her eyes and crinkled her nose. "What's your name?"

The pained smiled returned. "John. John Boone."

Returning the smile, Virginia started to turn back inside the building. Over her shoulder, she shouted, "my name is Virginia. Thanks, again, Mr. Boone." He nodded as she quickened her stride, returning to the vestibule to glance at the directory and board the elevator to the third floor.

When Virginia arrived at the conference room, she'd learned—by the detailed description her client offered—that John Boone had actually given him directions, as well.

The deposition dragged on for an hour and a half. Virginia's client had done a great job. Now, Virginia was anxious to get done so she could go home to relax. It'd been a long day, and thanks to all the pacing earlier, her feet hurt.

As they were wrapping up, her client stopped to use the restroom. Virginia found herself thinking about the man who'd helped her earlier. Actually, she was wishing she'd have thought to give him some money or something, knowing full well she'd have never found this place without his help. Doubting he'd still be loitering on the street below, Virginia decided if she were lucky enough to see Mr. Boone, she'd give him some money and thank him again.

When she initially stepped out onto the sidewalk, Virginia was certain she'd lost the opportunity to help Mr. Boone. As she headed to the parking garage, she caught a glimpse of someone crouched in a doorway, no doubt trying to avoid the increasingly severe cold that had fallen over the city.

Virginia picked up her pace and tightened the black, knit scarf she wore wrapped around her neck, trying to seal in some warmth. There were even fewer people than earlier on the street, and it was getting dark.

A man's voice rang out. "Did you get where you needed to go, okay?"

It took a few seconds for Virginia to realize she was being spoken to. Once the voice registered in her head, she stopped and turned back. Peering into the portico, Virginia recognized John Boone as he stood to greet her.

"Yes. Yes, I did, John. I was hoping I'd see you again." Virginia reached into her purse and pulled out a twenty-dollar bill. It was the only cash she had on her. "I wanted to give you this. To thank you for your help. You were a lifesaver this afternoon."

John reached for the cash. "You didn't have to do that. But, thank you just the same." John glanced up and down the virtually empty street. "It's pretty dark for you to be walking all alone. Where are you parked."

For reasons she didn't understand, Virginia's guard was completely lowered with this stranger. "I'm parked in the garage at the end of the street. I'll be okay."

John turned back toward the entrance way. "Just let me take care of my stuff, and I'll walk you to your car." Grabbing the suitcase and the duffel bag, John walked a few feet away to where there was about a three-foot break between the buildings and tucked his bags out of sight. "There. They'll be okay in there." John swung his hand out in the direction of the garage. "Shall we?" His frail smile returned.

Without hesitation, Virginia smiled and moved to walk alongside John. "This is twice in one day you've rescued me."

"It's no trouble." John shrugged his shoulders and waved his hands in the air. "It's not as though I have anything else to do."

It wasn't lost on Virginia how well-spoken John was. She couldn't imagine what might have happened to this kind man that had him living on the streets of Philadelphia. When they arrived at her car, Virginia opened the car door and thanked John again. He nodded and smiled, rubbing his hands together, apparently trying to warm them.

Virginia thought to offer him a ride but to where? Quite likely, where she'd met him was likely his home. She reached both hands behind her neck to remove her scarf. She stepped forward and draped it around John's neck. "Take this, it will help keep you warm." She knew she had plenty more of those at home.

John nodded, reached into his pocket, retrieved the twenty-dollar bill, and held it in front of his chest. "Thanks for the help. You have a good night." He shoved the bill back into his pocket before turning away with a smile that his eyes didn't share.

Virginia started to get into her car but, suddenly backed herself up. She reached into the outside pocket of her handbag and pulled out one of her business cards. "John!"

John was a few parking spaces away. He turned back and raised his eyebrows. "Ma'am?"

Moving toward him, Virginia extended the card. "If you ever need anything, you can reach me at the address and phone number on the card."

John glanced down at the card before returning his gaze to meet Virginia's. He tipped his head to the side, his eyes glistened. His words were hesitant. "Thank you." Before he turned and walked away, John held the card up in the air. "This means a lot."

"You take care of yourself." Virginia had read somewhere that the average human being makes thirty-five-thousand decisions a day. She had no idea how far reaching the decision she'd just made would turn out to be.

Available November 2019 on Amazon.com

Karma Debt, Book One: The Awakening

A near-fatal motorcycle accident nearly claims the life of the handsome Donovan McBride. Instead, on the day he is to be removed from life support, he is granted a miracle. The black-winged angel who'd appeared in Donovan's hospital room likely provided an explanation … if only he could remember what had been said to him. He can't.

Donovan does recall waking up to the beautiful Doctor Josephine Kenneth by his side. Her voice calmed him as he'd tried to digest how the last three months of his life had been spent in a hospital room. Within a few days of waking, Donovan was transferred to a rehabilitation center, dashing any hopes he'd had of getting to know Doctor Kenneth better.

A year later, a chance run-in—while Christmas shopping—reunites the two. As Donovan falls for the stunning doctor, he can't help but feel that his accident brought them together once and now fate was giving them a second chance.

Enjoy the ride as *KARMA DEBT, The Awakening* shares an amazing journey of love. But, don't be fooled by it ... second chances simply don't come free.

Excerpt from Jeanne's
Award-winning and Best-Selling novel,
Karma Debt, Book One: The Awakening

Chapter One

August 2014

When a soul re-enters a person's body—long after it had obviously departed—it's just not the type of thing you witness and, well … somehow forget.

Doctor Josephine Kenneth had just come on duty at Cooper Hospital when she was paged to report to the trauma unit to provide much-needed respite for the doctor on call.

She'd already been advised the department had been alive with alarms, bells, and buzzers all evening. Owing thanks, no doubt, to the dreaded impending full moon.

Answering the call, she made her way past the nursing station where a busy secretary was typing on a computer keyboard while speaking into a phone propped between her ear and shoulder. Her words … *yes, doctor, I've got it. Now, about the guy in room 333 …* faded as Josephine passed, growing nearer to the exam room at the end of the hall.

She entered quietly and watched as Doctor Lara Bruneau, the senior trauma physician, was going over every inch of the body of a comatose man. He was stretched out on an exam table—unconscious, intubated, and completely naked. Josephine had learned he'd been in a serious motorcycle accident. As is standard, to achieve the most thorough exam possible, the trauma team had cut off what clothing remained after the asphalt had claimed its take.

Doctor Bruneau shouted out STAT lab orders and imaging requests—over the rhythmic sound of the respirator—to the nurse who was assisting her.

The doctor was a woman in her late forties with blond hair and a petite build. From all Josephine had witnessed, it was apparent she'd never allowed her small size to define her. Like a jaguar, her moves were quick and calculating, but most importantly ... accurate. As a top healer in the world of life-threatening injuries, she was highly respected.

Josephine observed her steady and capable hands at work. During her time as a resident, she'd spent hundreds of hours working alongside the skilled surgeon and only hoped she'd someday acquire even half her talents.

Once she realized Josephine had arrived, Doctor Bruneau prepared to turn the stranger's care over to her. Oddly enough, even though Josephine was in her third year of residency, he was actually her first authentic *John Doe*.

Doctor Bruneau dismissed the nurse who'd been helping her and turned toward Josephine. In a soft, compassionate voice she requested, "Hang with this one if you can, Josie. It's going to be touch and go for him. Try to make sure he's not left alone." Cases like this wore heavy on their hearts. However, they'd each understood, when choosing this field of medicine: they simply wouldn't be able to save them all.

Doctor Bruneau headed for the door. She paused at the trash can to peel off her purple non-latex gloves. Tossing them in, she turned back toward Josephine and sighed. She lowered her chin, closed her eyes, and shook her head, before leaving her alone with him.

Tentatively, Josephine moved in closer to study the mystery patient. She tried not to notice his amazing build. His hair was so black it almost appeared to be a deep blue. A late summer tan accentuated some very well-defined muscles. No wedding ring and no interruption in the bronze of his left ring finger told her he was probably single. She looked him up and down trying to concentrate only on surveying his injuries.

Frustratingly curious, she bent over, her lips close to his ear. "Who *are* you, *John Doe*? Who, out there in this big ole' world, loves you? And who's going to feel absolutely devastated when they find out you're in here … with me?"

Assessing him again, she guessed he was in his early thirties. Hospital personnel usually relied on driver's licenses of unconscious accident victims, but no documents were retrieved at the scene. His motorcycle had hit a tree and caught fire after he was thrown from it. The police assumed his saddlebags would probably have contained his identification. However, they were no more than ash when the firetrucks arrived to extinguish the bike.

Considering the amount of road rash and the mangled condition of his limbs, it amazed her how well preserved his face appeared. His helmet had surely done a good part of its job. The skin on his face was perfect—soft and flawless. But, she was all too aware of the God-awful destruction hidden beneath his unblemished façade.

Preparing to take him down to Radiology, Josephine snatched a sheet from a linen cart on the side wall and draped it over him. She propped a portable respirator on his chest so it would be ready to breathe for him when they traveled between floors.

Leaning in, she pressed her thumbs against each of his closed eyelids—raising them. His deep blue eyes were as vacant as sea glass on a barren beach. She'd seen it before. She could always tell when a patient's lifeforce had left their body. It was usually long before the heart got the message to stop beating. Yes, the eyes were always the first to know when the soul departed. They would harden like ice on a lake with no reaction to light or activity—empty and soulless interpreters of nothing.

She realized transport had arrived when she heard the racket in the doorway. The noises were caused by a stretcher being jammed through a scarcely-big-enough entranceway. Its navigator was a tall, lanky male orderly. Once he'd cleared the threshold, he rolled the gurney across the room—bringing it to a halt next to the exam table.

John Doe didn't flinch as they grabbed him and shifted his body over onto the stretcher. Limp and motionless, he was no more animated than a rag doll.

Once he was transferred, she tugged on the sheet to pull it up and had tucked it under his chin. Doctor Kenneth placed her lips close to his ear. "Okay, *John*, we're going to take you down for some testing now."

She reached back and grabbed his IV pole, which had several liquid sacks hanging from it. She inserted the rod into a port on the side of the stretcher.

She addressed the attendant with the mop of thick, messy brown hair by the name on his lab coat. "Harry, I'm Doctor Kenneth. I'll pump the respirator bag and push from this end. You just pull and steer from the bottom there. We have to get him downstairs quickly."

Not waiting for his reply, she moved some tubes around. After hooking up the device that took over the job of his lungs, she began pumping it with one hand. She reached back with the other and flipped the stationary respirator's switch to *off*. The room went eerily quiet. Finally, she grasped the corner of the stretcher, thrust her hips forward against the frame, and started moving.

She and Harry maneuvered down the hall and onto an elevator. When they arrived on the basement level, they maneuvered through hallways and around corners until they reached an overhead sign that read RADIOLOGY DEPARTMENT. A tech greeted them and directed the way into the MRI suite.

At every turn, Josephine gently spoke to her patient. *Just a little bump*, she'd warned as they rolled him onto the elevator and again when the doors opened, and they'd rolled him off. *Just a sharp turn here, John … We're going to transfer you over to the stretcher connected to the MRI machine … Now, this table moves so don't be alarmed … It's going to be loud, so I'll be putting these foam plugs in your ears before the test begins … I'll remove them when you're done … You're alright, John.* She placed her hand on his shoulder … *We've got you … You're gonna be alright.*

She continued to explain everything that was happening as they took him to X-ray, CT scan, and back upstairs again. Josephine had warmly referred to him as *John* all the while. Relief followed when he was safely hooked back up to a vent and re-attached to the monitors in the trauma unit.

Josephine stayed by his side. She'd periodically checked in with the emergency department, but each time they'd advised her things had grown unusually quiet; therefore, she wasn't needed. Lucky for *John Doe*—otherwise she'd have had to leave him on his own.

When the hum of the ventilator threatened to lull her to sleep in the dimly lit room, she sang to him … ♫ ♪*Are you sleeping, are you sleeping, brother John, brother John* … ♪ ♫ He didn't move an inch. On one stanza of ♪ *Morning bells are ringing … Morning bells are ringing,* ♪ his night nurse, Megan, had wandered in before Doctor Kenneth had heard her coming. The amused RN merely offered a nearly glow-in-the-dark smile before leaving her alone with him once again.

She'd never been much of a singer, so when she bored with the English version, she'd start … ♫ ♪ *Frère Jacques, frère Jacques, Dormez-vous? Dormez-vous?* ♪ ♫ It was the only French she'd ever spoken … if it could even be counted as *speaking* French.

In the wee hours of the morning, Josephine, needing to stretch her legs and get a second wind, went out to the nursing station. She found a weary Doctor Bruneau there—reading the reports containing the lab and testing results on their *John Doe.*

Doctor Bruneau dropped her eyes and frowned when she spotted Josephine. She shook her head. "It's all bad news, Josie. He doesn't have a tub of butter's chance in hell of surviving this. As I feared, our *Doe* has a Diffuse Axonal Injury. On the first look at everything—and you know how hard DAIs are to predict by scans alone—it looks like a grade III. On the Glasgow Coma Scale, he was already a 3T when he was brought in. Sadly, we won't have good news for his people—whenever we finally find them. Wherever they are, they'll have to agree to discontinue life support. He's simply never going to wake up from this. Ever."

Josephine's heart sank. She'd already known—by the vacancy in his eyes—he wouldn't make it. They'd even expected it would turn out to be a DAI. But, it didn't stop her from wanting a miracle for the good-looking guy she'd spent all night serenading. Poor *John*.

Leaving Doctor Bruneau at the desk, Josephine returned to his bedside. She sat on the black vinyl chair with the chrome armrests where she'd been sitting earlier. Reaching between her legs, she grasped the edge of the seat and walked her feet forward to scoot closer to him. With a sigh, she gazed at his beautiful, perfect, and youthful face.

Josephine never prayed anymore. She had a sixteen-year long beef with her Creator, and she had no doubt He knew it. But, she was calling Him out on it tonight. She leaned her elbows on the edge of the bed and wrapped a hand around her *John Doe's* wrist, grasping it.

The next words she spoke were tender and soft and floated in the air like feathers in that dark, lonely room. She raised her eyes to the ceiling. "God, I'm still madder than hell at You. We both know You owe me some answered prayers. Well, I want to cash in on one of those tonight … for this guy. All the medical science in the world won't save this one. I know a miracle is a big order, but with all You've done to me—it's the least You can do right now." As nearly an afterthought, she added, "Amen."

Josephine looked back up at the face of the man in the bed. She released his arm, leaned back in her chair, and audibly exhaled. For the first time all night, she felt the tiniest bit of hope for her handsome *John Doe*.

Chapter Two

October 2014 ... Three Months Later

Wide-eyed and gasping, Ann Marie McBride fell straight to her knees after rounding the corner to enter her son's hospital room. The poor woman groaned, just before crying out, "Oh, dear, God!"

Startled by the commotion, Doctor Kenneth glanced up from the chart she held in her hand and hastily tossed it onto the bottom of the bed before dashing across the room to Ann Marie's side. She'd moved so quickly, her lab coat had taken flight behind her like a bright white cape.

Ann Marie's husband, Albert, had been a few paces behind. When he entered the room, he immediately stumbled backward—his back and palms coming to rest on the wall behind him— as he fixed his eyes on their eldest son, Donovan, sitting upright on his hospital bed.

Bending over and tucking her arm under Ann Marie's armpit, the doctor slowly eased her onto to her feet. Her long red hair fell forward, practically covering up the blue monogram on her jacket, which read DOCTOR JOSEPHINE KENNETH. Her heart raced as she tried to explain to the woman in her grasp, "I didn't call you because we wanted to surprise you. But I'm afraid we didn't consider the risk of nearly shocking you to death instead. I'm so sorry!"

With eyes still bulging and mouth wide open, Ann Marie glanced up at Doctor Kenneth. "Why ... I ... oh, my goodness ..." Rapidly blinking and scrambling to her feet, she directed an incredulous gaze toward the bed. After glancing back at her husband—and appearing to suddenly trust her eyes—she stumbled, recovered, and ran toward Donovan with open arms.

Josephine smiled as she witnessed the mother and son reunion. Ann Marie wrapped her arms around Donovan, paused, leaned back, cupped his face in her hands and smiled through her tears as if she'd believed she'd never have had the chance to gaze into the open, alert eyes of her boy again. Technically—and medically—she'd been right. Albert joined her at the bedside and encircled his arms around his wife and son.

Crossing the room to join the trio, Doctor Kenneth reached out and grabbed the backs of two side chairs—one in each hand—and dragged them over near the bed. "Mr. and Mrs. McBride, why don't you both have a seat, so Donovan can try to explain what happened here last night?"

Mr. McBride spoke, "Oh, yes, ma'am. Thank you." He slid one of the chairs over toward his wife and closer to Donovan. He extended his hand out, waving it in the direction of the chair. "Sit here, dear." He dragged the second one next to the first and sat down.

It still surprised Josephine when someone referred to her as *ma'am*. After all, she'd won a game of beer pong only a few weeks back while playing with a group of friends from college. *Ma'am* felt like a lab coat she might grow into—one that didn't exactly fit her yet.

Ann Marie hesitated, as though she'd considered not moving away from her son. She leaned closer to Donovan, glanced at the chair, and sighed before sliding from the edge of the bed onto the nearby seat. She reached forward and grasped her son's hand and gazed intently at him. "You must tell us what happened! I mean … this is a miracle! I can't believe it! Today was scheduled to be the worst day of my whole life!"

Josephine knew no truer words had ever been spoken. This was to be the day Donovan McBride took his last breath. His parents had been coming in to say goodbye. After three months in a coma, with no hope of recovery, all the machines keeping him alive were to be turned off. Even Dr. Kenneth's personal request for Divine intervention several months ago seemed to have gone unanswered.

"Oh, my God, what the …?" All eyes shifted to the doorway where a visibly shocked, thirty-year-old Liam McBride stood with both arms extended, gripping the matte gray door jamb on either side of where he stood. His eyes were as blue as mood ring stones, but each upper and lower lid was encircled with red rings, disclosing the emotional hell he'd experienced. Obviously shocked, he shuffled with the gait of an old man as he crossed the room to the bed, never shifting focus off his thirty-two-year-old brother. "Donnie? Mom and Dad?

What's going on? I thought...."

Donovan smiled at him. In a raspy, soft voice he said, "I'm no quitter, little brother. I hear you were supposed to be attending my funeral this week. I wanted to surprise you all by being a no-show!" He stiffly reached out and welcomed an embrace, as Liam leaned in. Their hair blended perfectly. An identical match, you couldn't tell where one mane ended, and the other began.

Liam leaned back and looked at his parents before turning his head and acknowledging Doctor Kenneth. "Hey, doc! This is something else, right?" He grinned like the Cheshire Cat.

Josephine bobbed her head up and down, smiled, and raised an eyebrow. "It's quite a story ... he's pretty darned amazing."

The good doctor had gotten to know the family quite well over the last three months as they'd kept a daily vigil by Donovan's bedside. It'd taken the police a full three days to locate them using a partial license plate retrieved from the scene of his accident. But, once his parents were located, the police had driven them over to Cooper, so they might learn of the fate of their oldest child.

She'd never forget the night the McBride's arrived to see her *John Doe* for the first time. Sadly, it was a scene all too familiar to Josephine. The family had fallen completely apart while trying to absorb his fatal prognosis. The attending doctors failed to offer anything other than advising them to *pray*. She could still hear Ann Marie's cries and Albert's choked sobs—it had been heart-wrenching. Soon after arriving, and once Liam was there, they'd even called for a priest to perform the Anointing of the Sick ... a Catholic sacrament reserved for those believed to be dying.

She'd routinely witnessed the appearance of sheer terror on the faces of many of the visiting loved ones of patients in her three years as a resident here. Mothers who refused to leave the side of a comatose child, not even to shower … grown men crying like babies at the bedside of a dying brother … the trauma unit was indeed a scary place. Looks of profound grief, expressions of immense pain, and copious amounts of tears flowed everywhere one looked. It was an environment in the hospital that severely contrasted with the bouquets of flowers, boxes of doughnuts, balloons, and laughter one would be sure to find upstairs on the maternity floor.

While the surgeons here could save a good deal of the people who were brought in, as soon as a patient was stable, they were transferred to a step-down unit, making room for the next long shot to be provided a bed. So, the mood on this floor was always one of high alert, master skill and, well, quite frankly … prayer.

Today was pure evidence the McBride's had made the right choice to take a *wait and see* approach to Donovan's care. While the suggestion had been made for the family to discontinue life support, Mr. McBride had been adamant. "If our son's going to be dead, then he's going to be dead. But I want to allow ample time for a miracle to reach him. I don't see how anyone could object to that. We have money—if that's what the concern is—but, we won't be making any decisions to give up hope anytime soon. Hell, hope is all we have." Even at the time, it was an alternative Josephine had been grateful for, as she'd become pretty attached to her first *John Doe.*

Josephine learned—as she'd suspected—he wasn't married. Therefore, his parents had every legal right to choose to keep him on life support. In situations like this, the doctors didn't argue with the family because they were usually empathetic enough to give them time to realize their loved one was, in essence … already dead.

Doctor Kenneth moved to the head of the bed, gazed into his eyes, and grinned as she rested a hand on Donovan's shoulder. She nodded. "Now that everyone's had time to catch their breath, how about telling them what happened here last night?"

She stepped back and rested her behind on the wall-mounted air conditioning unit. While she knew the comatose mind could imagine all sorts of crazy things, she'd have to admit—it was a great story and she was eager to hear it again.

Besides, she wanted to believe the Big Guy had granted her … an honest to goodness walking, talking miracle.

Donovan gingerly settled back against a pile of propped up, crisp, white pillows and waited as Liam moved away and seated himself on the bottom of the bed near the footboard. Donovan scanned the faces of his family. They all looked so strained. He was only beginning to understand what they'd endured. As the one who'd been in a coma, he wasn't even aware he'd been gone for three months. In his memory, he'd just been with them for a family dinner the week before. The time he'd spent in this room didn't exist for him.

If he thought about it, he'd have to admit there were periods of time where he could recall being in a black space. A peaceful place.

But, there was no rational thought about it. He never wondered why he was *there*. It never occurred to him that he wasn't *here*. But, by the look on their faces, they'd felt his absence. Every. Single. Day.

Realizing they were all staring at him in anticipation, Donovan began, "Well, I opened my eyes sometime in the middle of the night last night, and a man was sitting right over there." He pointed to a dark blue, empty, reclining Geri Chair in the far corner, situated underneath the wall-mounted television.

Everyone shifted their gaze to where he directed. Donovan rubbed the front of his neck. It was hard to swallow; his throat was raw.

Doctor Kenneth must have recognized his struggle because she shifted and poured him some water. Reaching across and raising the cup to his mouth, she offered his lips a straw she had fixed between her thumb and forefinger. She explained to the group, "His throat is very sore from being irritated by tubes for so long. It will be that way for a while." Donovan's family nodded in unison as he took a sip of the welcome remedy and wrapped his shaky hands around the cup, taking it from her.

He swallowed and began again ... "The guy was surrounded by this incredible glow of white light. It was so warm and inviting and even sorta bluish in some spots. I wanted to stand up and get closer to it. It was as though a magnet was trying to pull me closer to him." The memory still made him tingle. "Then, behind the dude, there was this huge ladder. It looked like it was propped up on that windowsill ..." He balanced the cup in one hand and pointed to the window to the right of the chair. "... I could see the bottom rungs, but I couldn't see the top. It seemed to go up into infinity. The ceiling over the ladder was gone—there was just emptiness. Just warm, safe, calm emptiness." He paused and took another sip.

Ann Marie, Albert, and Liam each had their eyes fixed on Donovan. Not one of them had moved when Donovan had been speaking. One could hear a pin drop.

Albert leaned forward, "Do you think it was a dream, son? I mean … you've been pretty out of it for a long time."

Donovan sat up taller in the bed. He knew they'd have trouble believing him. It was a pretty big story, and he hadn't even gotten to the crazy part yet. "No, pop, I don't. He was as real to me as the three of you are now. I'm telling you …"

Tilting her head, Ann Marie interrupted, "Did he *say* anything to you, Donnie? Like, did you actually *talk* to him, honey?"

Slightly shifting on the bed, he nodded. "That's kinda the wild thing, mom …" He could picture the whole scenario but struggled for the right words to describe it. "The silence in my room was deafening. It was like coming out of a rock concert after sitting too close to the speakers. You know, like when you can hear but everything seems so far away and hollow? It was like being in a vacuum. I could see he was talking. His mouth was moving, and his face was lively. Sometimes his expression went from looking extremely serious to looking as though he was laughing out loud."

His mother furrowed her brow. "But you don't know what he said to you … like why he was here?"

Donovan shook his head and glanced at Liam who was being unusually quiet and stroking his chin. Using his big toe, he poked his little brother's thigh. "You're not saying much …"

Liam dropped his hands into his lap, folded them, and used his fingers to create a steeple. He wagged it as he used it to point at Donovan. "Well, brother, this is a lot to take in. I came here today thinking I was saying goodbye to you, and here you are …" He unlocked his fingers and threw his hands in the air, "… sitting up and telling stories about some white-winged angel coming …"

Donovan interrupted. "They were black." He realized he'd forgotten to tell them that crazy detail. The guy in the corner had an enormous span of beautiful black wings. He could picture them as clear as day. They'd expand up and out with the man's movements and then flutter down to rest behind him when he remained still.

Liam furrowed his brow. "Black? What? Jeez, you're killin' me, Donnie!" He smiled.

"No, no … I mean it. The guy had black wings! Oh! And he looked just like Michael Douglas!" He glanced back at Doctor Kenneth for support. While she was nodding and smiling, he understood she'd only known what he'd told her, too. Like the rest of them, she'd only had this second-hand accounting after the fact.

Liam let loose a laugh, threw his head back, and smacked his hand down on his thigh. "Come on, Donnie. This *had* to be a dream!?! Michael Douglas?!?"

Before they'd all arrived today, in the little bit of time he'd had to prepare, Donovan recognized how crazy his story sounded— outrageous even—but he felt certain it had happened exactly as he shared. This was no dream. He could feel every minute of the entire experience. He stiffened his lips. "Well, choose to believe or not to believe … I can tell you an angel with black wings was right over there—in my room—and now, here I am … alive and talking with you."

Ann Marie rubbed his arm. "I'm so very, very grateful for that, sweetie." She leaned in closer to her son. "Did he stay with you all night?"

He smiled. He'd known his mother would be the one to believe him. He appreciated her validation. "The last thing I remember I was nodding, my lips were moving as though no tubes were present, and he was beaming in response to what my mouth was saying. I still have no idea what that was. I couldn't even hear my own words. Then, the angel stood up, and it was as though a huge gust of wind blew across the room. The draft stung my eyes so, instinctively, I'd closed them."

He paused and took in a breath. "When I opened them, he was gone, and I was gagging on the tube in my throat. The alarm on the ventilator went off and—before I knew it—Doctor Kenneth here …" He turned and reached a hand toward her—she stood and grasped it. "… and a nurse came rushing in! Next thing I knew, my room was full of people, someone was yanking at the tube, and I shot straight up in my bed, taking in a huge—life-giving—breath of air. The trauma team in my room began clapping, crying, and laughing! I didn't even realize why everyone was so emotional until things settled down and Doctor Kenneth told me what had happened to me and how long I'd been here." He squeezed her hand before letting it fall away.

Albert clapped his hands together. "Well, that sure is some story, son. Whether it happened or if it was a dream doesn't much matter. We're just happy as hell you're back with us! This is an answered prayer!"

Dr. Kenneth moved to the foot of the bed, next to Liam, and picked up Donovan's chart. Holding it to her chest, she wrapped her arms around it. She addressed Donovan. "I'm going to finish making rounds. I know you all have a great deal of catching up to do! I'll be back to check on you before I leave today." She grinned and nodded at the group before heading for the door.

Donovan watched her leave. The fact that she was beautiful didn't go unnoticed by him, nor did her kindness. He would never forget how calm and soothing her voice had been last night as she tried her best to tell him about the last three months of his life. She'd even stayed by his bed when sleep beckoned him because he'd been afraid to close his eyes again. Her words flowed like a lullaby when she reassured him … *You're alright … I'll be right here … I promise you—you'll wake up.* He leaned forward to catch the last glimpse of her as she rounded the corner out of his room.

Grinning ear to ear, Liam jammed his finger into his brother's leg. "She's easy on the eyes, isn't she, brother?"

Donovan smirked. "I'm calling dibs!"

Liam nodded and threw his open hands up in the air. "After what you've been through for the last three months? She's all yours!"

Chapter Three

November 2015 ... One Year Later

Reading Terminal Market in Philadelphia was jam-packed with Christmas shoppers. Josephine was kicking herself for leaving so much of her shopping for the last minute this year. Black Friday—what had she been thinking? Actually, she'd been so busy at the hospital there wasn't anything else she could've done. At least coming and going would be easy because the trains running into the city from New Jersey ran more frequently around the holidays.

Having no immediate family should have made Christmas gifting a breeze, but Josephine had managed to adopt people when it came to the holidays. There was her neighbor, sweet Mrs. Wilson, the lovely widow next door, with whom she'd become friendly with years before.

Not to mention half the staff in the trauma unit, and there was no forgetting the long-term patients in her care at the hospital.

The smells of delicious eateries, bakeries, and fruit markets collided in the air, causing Josephine's stomach to grumble. Her navy double breasted pea-coat felt heavy, and the shoulder-to-shoulder crowd was making her perspire. Sandwiched in the mob, she struggled to keep her purse strap balanced on her shoulder.

Gripping two large shopping bags, she'd almost made it over to the Amish section when a man slammed into her, knocking one of the bags to the ground. As she bent to retrieve the bag, a woman ran into her from behind, knocking her forward and nearly onto her knees. Just as she thought she might be full-out trampled, a man stepped forward ordering, "Hold up, here," as he extended his arm out to protect her from further collisions.

Josephine scrambled upright, shifted her bags to her left hand, and looked up to shake the hand of the man who had come to her rescue. In doing so, she found herself gazing into an amazing pair of mesmerizing sapphire eyes. Familiar eyes. She stepped back and felt her pulse quicken. It was no other than her *John Doe*, Donovan McBride.

He froze in place and then shot her the cutest smile. "Oh, my God! I can't believe it! It's you! How are you, doc?" He reached out and grabbed her by the arms. He slightly rocked her back and forth and—appearing to think better of having done so—blushed as he let her go. "I really can't believe it's you!"

"Donovan! Oh, my gosh! Look at you! You look great!" She beamed and used her free hand to drag her fingers through her hair, before flipping it over to one side. She stepped closer to him to accommodate the human traffic jam trying to shove past her.

He looked down and away. When he glanced back up, his eyes were warm. "Thanks. It's Donnie, and it's amazing what a year of physical therapy will do for a guy who took a three-month nap, huh?"

Josephine was all too aware he'd been gifted a miracle. She'd seen it for herself. How could she ever forget the night she'd heard all the alarms on his ventilator sound—piercing the middle of the night silence in the hallway? Her heart had skipped a beat because she'd believed he was dying. So much so, she'd sprinted to get to his side to say goodbye. Both relief and shock overwhelmed her when she'd realized he was awake and trying to pull his tubes out. Josephine calmed him and stayed by his side until the respiratory team arrived to extubate him.

Remaining with him after he'd woken up that night, she'd had the daunting task of explaining what had happened to him. He'd had no memory of the accident at all. In fact, he had no memory of the whole week before the crash. A chunk of his life was gone from his memory forever. Josephine disclosed she'd sat with him the first night after they'd brought him in—when they couldn't find his family.

She'd purposely left out the part about her returning to the hospital the subsequent two nights despite not even being on the schedule. He'd won a place in her heart for reasons she didn't comprehend. So, she'd stayed with him as often as she was able until the police were finally able to locate his parents.

Josephine couldn't explain her feelings then, any more than she could explain them now. Bing Crosby was cooing *White Christmas* across the overhead sound system. The crowd buzzed around them, and her heart danced like a giddy schoolgirl inside. At thirty-two, she hadn't had these feelings in years. She wasn't even sure she wanted them. Ever again.

A woman pushing a stroller loaded down with a toddler and a ton of packages bumped into the back of Donovan's legs. He stepped in closer to Josephine and shook his head. "Hey, do you want to get out of here? Grab a drink or something?"

Feeling her face flush, she tilted her head. "Sure! But I need to exit at 12th Street if that's okay." She looked down at his hands. They were empty. "Wasn't there something you came in here to buy? It doesn't look like you've done any shopping."

Grinning, he shrugged and spread his arms out, palms up. "Hey … life's short. Have drinks now, fight crowds later." He winked and leaned forward to relieve her of the bags in her hands. "Lead the way to the exit you need, then we can walk around the corner to Filbert, and we'll hit the Pub there."

"Deal! I just need to make a brief stop once we exit. Then, I'm good to go." She hadn't finished her shopping either. It had been so long since her heart had felt joyful, she wasn't about to let this moment get away from her. Besides, she'd already had a sneak preview of the delicious Donovan McBride, and she wanted to know more.

They wove through the crowds. Each time they had to bob and weave, Josephine felt Donovan put his hand on the small of her back—guiding her through the obstacles. Something about his mannerisms made her feel so safe. When they reached the 12th Street exit, he stepped ahead of her to open and hold the door.

Josephine stepped out onto the busy sidewalk and moved to the right. Donovan wasn't far behind. About a half a block down, she spotted the homeless man she'd seen on the way into the market. He was still sleeping on the sidewalk grate. Josephine turned to Donovan and asked for the yellow shopping bag he was holding for her. He furrowed his brow before handing it to her. She didn't offer an explanation. She reached into the bottom and retrieved a thick quilt. Without saying a word, she tore the tag from the cover, tossing it into the bag. She gave the blanket a good shake—unfolding it—and gently placed it on top of the man. He lifted his head and looked at her with eyes void of hope. He nodded and pulled the blanket up under his chin before resting his head back down on the dirty backpack serving as his pillow.

Unblinking, she felt Donovan watching her. He half smiled and nodded as Josephine straightened and walked back over to him. "Wow, that was super cool to watch, doc. What an incredibly kind thing to do."

"It's Josephine ... or Josie. Take your pick—and thanks. I saw him on my way into the terminal. He looked cold, and I felt bad. It's Christmas time, and people were just stepping over him." Unexpectedly feeling excited, and trying not to appear as captivated as she felt, she said, "Let's go have that drink now, shall we?"

Donovan nodded and led the way. The crowd on the sidewalk forced them to walk in single file. When he reached the entrance to the tavern, Donovan opened the door and held it for her. *And to think they claim chivalry is dead,* she thought as she passed by him.

Josephine squinted when she entered the dimly lit bar. As he came in behind her, Donovan again placed his hand on the small of her back and guided her across the room to where the hostess stand was situated. He gestured to a long wooden bench to their left. "Have a seat, and I'll get us checked in."

She sat down and gazed at the gorgeous man across the aisle. Josephine reminded herself to keep her emotions in check. Donovan was simply a man who she'd helped in his time of need. It was her job. *Beware the Florence Nightingale effect*—the words of her professors warning their students against falling in love with patients—haunted her right now. She argued back with the ghosts—*he hasn't been my patient for over a year*.

Donovan joined her on the bench and placed her bags in the space next to where she sat. He extended his hand. "Can I take your coat for you?"

He was just full of surprises! She hadn't had the opportunity to get to know *this* Donovan. Josephine had only been acquainted with the injured one. Within a few days of waking up, he'd been transferred to a long-term rehabilitation center to regain his strength. She hadn't seen him since the day the ambulance team rolled him out of his room and off to rehab.

Josephine unbuttoned her coat as she stood up. Donovan slipped in close behind her and reached his hands around to grasp the front of the lapels on either side of her coat. He slipped it off her shoulders and slid it down her arms. It gave her goose bumps to feel his breath so close to her neck. Without saying another word, he crossed over and hung it on a community coat rack. He removed his jacket and hung it next to hers. She grinned as he returned to where she stood. "Did your folks send you to some sort of male finishing school or what?"

His smile was sheepish. "No. I'm just a gentleman raised by a gentleman."

Her heart skipped a beat. Donovan was fabulous, and it was becoming increasingly difficult to hide the fact that she thought so. She tucked her hair behind her ear, looked up into his eyes, and bit her lower lip. Releasing it, she teased, "I could get used to this kind of treatment."

Donovan raised his eyebrows. "Oh, please do."

McBride party of two? The hostess called out.

Donovan raised a finger in the air. "That's us." He collected Josephine's bags and glanced at her before jerking his head toward the girl standing a few feet away holding menus propped against her chest … "after you."

Josephine started to walk toward the girl. As she passed Donovan, she glanced at the floor and slowly raised her eyes to look up through her lashes. "By the way, be careful what you wish for!"

They were led to a booth at the far end of the room. All too aware they'd both been flirting, Josephine couldn't help but wonder if it was even ethical to be here with him. She slid into one side of the booth and noticed his flexed bicep as he leaned onto the table to reach across to place her packages at the far end of the other. Donovan slid into the booth opposite her, next to the bags, folded his hands on the table, and fixed his eyes on hers. Under the heat of his stare, Josephine felt all her concerns about ethics … rapidly fading away.

Chapter Four

Donovan stared across the table at Josephine. He couldn't believe his good fortune in having run into her. Ever since he'd completed rehab and started living a normal life again, he'd wanted to go back to Cooper and see her. He just hadn't mustered the nerve. It felt too much like going back to your old high school to visit your teachers, and he knew he was way too old for that kind of thing.

But, just like a Christmas miracle, here she was in the flesh, and she was dazzling. He watched how energetic she was and felt completely infatuated with her. She was reminiscing about the day they'd tried to surprise his parents, nearly shocking them to death instead. She threw her head back as she laughed and reached across the table, placing her hand on top of his. "It would have been my first *deceased due to poor planning* case!" She slid her hand off his and drew it across the table, tucking it onto her lap. She leaned back and laughed again.

He wanted to freeze time. Donovan couldn't remember when he'd ever felt this alive. It felt as though she gave off some powerful aura of energy and he wanted to absorb every ounce of it.

A waitress, wearing a red, fuzzy Santa hat, stopped at their table. "Can I start you off with some drinks?"

Donovan pointed at Josephine. "Ladies first."

She raised her eyebrows and nodded as she spoke, "You know, I think I'll have a seven and seven."

Slowly, a smile came across Donovan's face. "I'll have the same—with a slice of lime." He couldn't believe they both drank the same cocktail. He liked her more by the minute.

Santa's little helper tapped the edge of their table. "I'll bring you both a lime. I'll be right back."

Donovan leaned in and crossed his arms on the table. "So, where are you from anyway?"

"Depends, kind of everywhere. I started out in a little town over in 'Jersey—Maple Shade. At sixteen, I moved in with my grandparents in Haddonfield until my grandma died. After that, I moved in with my aunt, her husband, and my cousins in Audubon until I went to college. A few years ago, I bought a house in Collingswood. So, I guess if you're asking about now, the answer would be Collingswood. You?"

The hum of the crowd was getting louder as the booths filled up around them.

"Wow! I know exactly where all those towns are … I grew up right in Cherry Hill. I lived in the same house my whole life. After college, I bought a place not too far from the local mall. Pretty boring life, I guess." He shrugged his shoulders.

Josephine raised her eyebrows. "I'd say your life's been anything but boring!" Her smile faded. "Actually, my life *had* been somewhat on the boring side until my parents were killed—that's when things got shaky."

"Oh, my God!" Astonished, Donovan shifted in his seat. "I'm so sorry to hear that. Killed?"

She was nodding. "Yes, in a freak accident. They signed up for a hot air balloon ride to celebrate their twentieth wedding anniversary. They were getting ready to land when a fluke gust of wind knocked them off course. The pilot lost control of the balloon, and it crashed into the tops of some trees. Several of the tethers had been severed by the branches. Before any rescue attempts were made, the basket—with my parents in it—plunged about a hundred feet to the ground."

Donovan had to close his mouth. "That's ... that's terrible." He noticed the light in her eyes had dimmed.

Josephine looked off in the distance. "It was." She glanced back at him and drew in a breath. "Still is. My dad was killed instantly. My mother lived ... briefly. She was in the trauma unit, at Cooper, just like you were. She was brain dead. I was just a sixteen-year-old kid. The hospital staff allowed me to stay by her side. I sang lullabies to her the whole time. It took two nurses, my grandmother, and a janitor to pull me off her when they pronounced her dead." She blinked back tears.

Donovan wanted to hug her. His voice caught, "I'm so sorry! That's so profoundly sad. Do you have siblings ... was there someone there for you?" He couldn't shake the vision she'd painted of the teenage girl clinging to her dead mother.

She leaned in to put her elbows on the table. Locking her fingers together, she rested her chin on her hands. "Nope. I ended up an only child. I had my grandmother, but she was as brokenhearted as I was. My grandfather was an alcoholic, so he wasn't much help." She deliberately left out the details of becoming an only child. Instead, she smiled. "I guess this is a little heavy for a first date!"

He grinned and shook his head. "Nah." He paused, blinked, and jolted back against the bench. "Wait! First date?" Donovan raised his brows. "Is this a *date*?" He watched as she went crimson.

She stammered, "I mean … I meant … oh, I don't know what I meant!" Josephine opened her hands and covered her face with them. Peeking between her fingers, with a grin in her voice, she said, "Can't you just let me off the hook here?" She lowered her chin and dropped her hands into her lap, revealing a huge, coy smile.

Donovan chuckled. "No way." I'm kind of enjoying this upper-hand thing I have going on here."

Josephine rolled her eyes. The gleam had returned. She used both her thumbs and forefingers to form the letter "W." "Whatever! Call it what you want!"

He noticed she was no longer blushing. "Ha-ha, but in all seriousness, I'm really sorry about your folks. It must have been rough."

The smile left her face. "Thanks, it was. But, it led me into this field, and that's how I met you. From every storm comes a rainbow." Her eyes flashed.

The waitress returned, placing drinks in front of them. "Are you ready to order?"

The menus were on the table, unopened. But, Donovan didn't need one. "I know what I want, but she may need a minute."

Josephine perked up and tapped her hand on the table. "Actually, I do know what I want. I'll have a cheesesteak."

Donovan grinned. He should have known. No one from 'Jersey came into Philly without ordering a cheesesteak. "I'll have the same." *Two for two*, he thought to himself. The tantalizing doctor was winning him over a menu item at a time.

Their food came much too fast for Donovan. It was outstanding, and so was the company. He was grateful when they'd finished up, and Josephine agreed to order another drink. But, even after nearly two hours of chatting and laughing, he wasn't ready to let her go. As they finished their second round of cocktails, a standing-room-only crowd formed around them. He reluctantly signaled for their check.

While they waited, he asked, "Are you going to do more shopping or are you headed for the train?"

Josephine used her straw to spin the ice around in her glass. "After two of these? I'm headed home. I'll need a nap!"

He nodded and twisted his mouth to the side. "I hear that. Did you take the train in from Collingswood?"

"Always! I'd never drive into the city. Parking is murder over here."

"Well, how about if I take the train back with you? You'll get off before me. I parked at Woodcrest Station." Donovan held his breath.

Josephine's sat up straighter and bobbed her head. "I'd love that."

The waitress dropped the black waiter's wallet, containing their check, on the table. "I'll take that when you're ready."

Josephine reached for it. Donovan lunged his arm forward and grabbed it from under her hand, pulling it toward him.

He looked at her and raised his right eyebrow. "What? Go Dutch on our first date? No way. What kind of gentleman would I be if we split the check?" He rocked both brows up and down and grinned playfully.

She busted out laughing. "So much for hoping you'd let me off the hook."

He leaned in and smacked both his hands on the table in front of her. "I just have one question for you …"

Josephine pretended to let out an uninterested sigh when she spoke. "What's that?"

Donovan grinned mischievously. "How soon can I get you on a second date?"

The Complete Karma Debt
Two Book Series is
Now available on Amazon.com!

My Sister's Secrets

Drew Wallace is there for every important event in his younger sister, Lily Finnegan's, life. He's spent a lifetime fixing her problems and keeping her secrets.

Lily finds out she has breast cancer on the same day that she finds out her husband has some hefty secrets, too.

 As a child, Drew made many promises to his younger sister. They were easy promises to keep. Decades later, Drew must come to terms with the fact that despite always being there for her, he may not be able to keep her alive. In fact, he may be forced to be an active part of her death. But how can Drew carry this burden? How can he be the one who decides to end Lily's life? How will he find the strength when, every time he thinks of her, he's reminded of a lifetime of memories they've shared together?

My Sister's Secrets eavesdrops on the raw emotions of this brother sister duo when cancer rears its ugly head and it accentuates the depth and loyalty found in the family dynamic.

This touching, emotional journey shows the true power of sibling love and friendship and highlights the importance of showing appreciation for those in your life who mean the most.

Excerpt from Jeanne's Award-winning and Best-Selling Novel,

My Sister's Secrets

PROLOGUE

Before Lily had time to scream, she tumbled headfirst into the massive hole. Rocks and dirt showered down as Drew struggled to remain upright on the edge above her. With arms flailing, her brother recovered his balance.

The night was dark. The dense, musty brush was made passable thanks to the pale light of the full moon. The eerie song of wildlife lurking in the shadows traveled on a sinister breeze. The children were lost. Spotting a break in the thickness up ahead, Drew and Lily had broken into a sprint. Focused on the horizon, they were caught off guard by the den of snakes concealed by the murky night.

Drew knelt to peer into the opening. He spotted Lily at the bottom, surrounded by a cluster of hissing reptiles. His body tensed with panic and his eyes filled with tears. He leaned over and shouted, "Lily, it's too deep! I can't reach you. I have to go find help!"

With that mission, Drew disappeared into the night, leaving Lily behind to face her serpent-laden prison alone. She could feel their scales dragging against her bare arms, and their soft whispers had elevated to a roar. One snake coiled around her midsection. She squirmed against its power. Another long, slithering body wrapped itself around her neck. As the duet gripped and squeezed, Lily felt life leaving her body. She envisioned herself as a bright orb, mirroring the rapidly fading moon.

Just as death was about to carry her away, seven-year-old Lily shot upright. Blinking in the darkness, sweating and sucking in air, she wiped the perspiration from her face. Familiar surroundings became clear. An adjacent nightlight illuminated her dresser, which was topped with a white and pink ballerina jewelry box. Barbie's Dream House, with its occupants tucked in for the night, offered Lily assurance— she was indeed in her own room and in her own bed.

With her heart still racing, she gathered her pillow and tip-toed across the hall. Drew's door was closed. As quiet as a moment of silence, Lily turned the handle and nearly floated across the threshold. She crept past the cedar toy box filled with GI Joe's, Tonka trucks, and Matchbox cars and approached the edge of his bed. Drew was asleep on his side, with his sheet tucked up to his nose. Practically all Lily could see was his mop of auburn hair. She clutched her dusty rose pillow to her chest with one hand and reached to tap her nine-year-old brother's shoulder with the other. Nothing.

Persistent, Lily grasped his shoulder and shook him.

A drowsy Drew tried to focus. His little sister stood before him; her brown eyes wide with fear. Damp cascades of curls were matted to her forehead.

"What's the matter, Lil?"

She was still trembling. "I had a bad dream."

Drew rolled onto his back, lifted his behind while scooting over to the far edge of the bed, and raised a corner of his comforter up in the air. "The witch's flying monkeys again?"

"No. You and me were lost in a forest. I fell into a pit of snakes. You left me there alone… to die. Then, I woke up."

Lily accepted the raised blanket as an invitation to climb under the covers. "Don't tell Mom and Dad I slept in here again, okay, Drew?"

Drew scooted back a little further. "It's *our secret*, Lily."

She slid close to Drew and settled in. He'd already resumed his position on his side, facing her. In the safety of his presence, she felt her heart rate returning to normal.

After a few minutes, when silence had fallen over them, Drew's voice sliced the stillness. "Hey, Lil?"

She squinted to find Drew's jade eyes staring intently at her. "Yeah?"

"I promise I'll never leave you alone in a forest, and I promise I'll never let you die."

Satisfied, Lily allowed sleep to carry her away.

In the precious innocence of that moment, neither child could possibly have realized… sometimes there are promises you just can't keep.

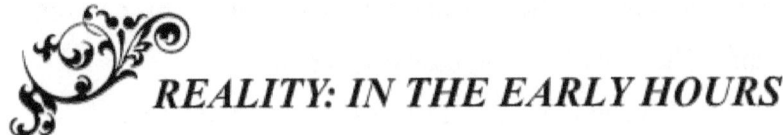

REALITY: IN THE EARLY HOURS

ONE

You know, it wasn't supposed to be this way. She wasn't supposed to be here, all hooked up to machines like this. I'm telling you, just like I told the doctors this morning: she has a Living Will. I know because she made me fill the damn paper out for her. Her answers were *no*—no tubes, no machines, no feedings. No. No. No. Then, she signed it.

They brought her here in the back of an ambulance, unconscious. The doctors didn't have a clue what the hell her wishes were, so they implemented all emergency life-saving measures. That means they hooked her up to life support. Now, it's someone else's problem. And that someone else is *me*.

She'd promised me... you'll *know*—that's why I'm picking you. I don't know a damn thing.

Maybe it's easier to tell you what I do know. I know this disease is a vile beast. I wish I knew a grimier, more repulsive word than vile. Because, if I did, then this disease would be that word.

I hate cancer.

Something grumbles in my stomach. I can't tell you if it's hunger or grief. They both feel the same. Empty.

I've been sitting on this sparsely padded side chair for hours now. I find myself leaning forward because my back is killing me. I have my arms draped over the raised side rail on her hospital bed, and I'm nearly in a trance from the a cappella solo performed by the ventilator. *Whoosh-bump-shoo. Whoosh-bump-shoo. Whoosh-bump-shoo.*

Lily always believed I could fix anything in her life ...always said I was her *hero*. I'm so pissed off the doctors screwed this up. I mean, really, don't heroes save lives? Some Superman I'll have turned out to be.

They're gathering outside of her door, and the sound of their hushed cries makes the hair on my neck stand up. I feel like I've swallowed a rhinoceros.

Evening is rushing through the window—our time is short. I've been praying for her to wake up and give me some sort of a sign. I tried to send a message from my mind to her mind. It didn't work when we were kids, and it didn't work now, but damn ...I really needed it to.

Years ago, she started calling me *asshole*. She swears like a sailor, anyway, but I can be pretty sarcastic, which probably means I earned the nickname. Right now, I can almost hear her voice teasing me. *Hey, asshole.* Inside, it makes me feel warm, and sweet, and satisfied—like I just ate the best piece of chocolate I've ever tasted.

The salty tears sliding down my cheeks work hard at dissolving the memory's sweetness.

When I can't look at her in this bed anymore, I project pictures of her on the inside of my eyelids, and she still looks the way I need her to. She's a small child, running across a field of wildflowers in the blazing July sunshine. I see her ponytail rocking from side to side as she's skipping along the trails in the woods we explored when we were kids. I see her coming down the stairs all dressed up for the prom and looking just like a princess. I can see her glowing with brand new life in her belly. I see her smile. Her eyes shine when she smiles. I watch as she jerks her head to the side to toss her long, chestnut curls back over her shoulder. I'll tell you, in every image she's beautiful, she's vibrant, and, well... *she's alive.*

The nurse just came in to check on her. Just like the others, she nods at me but doesn't speak. None of them have to; their expressions tell me everything.

I'm sick with loss.

I search my mind for the good it will relinquish. I focus so much on what is tragic about all this— I fear the joy will become buried so deep, I can't find it.

I'd like to tell you I've learned something bold or brilliant from enduring this journey with her... I haven't. I'd like to tell you walking this road with her exposed a greater purpose for me... but it really didn't.

What happened when this monster barged in and took over my sister's body? What did it leave me with? Well, I'll tell you... our past. Nothing can take that from me. Colors, and smells, and places, and songs will always be part of her and me. Now, the memories just belong to me. Lily may have been robbed of her future, but I still own every memory we've ever made and every secret we've ever shared. Secrets I've never told to anyone.

Well, never told... until now.

HER SECRETS ...

TWO

As she tried to move away, Drew grabbed hold of Lily's arm and spun her to face him. "Oh, come on, Lily, please. Can't you just take a quick look?"

"Drew, let me go! Knock it off, I mean it! Go see your family doctor! I'm not looking at your junk, for Christ's sake! I'm your sister! Lesions on your penis? Damn! Who have you been sleeping with anyway?"

Appearing flabbergasted, she pushed him away and turned back to face the black granite countertop, which was full of dirty dishes. She argued, "This isn't helping you change a grade on a report card or letting you in the house after Mom locked you out for being late. I mean... brothers just don't ask sisters to do something like this for them!"

Drew fired back, "Maybe a brother can ask his sister for a favor like this when she happens to be a *nurse!* Jeez, Lily. You don't have to make it sound so damned incestuous! I'm just too embarrassed to go to my doctor, okay?"

He studied her for a minute. She rinsed the dishes and aligned them, precisely according to their sizes, in the rack situated in the open mouth of the dishwasher.

Earlier that afternoon, Drew had phoned Lily to ask if he could come by after work. Her husband, Peter, happened to be out of town. Sounding happy for the company, she'd offered to cook dinner for him. Lily's meatloaf tasted just as good as their moms once had. Tonight, it melted in his mouth, and he'd devoured it like a hungry twelve-year-old boy. It warmed his heart to remember their mom. He would have embraced an opportunity to reminisce about her, but it was one of the few things he couldn't share with his sister. It frustrated him. *Mom's death was an accident... if only Lily could forgive herself!*

First to break the silence, Drew confessed, "Okay. I may have suffered a lapse in judgment and spent the night with a woman who was far more attractive under the camouflage of bar light than she was the next morning!" He smiled sheepishly and waited to be scolded.

Lily's sarcastic laughter filled the kitchen. She put her hands on her hips. "Well, brother, how about the gold standard in safe sex? Maybe you remember it—a condom!? It might be a real necessary garnish if you're ordering up dirty girls to go with your dirty martinis!" As she turned her back to him, he saw her smirk at her own stupid joke. She picked up the ranch dressing and put it in the refrigerator.

Scolding rendered.

"You're a real comedian, Lil! Actually, after four martinis, there wasn't a single thought about a condom, pro or con. Not one thought! Okay?"

It was true. Several weeks back, he'd attended a happy hour with coworkers. He was finishing up his second martini when a blonde sat down next to him. She'd introduced herself as Ariel and engaged him in small talk. He was lonely and embraced the attention, ordering drinks for them both. After several, Ariel invited him to her place. One thing led to another, and not long after, Drew had discovered the open sores. Mortified, he'd tried every over-the-counter remedy he could find before relenting and calling Lily. He called her—instead of his physician—because the thought of having to explain his need for a doctor's visit to a fresh-faced twenty-year-old receptionist was more than he could bear.

Drew really didn't see how this was much different from the time Lily had scored him a prescription for his bronchitis. Okay, well maybe it's a little different... *but, she's a nurse, for God's sake!*

Lily closed the fridge and crossed back to the sink. She opened the cabinet below and grabbed a fresh package of yellow dish gloves. She tore the gloves from the package and tossed the empty wrapper onto the counter. They dangled from her hand as she sighed and crossed the room to stand in front of him. She motioned toward the floor with the gloves. "Drop your pants."

Drew's voice cracked, and his eyes widened. "What... what... are you gonna do with *those*?"

Lily slipped a glove onto each hand. "Look, Drew, it's bad enough I have to *look* at you, but I'm definitely not going to *touch* you!"

Drew went crimson. He nervously dragged his fingers through his dark hair, rendering it a tousled mess. "You know, this isn't a walk in the park for me either, Lil. It's not like I'm exactly comfortable with this!"

As Drew struggled with his buckle, button, and zipper, he babbled, "Lily, thanks so much for checking this out. This isn't nearly as bad as having a strange nurse judging me and all. I don't think I could take that. I really hate that this is awkward for you, but man, am I glad you're doing this for me."

By the time Drew finished rattling, he had managed to drop his slacks and boxers down to his ankles. He stood before Lily, half naked. He realized he must look like one of the geriatric patients she'd joked about. She shared stories of their shuffling down the hallway, bare-assed, after having walked clean out of their hospital-issued pajama pants.

Lily bent to look at the several red, weeping lesions on him. He noticed she went right into professional nurse-mode. She furrowed her brow and sympathized, "Oh, Drew, this looks so painful! You shouldn't have waited so long to address it."

Perhaps to lighten the mood, or perhaps because he knew how weird this was for the two of them, he grinned and glanced down at her, "You know, Lily... if we lived further south, this would be just an ordinary Friday night!" Drew burst into laughter as he watched her shock.

She straightened and rose to face him. "Drew Wallace, you are a complete asshole!"

"Oh, come on, Lily. I was just trying to lighten it up a bit. By the look on your face, you might have thought I was a leper!" He scooped up his boxers and slacks, buttoning them.

Lily barked, "No, Drew, I was looking at carelessness, and you'll be lucky if your whole penis doesn't fall off!" She snapped off the gloves with the skill of a surgeon.

Drew's laughter halted. He paused while buckling his belt, the humor on his face replaced with skepticism and maybe just a little bit of fear. "It can't fall off... right, Lil? You're just bullshitting me, right?"

Lily was standing only inches from her brother. She stared him down, allowing him to suffer for his tasteless joke. Finally, she answered. "No, asshole, it can't fall off. I'll get one of the doctors at the hospital to prescribe something for you tomorrow. I'll have to lie and say it's for me." She crossed the room, dropping the gloves into the trash can as she passed.

The next day, when Drew picked up the phone, he was relieved when he heard Lily's voice on the other end. She whispered, "I spoke to Doctor Robinson, and he agreed to call in a prescription. You can pick it up this afternoon at the pharmacy. It's under my name. You owe me big time! I had to listen to a twenty-minute lecture on safe sex and how to spot a sexually transmitted disease." Her voice elevated several octaves. "You know, I wanted to die!" Then in a hushed tone, she cautioned, "And whatever you do... not a word about this! I could lose my license!"

He was lucky she couldn't see him sitting at his desk. He had his phone propped between his ear and shoulder. Leaning back in his chair, with his arms folded across his chest, he was grinning ear-to-ear at the visuals of responsible, loyal, safe-sex Lily taking the fall for him. She must have been horrified. He tried to hide the sound of his smile and bit down on his back teeth. "Lily, it's our secret, and this won't ever happen again. I promise!"

"Drew?"

"Yeah?"

"If it does, you're on your own. I'm not helping you. If you sleep with trash, expect to wake up smelling like a Dumpster."

Drew couldn't help himself any longer. He and Lily were longtime country music fans. He started singing, "*Almost heaven... West Virginia...*"

Lily gasped and hung up, but not before a bellow of Drew's laughter rang through the phone.

THREE

Drew nearly pulled his black, king cab pickup truck into the parking lot on two wheels. He took notice of Lily's brilliant yellow Mustang convertible already parked in the lot and knew she'd be waiting for him inside. She was never late.

Yanking the keys from the ignition, he pulled the door handle and jumped down from the seat. He barreled forward, slowing to a walk as he passed through the double glass doors. He surveyed the room for Lily. He spotted her seated in a dark, heavily varnished booth to the left.

She shook her head when he approached. "Well, hello, Mr. Minute Man!"

Drew leaned in and kissed her on the cheek before sliding onto the bench across from her. He was late more often than he was on time, so he owned it. "Alright, alright, but I have a good excuse." He glanced around and spotted Seth, a waiter they'd known for a while now. He motioned for Seth to come over. Seth mouthed *be right there* and Drew nodded. The waiter was clearly more comfortable in his apron these days, which reminded Drew of how creative Lily had been on the day they'd first met him.

Drew quickly realized he'd only had half of Lily's attention and turned his head to see what had captured her gaze. Just across the restaurant, Drew saw a young man with shoulder-length blonde hair. Drew guessed he couldn't have been more than eighteen. The apron wrapped around his waist indicated he was one of the servers. Even though Drew and Lily came here often, he couldn't recall having seen him before.

"I don't think he's on the menu, Lil," Drew quipped.

"Don't be ridiculous, Drew! He's merely a child! I was watching that group of young waitresses ignoring the poor boy. Girls always have to be so mean!"

Drew turned again, noticing a small circle of girls wearing matching uniforms, clearly excluding the kid across the room. He wasn't overly tall, maybe five-nine. He was handsome, a surfer type with a deep tan, and eyes that sparkled aqua. He shuffled across the room, never losing track of his shoes.

He placed two menus on the edge of the table. "Hi, I'm Seth. Can I get you something to drink?"

"Raspberry iced tea, please," Lily answered, reaching for the menus and sliding one across the table.

Drew picked it up. "I'll have whatever dark beer you have on tap."

"Okay. I'll bring those right out for you!" He left them with a rehearsed smile.

He quickly returned, awkwardly balancing a small brown tray. After putting their drinks down, Seth glanced from Lily to Drew. "Ready to order?"

"I think I'm ready. How about you, Lil?"

Lily slid her menu to the end of the table. "I'll take the chicken Caesar salad. I don't think we've met before. Are you new?"

"I started a week ago."

Drew stacked his menu on top of Lily's. "I'll have a burger, medium-well, and fries. Don't worry about us. We're pretty low maintenance."

Seth collected the menus and tucked their order ticket into his binder. "Your food will be up soon."

Just as Seth started to walk away, Lily grabbed his wrist. "Don't let those girls over there intimidate you. Girls are so petty. You'll do just fine here!"

Confused and casually trying to reclaim his arm, he mumbled, "Umm... thanks, ma'am."

Drew looked amused as Seth scooted away from their table. "Counseling our waiter?"

Lily half-heartedly laughed. "I have daughters. Some teenaged girls made their lives miserable, and they didn't deserve it! It still makes me mad." She was staring at the group of waitresses deliberately ignoring Seth when he passed by them to enter the kitchen. Lily suddenly jumped up. "I'll be back."

She headed toward the restrooms. Drew watched as she stopped and spoke to the circle of girls. When Seth returned from the kitchen, their expressions had completely changed to those of obvious delight. He'd appeared notably puzzled—not even speaking—when he placed their food on the table.

After dinner, Drew and Lily walked toward the exit, passing the group of waitresses gathered around Seth. A few of the girls glanced at Lily as they passed. They smiled as though they were having their picture taken. In return, Lily winked.

Drew raised an eyebrow. "What did you say to those gals?"

Lily shrugged her shoulders and smirked. "Nothing much. I just told them to keep it on the down-low, but the word was out that Seth wasn't letting on as to who he really is ...and that I'd heard his cousin happens to be the lead singer in the popular new boy-band all the girls are crazy about."

Drew grinned, and now it was Lily who looked as though her picture were being taken!

As always, Drew was amused by her antics. He draped his arm around her shoulder and shook his head. "Lillian Finnegan... always the philanthropist, you are."

Drew clapped his hands together. "So! I'm really sorry I made you wait. I'm stuck on this ridiculous project at work, trying to design a home for a woman who doesn't know what she wants. There really is no pleasing her. She reminds me of Alisha!"

Drew was referring to his ex-wife, whom he had divorced years earlier. She ultimately couldn't make up her mind as to who she loved more: her husband or her boyfriend. She and Drew had two daughters, Sophia and Sora. Drew had caught Alisha with the guy, and when all was said and done, she got the boyfriend, the house, his daughters, his dog, and darn near half his income.

Lily casually waved her hand in the air. "Really, it's fine, Drew. I didn't wait that long." She was fidgeting, rearranging silverware and twisting her napkin between her forefinger and thumb.

He raised his brow. "What's going on, Lil?"

She took a deep breath and sighed. Drew suddenly noticed a manila envelope lying on the table. Lily reached for the envelope, retracted, and reached again as though she couldn't bear to touch it.

"Remember, I told you I was getting all these strange vibes from Peter, so I was hiring a private investigator?" Lily paused. Drew nodded and his heart sunk. "Well, I did it. Turns out, he's a pretty good photographer, too. He trailed Peter for about ten days. That was all the time he needed. He gave me these."

Her hands trembled as she pushed the envelope across the table to Drew. He didn't usually look at her hands, but as she eased it over, he noticed how much they'd aged. They told a truth her face concealed.

"And to think I thought he was gambling." Lily shook her head as Drew tried to guess at what was masked inside the envelope.

As he withdrew the contents—about ten black-and-white photos—tears carved tracks in Lily's rose-colored blush. He knew his expression transitioned from his original curiosity to utter disbelief as he realized the pictures were of Peter involved in various sexual acts with several different women—most of them Asian. He methodically stacked the pictures on the table as he looked through them.

Holding the last two pictures—one in each hand—Drew raised his eyes to meet Lily's. He finally managed to speak. "What. The. Hell?"

"Prostitutes, Drew. Can you believe it?" She defended, "I mean... shit... Peter didn't need to pay for sex. Hell, I love sex. And, to tell you the truth, I'm damn good in bed! And I don't do any of that *courtesy fake* stuff!" Her voice had risen.

Drew glanced around the somewhat empty establishment. He shifted in his seat and blinked to try to erase the overload of unwanted details about his sister's sexual prowess.

Normally, she'd joke about such things. However, right now, she was uncomfortably serious. Under different circumstances, Lily could be pretty quick with sexually loaded innuendos. On such occasions, Drew would teasingly bug his eyes out, hold a finger up in the air, and say, "Check please!?!" But there was no room for laughter right now. *Prostitutes... damn.*

Lily turned her face toward the window as Seth approached their table. "The usual, folks?" Drew nodded for them both while scrambling to tuck the X-rated pictures into the privacy of the envelope. He slid it back over to Lily. Seemingly unaware anything was amiss, Seth turned and announced, "Coming right up!"

Drew desperately tried getting a grip on the unimaginable. *Peter Finnegan was stereotypically good-looking—tall, dark, and handsome ... and he's actually paying for sex?* Why on earth would he risk losing his family, who he seemed to genuinely love? In reality, Lily was right—he *was* gambling. *Surely, Peter understood the stakes?*

Drew was sympathetic. "Have you had a chance to think about what you're going to do, Lil?"

Lily took a deep breath. "I have. When I decided to actually have him investigated, I thought long and hard about what I would do if it turned out he was guilty. I'm leaving him, Drew. There is no way I'll ever trust him again. Ten minutes late and, where is he? Ten dollars missing and what's he doing? And, if there's a strange smell on him when he walks through the door at the end of the day? I'd have to wonder if it's the Chinese food he had for lunch or the Asian whorehouse he went to for dessert. I can't live like that."

She slammed her fist down on the table. "I won't. Dammit, I'm worth more than this. More than twenty years of my life dedicated to that man! How could I not have known? When did I get so stupid?" She looked totally exasperated. "Why are they all so ...*young*?"

When Seth reappeared, he was carrying their drinks. Lily rose from the table and avoided eye contact. "I'm going to splash some water on my face."

She looked so... broken. Drew couldn't believe he hadn't noticed it the minute he'd sat down. He would never have gone on about work.

Seth glanced at Lily and raised his eyebrows. "Will you be ordering any food today?"

Drew shook his head. "No. Probably just this round of drinks, but I'll let you know if we need anything else."

Before long, Lily returned, looking a little more refreshed.

Drew paused while she sat down. He leaned forward. "What will you tell your girls?"

She swallowed hard. "A lie, of course! It would be the grossest thing in the world for them to live with the disgusting images of their Dad with . . ." "She hesitated, waving her hand dismissively. "... those women." I'm sparing the girls that visual. I'll find some good divorce term like *irreconcilable differences*."

The *girls* were Lily's daughters. Amanda, at twenty, was a blue-eyed version of Lily. She had Lily's confidence, poise, and spunk. She was beginning her junior year at Virginia Tech. Eighteen-year-old Rebecca had beautiful red hair and blue eyes. She was the bashful one and would be entering her freshman year at Albright the following week.

Drew tried to imagine how this would all unfold. "When are you telling Peter you're on to him... he's been caught?"

Lily coiled a napkin in her hands as she spoke. "Actually, my plan is to get the girls off to school next Saturday. I will confront him once they're safely out of Dodge. I can't fathom dumping this on them right now."

She paused, gazed away, and finished her thought. "Also, I've decided I'm telling Peter that he and I are going to behave as though everything is normal this semester. This is Bec's first time away from home. She'll probably be a little homesick, and I'm not having her deal with this mess, too."

Drew furrowed his brow. "When do you think you'll tell Amada and Bec?"

Lily glanced out the window with tear-filled eyes, seemingly envisioning that scenario. "We can tell them when they come home for the holidays. Actually, we really won't end up telling them until after the first of the year. The girls have a ski trip planned in Colorado, right after finals. They're meeting out there and then flying home together on Christmas Eve, and we certainly won't be telling them then."

Lily smacked her fist on the table again, this time hard enough to make the silverware take flight. "Dammit, Drew. This just isn't fair. Now, we're all stuck with Peter's choices. How could he be so selfish? What was he *thinking*?"

Drew wanted to offer that there were no shots of Peter's brain in those pictures, so it was unlikely there was any *thinking* going on. Instead, he reached across the table and grasped her hand. He felt helpless. He'd always believed most problems could be solved by throwing money, time, or love at them. He knew it wasn't the case now.

He let go of her hand and signaled for Seth to bring their check.

Seth placed it on the table. "I'll take this whenever you're ready."

"Let me take care of that now." Drew slid his credit card across the table. Seth scooped it up along with the check.

Lily's phone rang. She picked it up and glanced at the screen, puzzled. "I don't recognize this number." She paused and answered. "This is Lillian Finnegan." She listened before beginning again. "Yes, that is correct. Oh. I see. When? Tomorrow? Well, let's see. Noon? Okay, I can do that. Thank you. Thank you for calling. Bye."

Lily frowned and shook her head. Drew looked puzzled, so she explained: "I had my mammo today, and they didn't get enough images. Who has the time to do this? It's bad enough I have to get my boobs crushed in a vice annually, never mind an encore a day later!"

"Are you sure there's not more going on?" Worry about Lily quickly replaced Drew's anger at Peter.

"Oh, Drew, honestly, I have so many friends who get called back for additional views after mammograms. It's almost never cancer. If an image is remotely questionable, they bring you back, even if they believe it's nothing. They cover their asses. It's medicine dictated by lawyers." Drew failed to notice Lily's lower lip slightly quiver as she turned away.

Instead, he released a sigh of relief. He picked up his card and signed the receipt Seth had dropped.

Lily passed the envelope back across to Drew. "Please take this and keep it in your safe until I'm ready to confront Peter."

He picked it up. "I'm always here for you to talk to... whatever you need. That is, except for killing him. Don't ask me to kill him. I wouldn't do well in jail. I'm too pretty." Attempting a smile, he slid out of the booth.

He wished this had been one of their light-hearted dinner dates. Drew reached a handout to Lily, and she grasped it. He helped her move to the edge of the booth and stand.

She looked into her brother's eyes. Her expression was sober. "I know, Drew... believe me... I know."

Drew stepped aside, motioning for Lily to go ahead of him. Instead, she locked her arm into Drew's and leaned her head onto his shoulder. They started toward the exit. With Lily on one arm, he was all too aware... he had the destruction of her marriage tucked beneath the other.

Available on Amazon.com !

ABOUT THE AUTHOR

Readers can find Jeanne at:

Website: www.Jeannemcnamee.com

Twitter: @jeannemcnamee

Facebook: https://www.facebook.com/jeanne.mcnamee.7

Join Jeanne's mailing list for future releases, promos, and chances to win
Kindle Fires and Amazon gift cards!

Sign up today!

@

www.Jeannemcnamee.com